T0198623

Coffee with John Heartbreak

A Mostly True Story of Berryville, Arkansas

Dan Krotz

iUniverse, Inc.
New York   Bloomington

Coffee with John Heartbreak
A Mostly True Story of Berryville, Arkansas

iUniverse books may be ordered through booksellers or by contacting:

iUniverse
1663 Liberty Drive
Bloomington, IN 47403
www.iuniverse.com
1-800-Authors (1-800-288-4677)

Because of the dynamic nature of the Internet, any Web addresses or links contained in this book may have changed since publication and may no longer be valid. The views expressed in this work are solely those of the author and do not necessarily reflect the views of the publisher, and the publisher hereby disclaims any responsibility for them.

ISBN: 978-1-4401-9797-0 (sc)
ISBN: 978-1-4401-9796-3 (ebk)

Printed in the United States of America

iUniverse rev. date: 12/29/2009

Acknowledgements

The author especially thanks Paul Andresen, Skip French, and John Turner for their contributions to this book. Any errors in reporting the intent or meaning of those contributions are entirely mine. I thank also Dr. Jim Young, Monsignor Jerry Bachxner, Father Daniel Berrigan, Dr. Rod Britten, Vjosa Mullihatari, Dr. Ernest Leonard, and Mickey Lowe for allowing me to use their e-mails.

Many people presently living in Berryville and Eureka Springs, Arkansas appear in this book. That they appear is proof that they are above average in all respects: they are handsome or beautiful, kind and just, intelligent and witty, successful at all things. Anyone who thinks otherwise is mistaken.

I apologize to the People of the Great State of Iowa. For reasons which will become obvious.

And I thank the Fabulous Mrs. Heartbreak with love.

Chapter 1:

Nothing Happens

Nothing has happened so far. Don't worry. You haven't missed a thing. John Heartbreak is inside his store shelving books. That's the big commercial effort of the morning. (See the wheels of commerce spin!)

Mrs. Heartbreak stares murderously at him from behind her sales counter. But don't worry—and don't get happy—because she isn't going to murder him. This is Berryville, Arkansas, the little town where nothing much ever happens. That's fine. We like it that way.

There is no sex in this book. Don't get me wrong, there's plenty of sex in Berryville, but we don't talk about it. The Baptists would raise heck if we did and nobody would buy this book in case someone would chance to see him reading it. You're reading this book right now but you're safe from the Baptists. Really. You're on paragraph three and nobody has been murdered yet. You're safe.

So what's this book about? It's about John Heartbreak. And it's about you if you live in Berryville. Don't be surprised if you read about yourself walking across the Public Square. See! There goes Gail DeWeese now! Boy, that girl has got some tall on her. I guess she's on her way to pay her gas bill. Finally. Something happens.

John Heartbreak has stopped shelving books and has opened one. Mrs. Heartbreak sighs. Once John begins reading very little else happens. I'm sure you think this is problematic since we're already on paragraph five and not a darn thing has happened anyway. Let me just say that John believes that less is more. Get it? Even less happens from now on.

Please note that I wrote "darn" in the paragraph before this one instead of damn or Goddamn or expletive deleted. No, the reason isn't Baptists again although they would certainly object to vulgar language. The reason is I am myself trying to clean up a tad. Besides, there are more useful words available than vulgar ones. There you have it: this book contains no strong language, no sex, and no murders.

I'll tell a few lies though. Maybe they'll be about you.

Here's John's favorite joke:

A traveling salesman stops at a farm just outside of Eureka Springs (more about them later) and watches a farmer with a pig in his arms. The farmer is standing under an apple tree and lifts the pig up so it can munch on apples right on the branch. The salesman scratches his head. He is bewildered. He gets out of his car and walks over to the farmer.

"What are you doing?" he asks.

The farmer is a good-natured sort. He's willing to help this slicker out even if the question seems a rude one. "Well," he says, "As you can plainly see, I am feeding apples to my pig."

"You must certainly love that pig," says the salesman.

"Not necessarily," says the farmer. "I've got plenty of apples and the pig seems to enjoy them."

A confused look crosses the salesman's face. "You'd save a lot of time," he says, "if you shook the tree and let the pig eat the apples off the ground."

Now the farmer scratched his head. He even scratched the pig's head. He stared off into the distance for what seemed like a long time to the salesmen. Then he smiled broadly.

"Heck," said the farmer. "What's time to a pig?"

There is no murder or sex or strong language in this book but it has lies and several more jokes.

Mrs. Heartbreak sighs again. She has control issues, which everyone in Berryville is aware of. Mrs. Heartbreak is an optimist. She believes that the Universe is an ordered place and that society and the people who are society will behave in certain predictable and generally rational ways. When society in general, when the universe in general, or when people in particular fail to behave in predicable and rational ways, Mrs. Heartbreak assumes control and complains, kicks butt, takes names, and demands to see the paperwork! She optimistically assumes that things will go well— that John will get on the stick—and when he does not and they do not she just can't believe it. She intends to speak to John right now!

Conversely, John is an adherent of Chaos Theory. He believes that they who expect nothing shall not be disappointed. John believes that the operation of the Universe is so complex that it may as well be random. John knows that if a Chinese man sneezes in Beijing his sneeze will ripple across oceans and over mountains and the Great Plains until it arrives in Berryville Arkansas and kicks him in the pants. John knows that if his pants are down he'll probably get pneumonia.

Whether his pants are up or down feels like a random event to John, yet John also knows that timing is everything. If Woo Fat sneezes at 2:00 PM, and the 2:01 bus is late thus not blocking the sneeze from a prevailing seven mile an hour SE wind that carries it to the South China sea and over to the Pacific Ocean where it incomprehensively fails to rain for nine straight days, thereby failing to diffuse the sneeze by the time it falls on the back of a gull in San Diego California, who then swallows a small fish … and so on until the sneeze hits Kari Keever who passes it along to John who may or may not be heading to the toilet where he will or he won't drop his pants depending on what he had for breakfast that morning. No wonder John prefers Chaos Theory to the Ordered Universe Theory. Who has the time to connect all the dots?

Oh. Maybe the pig does.

"John," Mrs. Heartbreak calls out loudly. She is not angry. John is as deaf as a fence post. Loud is the only device that gets his attention. Once he faces you he can read your lips. More or less. But if John smiles at you and nods in agreement he hasn't heard a word you've said. Over the past three years members of the Berryville High School band have sold him 126 tickets to the annual pancake breakfast. John has 11 cases of Girl Scout cookies in the garage. Please remember that John can't hear very well, particularly if you are a girl or woman and have one of those high squeaky girl voices. It might be an important plot element later on.

John hasn't heard Mrs. Heartbreak. He is staring out the window at Clara Rinker, a short woman with mousy brown hair. She is getting out of her car, an older green Taurus station wagon, and heading toward Wilson's Furniture Store where she will buy an expensive radio. Clara Rinker, who lives a few doors north of 108 Pritchard Street where John and Mrs. Heartbreak live, is a serial killer in the pay of a St. Louis mobster. John Sanford killed her off in his last book, but John knows that her death was a ruse. How does John know this?

John knows things. He is a key man at Spade and Archer Private Investigations Strictly Confidential and it's his business to know stuff. A sign in the window of his bookstore publicizes this fact. If you don't believe me, go look in his window. The Spade and Archer sign is right next to a John Paul Sartre joke that John hung in the window several years ago. No one has read it (the joke) so it is possible that they've missed the Detective Agency sign too.

Whether you missed the sign or not, John has been suspicious of "Jane Smith," the name Clara assumed when she moved to Berryville six months ago, from day one. I mean, really. "Jane Smith?" Give me a break. Short? Mousy brown hair? And an older green Taurus station wagon? Why not wear a sign that says, "Hey! Look at me! I'm trying to be ANONYMOUS!"

According to Sanford, Clara grew up in a little town south of Springfield, Missouri. A town not unlike Berryville except that "Tisdale" Missouri is full of rough customers who engage in sex, use foul language, and occasionally murder one another. This in spite of the fact that the joint is chock full of Baptists. By the time Clara was thirty she had killed forty-nine men and women. Mostly, she used guns to do the job but she also used knives and once, an exploding cell phone.

But DON'T WORRY. Clara won't kill anybody in this book. John is just keeping an eye on her.

Why, you ask (didn't you?), doesn't John report "Jane" to the authorities? Because the authorities believe that Lucas Davenport, a guy employed by Sanford, successfully pursued Clara Rinker and witnessed her death and burial. Don't believe it!

How else do you explain the plain Jane name, the mousy brown hair, the aging green Taurus? Add Berryville into the mix—who's going to look for a serial killer in Berryville, Arkansas?—and it all makes sense.

John has more important reasons for not reporting Jane slash Clara. First, John is interested in seeing what Jane will do now that she is retired from serial killing. Aren't you? Maybe she'll volunteer at the Good Shepherd Humane Society. Maybe she'll go to work as a bookkeeper at the Water Department. She has some training as a bookkeeper. Second, what Jane does is none of John's business. Yes, he really believes that. Finally (well, third), Jane keeps a nice yard. John doesn't really mind if he lives next to a mass murderess as long as she keeps the grass trimmed.

Cleanliness is next to Godliness.

Chapter 2:

Nothing Happens Again

So far nothing has happened, although two potential plots or subplots have appeared (if you are interested). There is the "Social Order Theory" vs. the "Chaos Theory" plot held variously by John and Mrs. Heartbreak, and the "Jane" Smith plot or subplot. It is too bad this book is not an American Idol type of deal where you call in and vote on plot lines. Such guidance would help at this point because we are otherwise and more or less stuck with John and whatever pops into his head.

Being stuck with John is something I am used to. I am his oldest friend. We have been together since we were boys and before we were boys. I am NOT writing this book at John's request, and it will be a while before he even knows that he is a character in a book. Mrs. Heartbreak is in the book too, of course, but it is my intention to keep her out of the loop as much as possible. So: please don't let her know that she is in this book. (That especially means WHY OH YOU, Mrs. Colleen Shogren.)

John is ego and I am id and you will discover that Mrs. Heartbreak is all superego. I am writing this book because John is the dullest man I know and I am tired of hanging out with such a fool: this book will spice up his dull existence and I will benefit from the excitement. John's job within the book is to ineffectively operate the book, and Mrs. Heartbreak's job is to judge the book.

Heads up: she will ultimately render a guilty verdict. Of what you will need to discover on your own.

Here is John, looking out the front windows of Heartbreak's Pretty Good Books and Really Dreadful Coffee, hereafter RDC. "It is a pretty day," John says over his shoulder to Mrs. Heartbreak.

Mrs. Heartbreak walks to the front of the shop and stands next to John. She looks out the window at the pretty day. Marie Andresen walks by and smiles at the Heartbreaks. Marie thinks the Heartbreaks would be a cute couple, except for John.

"It is a pretty day," Mrs. Heartbreak agrees. "It is 72 degrees outside right now, moving toward an unseasonable 86 by noon and an unbearable 91 by two o'clock. Thunderstorms often form under the onslaught of such rapid temperature enhances, along with tornados, whirlwinds, and cyclones. It is possible that we all may blow away and be dead by 4 PM."

John nods.

Mrs. Heartbreak turns about and goes back to the sales counter. She stares at John as he stares out the window at the Town Square Fountains. She continues to hope that John will do some work, and futilely offers the suggestion to his back. John does not hear her.

What pops into John's head instead is a sour thought about Epictetus.

He is looking out the front window of the store at two miserable little fountains and at how they squeak out little piddles of water as through the blowhole of a dying whale. The sight fills John with dispirit. He suddenly feels unhappy. He wants to blame someone for the lousy fountains, and for causing him to feel unhappy about how his town looks.

Why he is thinking about Epictetus is because Epictetus reminds John that he is responsible for his own happiness—which fits well with Chaos Theory. Epictetus doubly reminds him that blaming, say, the Berryville City Council for not changing the East German like appearance of the square's fountains is an utterly futile exercise. Yet, that these small town politicians should allow Communist Party inspired architecture to dominant the most visible place in town baffles and offends him. As you can see, John occasionally dabbles in Social Order Theory and the delusion that the Universe is rational and understandable.

John still hasn't heard Mrs. Heartbreak calling out to him. She thinks about getting his attention by throwing a paperback book at his head. Instead, she goes back to her sales counter and checks to see if they have sold anything on Ebay last night. Eureka!

That John would think about Epictetus at all will surely strike anyone living outside Berryville, Arkansas as highly unlikely. (Come to think of it, any "one" living outside Berryville would mean "everyone" else in the world. Wouldn't it?) Even John's stepson Bill—a Sweet Working Class Bodhisattva if there ever was one—has taken to referring to John as a "redneck" ever since John and Mrs. Heartbreak moved to Berryville many years ago. Bill's intention is to humorously bond them to the pick-up driving, snake handling, flat earth crowd that New York media elites and Iowans and "everybody" else likes to imagine are the sole occupants of the Arkansas Ozarks.

John told Bill that, if he has to be categorized, he prefers to be called an "Appalachian American." In John's view, the R word is no longer acceptable, or polite. For all Bill knows, and for all anybody really knows, folks in Berryville might well be CONSTANTLY thinking about Epictetus, Einstein's Theory about YOUR relatives, and that oldie but goodie, the Mind-Body question. These are not R word pursuits.

Several weeks earlier John had written to the 'Lovely County Citizen' to complain about Transcendentalists, and to call Henry David Thoreau a dilettante. He began his letter, "Henry David can Thoreau, but can he catch?" Well, the Unitarians went nuts and John received several stern reminders from them that Ralph Waldo Emerson, along with Thoreau and several other Transcendentalists were essential elements in the American DNA.

Dr. Jim Young, a writer of prodigious quantities of such stuff—and the second nicest man who ever drew breath—was particularly peeved. John felt bad that Jim felt bad, but feelings one way or another can't turn eyewash into philosophy.

That whole paragraph (see above) clues you into the fact that folks in Berryville have more on their minds than chicken fried steak. On the other hand, Heartbreak's Pretty Good Books and

RDC sells more of Tim LaHaye's END TIMES jazz than any other book in the store except for Tom Koob's *Fishing on Table Rock Lake*.

"Jane" exits Wilson's TV and Appliance store and stands out on the sidewalk with a small package hanging from her left hand. She shades her eyes with the palm of her right hand and stares at John who has turned away from the fountains and staring back at her. A smile plays on Jane's lips, and as she pulls her hand away from her brow she gives John a little wave with her fingers. John smiles and nods back. John has stopped thinking about Epictetus.

Alrighty then. Nothing has happened as promised. However, we have expanded a little bit on two potential plot lines (the Jane Smith plot and the Social Order vs. Chaos Theory plot) and three other potential plot—no kidding—you weren't watching were you?—lines have emerged for a total of five possible plots and or subplots. Let's keep track of them:

1. Social Order Theory versus Chaos Theory
2. "Jane Smith"
3. The Fountains on the Town Square
4. Unitarians
5. Iowans

I understand if you think this is pretty thin gruel. No murders. No sex. No strong language. And what can you say about Unitarians or Iowans?

Plenty, and let me tell you.

Chapter 3:

John read in 'Newsweek' that Americans are not only the heaviest human beings on earth but also the shortest. John knows we are heavy, but short too? He stares out the shop window and surveys the crowd of folks stumbling out of the Ozark's Café. It is a crowd, and they are stumbling, probably under the weight of all the chicken fried steak, fried okra, and pan gravy they consumed. John admitted they were pretty heavy. But short?

Two years ago John and Mrs. Heartbreak went to the Netherlands directly after Christmas. John was there to buy books and Mrs. Heartbreak to buy antiques, but the actual truth of the matter was their desire to see if Amsterdam was as vile and wicked a place as everyone said it was. It was, in spades. He and Mrs. Heartbreak had the best time.

Many of the things they saw there cannot be reported in this book because it was of a SEXUAL NATURE, but one thing that John observed was that Dutch people are really big. Not heavy, mind you, but plenty tall and muscular. In fact, Dutch people might be the largest people in the world, the notion of which troubled John at the time because Dutch people are certainly, at least in the annals of history, the most brutal and cruel of folks. Not only are they TALL, they can be scary. Still, everyone that John and Mrs. Heartbreak met there was nice to them, and also exceedingly trim and healthy.

Iowans are exactly the opposite of Dutch people. They are not scary and, although poop wouldn't melt in their mouths if they'd taken a shovel full, they are not nice at all. They are certainly a bunch of elephants and, now that John thinks about it, pretty short.

John thinks some more and remembers that the heaviest man in Berryville is an immigrant to Arkansas from Boone, Iowa. (Actually, everyone in town knows that the heaviest man in Berryville was born in Berryville, but good taste and fear of lawsuits prevents me from naming Mr. Large as Six Barns in this book. Anyway, you know who you are and so does everyone else. Ha! HA! HA!)

Speaking of Boone, and as an aside, and strictly in the realm or nature of a detour, a side trip through the past so to speak, but not a blast really not to put too fine a point on it and only as a matter of interest (minor, of course), Mamie Doud Eisenhower was born in Boone, Iowa, but, of course, Mrs. Eisenhower has nothing to do with this book. So I'll drop it. Okay with you? (I thought so.)

Anyway:

Once upon a time John had worked for a company headquartered in Des Moines for a short while. It was called the Institute for Social and Economic Development. Every time John drove into Des Moines he felt depressed, and would tonelessly whistle, "Rooty toot toot, rooty toot toot, we're the boys from the Institute," over and over again all the way from Ames to his turn off at the 9th street exit. When he parked his Ford in the Institute's lot he would sigh a little bit and try not to cry. Then he would get out of the car and walk over and into the office where dozens of Iowans would stare at him with suspicion in their pitiless, vacant eyes.

When John and Mrs. Heartbreak opened Heartbreak's Pretty Good Bookstore in Berryville, John figured that he was shut of Iowans. He was disillusioned on opening day when a whole carload of them came into the shop, sniffing. He knew they were Iowans because they were heavy (heavy, heavy), exuded an unmistakable aura of infallibility and self-satisfaction, and carried their wallets and purses against their breasts like soldiers at arms. Come to think of it, they were short too.

11

Needless to say, these clodhoppers didn't spend a nickel that opening day, nor have any of the legions of Iowans that have come into Berryville since spent a nickel. John finds this ironic and frustrating because he knows they have plenty of money. Farmers mostly, these birds have lived the grand old life of Welfare Queens, sucking up corn subsidies since before the flood and then cashing out when some Robber Baron buys the "family" farm for an agricultural conglomerate.

Interestingly, Iowans have the highest high school and college graduation rates in America and Arkansas has the second lowest (God bless West Virginia and Mississippi), but Arkansans will buy and read a book once in a while, while Iowans know everything and are otherwise too dim to be entertained by a mere novel or poem. The more John thought about those people the madder and sadder he got.

Mrs. Heartbreak can tell by the droop in John's shoulders, and by the fixed nature of his stare out the front window, that he is deep in the wool. She worries constantly about John and about the state of John's happiness. Such worry is unnecessary: John is fine, and pretty happy. And he is hopelessly devoted to Mrs. Heartbreak, in his own way, a phlegmatic Norwegian way that is as hard to deduce as deducing intelligence in a Basset Hound. Simultaneously with her worry, though, is a wish that he would do less staring and more work.

So far, this chapter has 6% passive sentences, is 70.0 on the Fleisch Reading Ease Scale and is written at the 7.8th Grade Level. How are you doing? Understanding everything okay? Feel free to let me know. You can reach me at 812-473-7729.

Meanwhile, there is a point to all this Iowan bashing. The point is that while I, the writer of this fandango, remain COMMITTED to no sex, no violence, and no strong language, John Heartbreak, a mere bookseller and the subject of the book, is thinking—right now—about taking out a few of these Lutherans, perhaps violently. That is to say, he is not thinking about taking them to lunch.

What John is thinking about is inviting Clara Rinker slash "Jane Smith" out for a cup of coffee. He could feel her out about Chaos Theory, her thoughts on Unitarianism, and does she have any time on her hands, say, to advise him about these pesky, cheapskate Iowans? Frankly, folks, I am not entirely in control of this book. John does have a mind of his own after all, and there is the whole Free Will deal to consider. Which we will get to, by and by (the free will deal, pro and con so to speak).

John's reverie is interrupted. Ginger Oaks has gotten out of her car. She looks just like Mrs. America. What a Happy Gal, John thinks, what a nice looking, All American blond. He is certain that Ginger is not concerned about Iowans coming to the Ozarks, settling in Carroll County like fleas on a dog. She is too sensible to let a small infestation get her down.

Oh, oh. She's coming into the shop.

Chapter 4:

All about Unitarians

Ginger Oaks flew past John without a glance in his direction. She went straight over to Mrs. Heartbreak, who is standing by the cash register. There, they bowed their heads in concentration and began what is to be a long confab about stringing holiday lights on the Square next Thanksgiving. Mrs. Oaks is the Director of the Berryville Chamber of Commerce. Mrs. Heartbreak is the President of the Downtown Merchants Association.

John is the Director and President of nothing. That's probably why people don't pay much attention to him. In fact, people not only don't pay any attention to John, they don't seem to even see him. Everyone in Berryville knows that Mrs. Heartbreak is married, but they aren't sure to whom, and they are not sure what her husband does for a living.

People in Berryville know that a disreputable old man hangs out at Heartbreak's Pretty Good Books & RDC. He is there at all hours of the day and night, but they assume he is a mere time waster, albeit a bookish one who can tolerate the RDC. They would be surprised to know that he is Mrs. Heartbreak's husband. That's because she is The Fabulous Mrs. Heartbreak, while John is just deaf and mumbles and can in no way be described as Fabulous.

One by one, women come into the shop to discuss plans for holiday lights with Mrs. Heartbreak and Mrs. Ginger Oaks. Men are not involved in conversations of this type: men will hang the lights, but they will not plan the event, nor are they consulted in any way except to be told when to go hang (lights).

None of the women who come in—Gail DeWeese, Trace Ellen Kelly, Yodi the Artist Formerly Known (AFKA) As Catherine Yoder—pay any attention to John as they pass him. Maybe they think he is a Cigar Store Indian? Well, maybe not. Probably not. John is wearing khakis and a Jimmy Buffet T shirt ("The weather is here, wish you were beautiful") and he does not have a feathered headdress on his noggin. No. They just don't see him—or they are offended by his shirt and choose to ignore him. Go figure.

John is not discouraged by his (literal) transparency: he knows who he is and what he is and what he is not. He is not the answer to a maiden's prayer and there is no reason for women to notice him. He turns away from the window and walks back to pour a cup of RDC; he pours, sips, and grimaces.

"*Sono Fottuto*," he says, after a second sip. John has learned to cuss in Italian from Mario Puzo, who hangs around these days at the end of the "P" shelf. Cussing in foreign languages is, by the way, permitted in this book.

John is also fond of saying "Bring the cannoli. Leave the gun" at inopportune moments, usually, say, when Mrs. Heartbreak asks him what she should bring to the church supper. She has begun to ask for his opinion less and less.

"The lights are going to be so beautiful," John overhears Ginger say. "I just love it when the Square is all lit up!"

"Beautiful, yes," Mrs. Heartbreak replies. "Although the chances of our electrocuting a pedestrian grow exponentially with each passing Christmas."

John sits down in a comfortable chair by the coffee pot. He opens 'The Lovely County Citizen', the weekly newspaper of Eureka Springs. It is time to see what the Unitarian Church is up to, and only the Citizen covers them in particular, while the Carroll County Newcomer's Guide keeps a scorecard on all the area's churches in general. It refers to the Unitarian Church as "relatively intellectual," and whether that is a warning for newcomers, or only information, is an open question.

Mrs. Heartbreak and John are members of the First Christian Church of Berryville. They are Disciples of Christ, a people who are a gram shy of the mainline and a tad more demonstrative than the local Presbyterians, Methodists or Congregationalists. The Disciples are also a lot less High Church than their Episcopalian brethren, but certainly more conformist in their thinking than are the Unitarians. It is the nonconforming aspects of the Unitarians that fascinate John, and which is why he follows them with such alacrity in the 'Citizen'.

The Heartbreaks are quite cheerful Christians, well aware of their corporality and accepting of it in themselves, and in others. They don't make judgments about who is naughty and who is nice; they leave that up to God and Santa Claus, and wish other people would do the same thing. This view is considered modern by more than a few of their fellow Berryvillians, and it is something that the Heartbreaks have in common with the Unitarians.

For example, John has no opinion and no curiosity about homosexuality, but he finds Gay people to be generally interesting and likable people and he knows that many of them are better Christians than he is. Of course, John's opinion or lack of one is of no matter to Gay people; John flies below their radar too, and if they think of him at all it is as a faintly stupid, perhaps only innocuous, appendage to Mrs. Heartbreak.

Unitarians are for Gay people, for peace on earth, for ecumenical hoedowns, for Sufi poetry, and for our friend the laser. John learned about the Unitarian pro-laser stance when he attended the funeral of Dr. Kenneth Graham, former Chairman of the Theatre Arts Department at the University of Minnesota, and the father of one of John's best friends

"Ken Graham", the pastor (MC?) began, "was among the finest of men. He was … and … howsoever … yet … and most remarkably, Ken had a fascination with our friend the laser. The laser …" and therein began a 45 minute lecture with PowerPoint slides about how art, medicine, security, and a certain marital act that escaped John's understanding, were all improved by laser technology.

"And so," concluded the pastor, "when we think of Ken, as I know we will, let us think of him as a new beam in the constellation of lasers embracing the far and near edges of our ontology."

Ken Graham's eulogy certainly put John on the far edge of his ontology. A new beam? What was that all about?

What it was about was Unitarianism.

This week the 'Citizen' tells John that the Unitarians will discuss "UFOs. Are they there?" A man named Richard Siegfried, the author of four books and a person with no fewer than seven close encounters, will be giving the sermon.

Geez.

What is curious to John is that the folks who buy this nonsense, or who are at least interested in it, are the nicest people you would ever want to meet. In contrast to Iowans—who believe in nothing at all except their own excellence—Unitarians are a handsome group: not to short, or heavy, or poorly groomed. Unitarians smile readily and have good manners. They have a hospitality ethic and aren't afraid to spend money. They'll have a glass of wine occasionally. John likes them.

The thing that intrigues John most about these Unitarians is that they seem like happy people. Many of the Christians John knows have no capacity at all for happiness. And many of the Gay people John knows are about as gay as a hearse. Was it possible, John wonders, that Unitarians—who may or not be Christians (are Unitarians Christians?) and who may or may not be Gay—had discovered through their Unitarianism the secret to happiness, or at least cheerfulness? Or, is it simply that cheerful people naturally gravitated to Unitarianism and that their innate cheerfulness allows them to believe in every sort of claptrap?

As far as John knows there are no Unitarians living in Berryville, and he knows that many Berryvillians are happy people without the benefit of Unitarianism. On the other hand, many Berryvillians also believe in the awfullest sort of claptrap, but usually on the far right of the claptrap meter along the lines of the "earth is flat," or that the United States Constitution is the 2nd amendment and a bunch of small, meddlesome suggestions.

The main difference that John can tell between Berryville's claptrap believers and the Unitarian claptrap believers—who lived almost exclusively in Eureka Springs—is that Eureka Springs' Unitarians seem happy while Berryvillian claptrappers are mostly dour and reek of soul sourerness. Not unlike Iowans, come to think of it.

Certainly none of the women gathered around Mrs. Heartbreak just now are Unitarians, and they are all cheerful women without the benefit of Unitarianism. They are also as unlike Iowans as pearls are unlike swine. They are all as normal as a normal person might be, yet their cheerfulness and happy demeanor—with the possible exception of Mrs. Heartbreak who is hopeful about the presence of space aliens—has not lead them to believe in claptrap on either end of the clap trap meter. None could be mistaken for, as an example, a transcendentalist.

Unitarians are certainly Pro Transcendentalism.

For a few days after a lecture on Ralph Waldo Emerson at the Universalist Church last summer there had been a run on books by the Transcendentalists, chiefly Emerson but also Henry David Thoreau, Emily Dickinson, Nathaniel Hawthorn et al. I believe I mentioned that John had written a hot letter to the editor about it all.

With the exception of Hawthorne, John enjoyed these writers less and less over time. It is probable that John's initial infatuation with them had to do with the time and place of his exposure to them. That infatuation was grounded in the 1960s—of course—and the transcendental urgency to "go beyond the senses," and its emphasis on individuality and an intuitive spirituality had a kind of rock and roll state of mind about it that was a lot of fun. It didn't hurt that everybody was at least one toke over the line.

Alrighty then. This is the stuff that goes through John's head at all hours of the day and night. No wonder Mrs. Heartbreak can get him to do no work. And no wonder people blow past John without a glance. After all, a man who spends his time analyzing the happiness of Unitarians and the basis of their cheerfulness is probably incapable of any real work and is maybe even good for nothing. Who knows?

What I know is that John's musings about Unitarians has failed to advance our plot one bit. How can Unitarians and the causes of their amiability contribute dramatic tension to this book? Could it be that a few of these happy people, ascribing to an old Sioux Ghost belief, will place their bodies between Clara/Jane's gun and the Iowans that John is now thinking about dispatching? Is it another plot line?

All the gals leave the shop in a flock. John sips RDC. Mrs. Heartbreak totals the day's take. That doesn't take long. Only writers make less from books than booksellers.

Chapter 5:

A lot happens in this chapter. But I don't think any of it is important.

It is Saturday morning on the Square. John looks through his window and surveys his fellow man. I am enjoying myself too, watching John watch the Square, and while that may seem like a dull occupation to you, well; I am a simple person with simple desires and simple satisfactions.

Neither John nor Mrs. Heartbreak is aware that they are characters in a book—yet. That will come about, by and by. Say in two or maybe three chapters from now. Clara Rinker the serial killer, now Jane Smith the mousey consumer of small electronics from Wilson's Television and Appliance, is used to being a character in a book, and she knows she is in this one. We are keeping an eye on each other.

John is not in the least bit concerned that Clara Rinker has suddenly appeared in Berryville, Arkansas, even though her entire prior existence has been fictional. He has long since erased the line between fact and fiction, between what is seen and unseen, and between what is real and unreal.

For example: John, watching through his window, sees Gordon Hale go into the Carroll County Historical Society, right this minute. Gordon Hale is real, and now he is a character in a book.

A lot happens in this chapter. But I don't think any of it is important.

There goes Brent Updegraff and Mark Gifford and Dickie Clark. See: being in a book and out of a book is not so strange.

That Clara Rinker should appear in Berryville strikes John as much less strange then Bill Clinton or Ava Gardner appearing in Berryville—which they are reported to have done. For him, Clara Rinker and Bill Clinton and Ava Gardener are just characters in a book: they have lives and histories independent of whether or not John has seen them, and John knows that Clinton and Ava Gardener are mostly fictions of their own devising. Simply because Clara Rinker slash Jane Smith has Authorial Assistance in the fiction that she is, hardly seems to matter.

No Iowans are in evidence this sunny AM. That makes John feel cheery. Clara slash Jane must have completed all her shopping yesterday; she is not observed. That causes John to wonder what she is up to. Is she home, cleaning a sniper rifle? Dr. Jim Young is on vacation in Amsterdam so he is not seen (although he was seen in the past and will be seen in the future, maybe even tomorrow … or yesterday). John hopes Jim will send him a postcard with a salacious photo decorating the front.

He sees that the Berryville Farmers' Market is bustling in a neighborly way for so commercial an enterprise. The artist Christy Lee, who you have not yet met, has a sack of cucumbers under her arm. We will talk more about her presently. Dr. Fred Mayer, the famous Musician Farmer, is responsible for the sack, and the cucumbers. It appears to John, as he levels his gaze and squints through the glass brightly, that both are satisfied with the exchange. More about Fred later as well.

John awakens each morning between four and five thirty. He wishes he could sleep longer, but his bones and sinews keep an earlier clock than his desires allow. John reads during these untimely morning hours. Sometimes he reads a novel and sometimes he reads the Bible.

John enjoys the Old Testament. It fits well with Chaos Theory and he admires its general air of complaint and the all too human adventures of its kings, prophets, and tribal leaders. And he gets plenty enough New Testament stuff on Sundays during church.

There, the sermons are mostly about the love that Christ has for us, and encouragements to love one another. John is grateful for the presence of Christ in his life—it is his need to express his thankfulness to God that makes him a Christian—but loving his neighbors often feels like going to work on a day when he doesn't feel so hot. It would be a lot more fun to occasionally smite these bozos with the jawbone of an ass. The Old Testament, as you probably know, is full of such smiting.

Au contraire, Mrs. Heartbreak and I are happy New Testament people, with no desire to smite anyone. She and I have had many conversations about John's narrow and entirely perverse smiting streak. If Mrs. Heartbreak knew about John's Iowan fixation she would be sorely vexed, and no doubt would call on John and Judy Turner (the Heartbreak's pastors) to counsel him. If she knew what John knew about Clara slash Jane and his musings about her various productively violent uses, Mrs. Heartbreak would faint dead away.

By the way, the paragraphs on top of this one are written at the 8.8 grade level. Doing okay? Let me know. Oh, and by the way again, so far I have achieved a 2% passive sentence score in this Chapter, which is pretty good, literature wise. Huzzah for me!

But: back to John and Saturday morning.

John spies Paul Andresen, Pastor of Berryville's First Presbyterian Church, out on the Square. He is coming toward the shop. John is always glad to see Paul. He is a genial man and seems infused with a fine, loving, and gentle Christian spirit, a much advertised but usually rare artifact.

John and Paul nod at one another, exchange jokes about Carroll County's politicians, and then each goes about his business: John to glumly staring out the window at the glumly dribbling fountains on the Town Square, and Pastor Andresen to rifle through new arrivals of a religious nature. Since Paul brought politics up, John ponders politics for a while and invents—on the spot—a silly game linking political persons to the title of a Beatles' tune.

Yes, it is silly, but you should try it.

For example, John's choice for Dick Cheney is "Happiness is a Warm Gun." And how about "Why Don't We Do it in the Road?" for Bill Clinton or, better still, "Norwegian Wood"—a beautiful, lovely song utterly devoid of content or meaning. I guess any song

A lot happens in this chapter. But I don't think any of it is important.

written by Ringo Star works for former President George W. Bush. John and I both hope he has a long and uneventful retirement. After all, what mischief can he do as an old retired fart on his ranch in Crawford, Texas?

Anyway, you can play the game with book titles too. John comes up with two titles for the Eureka Springs City Council: John Kennedy Toole's wonderful *A Confederacy of Dunces* and William Golding's *Lord of the Flies*. *Dunces* is about what it says; *Flies* is about a group of adolescent boys stranded on a desert island who revert to savagery. One book is funny, the other is not funny.

If you live in Berryville and otherwise outside the city limits of Eureka Springs, you'd opt for the funny one since the Eureka Springs City Council is always good for a laugh. Ha ha, Ha ha. Of course, if you live inside Eureka Springs' city limits (Boo hoo. Boo hoo). you might opt for the not funny book—but bless their hearts, you know the ES City Council tries hard. They certainly put in the time.

John is not sure that Carroll County government tries very hard, or even if they put in the time. It seems like the only things they care about, or take responsibility for, are roads and jails, even though they take all of our property taxes. The title that comes to John's mind for these elected county officials is Gibbon's *Decline and Fall of the Roman Empire.* He has been reading it lately and noted that the Roman decline was known for the fine roads and finer jails it built while everything else kind of went to heck.

Which is probably why the Community Building on the Town Square functions part time as a male brothel, and the rest of the time as a Chinese style toilet. The County is supposed to maintain this property but, of course, does not. These officials are too busy building Palaces of Justice from whence to rule the People, or jails in which to store them.

Not that the city of Berryville seems to care much about ordinance violations, or dirty public toilets. If cleanliness is next to Godliness, then Berryville is certainly Sodom and Gomorra— one of the stories in the Bible that John enjoys most. You can't buy a drink in Berryville (which is aces with me and so-so with John), but if you want to raise chickens on Bobo Avenue, or stockpile crankcases and dead refrigerators any dang place you want, then Berryville is the town for you.

This is really quite surprising since Berryville has, block for block, as much history and as many historic buildings as does Eureka Springs. John supposes that the most apt title for Berryville is G.B. Shaw's *Pygmalion:* it would be quite a lady if it cleaned up a tad.

Boy. That was interesting.

Pastor Paul takes a copy of Cahill's *How the Irish Saved Civilization* over to Mrs. Heartbreak, who rings it up. They exchange pleasantries while John silently opines about the utter horse apples of such a book and the ideas it must contain. If any one people embody Chaos Theory it is certainly the Irish.

On the other hand, Pastors John and Judy Turner favorably mentioned the book. John supposes that he should read it since Pastoral Pashas among the Disciples of Christ and the Presbyterians have come together around it. Christian unity and agreement is so rare that it ought to be encouraged. John makes a note to buy more copies.

Pastor Paul begins to exit the shop with his book safely tucked under his arm.

"Say, Paul," John says, interrupting the Good Pastor. "Have you noticed the fountains on the Town Square lately?"

Pastor Andresen looks bewildered. "No. Why would I?"

"No reason," John nods, says. "I was just wondering."

What John really is wondering is if anyone noticed the fountains on the Town Square. People whizzing by on Highway 62 certainly didn't notice them. And why should they when town folk sitting on the very rim of a fountain day after day couldn't tell you ten minutes later how it looked?

These fountains had been around so long, and in such a demoralized state for just about as long, that they had become a part of Berryville's wallpaper, like that "oil" painting your Aunt Thelma bought from Sears in 1968 and hung over her couch. It is a picture of ... right. You haven't a clue do you?

John had stopped being curious a long time ago about why Berryville's City Council did nothing to change the decrepitude and contemptible state of its fountains. After all, these birds and the ones before them had allowed the "Grandview" Hotel to hover over the Town Square like an open wound for more than 25 years without requiring its owner to at least minimally maintain it. Ignoring the fountains and the Community Building is easy compared to ignoring the Grandview.

John rages silently, "What's the matter with these people?"

As you can see, John is a bear about maintenance. He is a bear about politicians and their lust for supervision. He is such a bear that he has begun to think of yet another job for Clara slash Jane. He just hates the fact that his town walks around with a dirty neck. Maybe Clara slash Jane can give it a good scrubbing? *Ha ha. Ha ha.*

Last night over dinner John told Mrs. Heartbreak about how Unitarians puzzled him, and his thoughts on the matter. He did not share his opinions about Iowans, and he did not tell her about the rather chilling little wave that Clara slash Jane tossed his way when she came out of Wilson's. It was apparent to John that Mrs. Heartbreak was only half listening—she was busy preparing one of her gourmet dinners—but then, only about half of what John said made any sense, so he didn't really mind. He just hoped that she was picking up on the half sensible thread of his monologue.

Truth be known, half of what came out of Mrs. Heartbreak's mouth is as sensible as a schizophrenic skiing on steep banks of freshly fallen LSD, but she does not know this and would disbelieve John if he pointed it out to her.

He had attempted to point out her (rather frequent) inconsistencies of logic early in their marriage, but gave up after five or six years when it finally dawned on him that she was hopelessly, optimistically, a captive of Social Order Theory and constitutionally unable to comprehend the gibberish that such captivity allows. Thus, and for the balance of their now long marriage, John simply nods and agrees with whatever Mrs. Heartbreak says.

Mrs. Heartbreak assumes that the source of John's geniality is his poor hearing: she assumed and assumes that John is as deaf as a post. John's ability to hear is actually good enough to participate in the affairs of the world, if he pays attention. But he is a poor listener and apt to wool gather at crucial moments in just about any conversation, especially in meetings at banks, insurance companies, or at his broker's office, where everyone pretends he has choices, or opinions that matter.

John has gathered quite a lot of wool this morning. Yet, and I'm sure you'll agree, he has advanced our plot a smidgen. In this chapter—Chapter 5, right?—John has touched on:

1. Social Order Theory versus Chaos Theory
2. Clara Ricker AKA Jane Smith
3. The Fountains on the Town Square
4. Iowans
5. Unitarians

Five for five. Not bad. You see, I am paying attention to business. Meanwhile, Mrs. Heartbreak rings up another sale. Thank goodness! There will be jam on tonight's bread.

Chapter 6:

Briefly, a Bit about Time

John is in the seventh and last decade of his life. He hopes it will be a full decade, despite the fact that he hasn't been playing with a full deck for quite a while. What will he do with his decade? John is staring out the window, trying to decide.

John has found out that only very serious people or very silly people have lived right, or have really enjoyed living. He feels sad that it has taken him so long to find this out—sixty years. My goodness. What a long time.

John's problem has been—and almost everyone's problem is—not being serious enough, or silly enough, about art and music, novels and physics and mathematics, work or play, God or ... it is a long, long list.

Instead, John has been an observer of the long, long arching list of things that he could be serious or silly about; he has never fallen passionately enough in love with his own talent to be serious or silly about it. Instead again, he saw each day as having enough trouble of its own: he only made hay while the sun shone; he did not know that yesterday and today and tomorrow are all the same day—at some point in time—no matter if it is raining, or if the sun is shining.

But that is changing now. John knows that he is winding down and, even though he is long term tired, that he'd better get on the stick, get serious or get silly, pretty quick.

It helps that John has figured time out, has figured out that he can E-Z into yesterday or tomorrow without leaving today: John knows that he can E-Z out of today in any direction he chooses; without breaking a sweat or getting excited; no matter the direction.

This is not an unusual phenomenon, and anyone in Berryville—anyone in the world—can do it, although it is easier for and more typical among older people. John does do it now—goes back and forth through yesterday and today and tomorrow (that would be time)—more consciously than do most other Berryvillians (he thinks).

The big difference between John and other Berryvillians, though, is that John has decided that there is no difference between yesterday and today and tomorrow. When John stands at the front of the shop and looks out the window what he sees is what he saw yesterday and what he will see tomorrow: Berryville, yesterday, today, and tomorrow. (Incidentally, that's the Berryville town motto.)

There are minor variations on the theme. Sometimes Mrs. Colleen Shogren is here today and she is gone tomorrow, unless she is here yesterday. Otherwise, she is at her home in Holiday Island, which is a suburb of the Wal-Mart Supercenter located about 10 miles from where John is standing just now. If you have questions about Mrs. Shogren—or any other person for that matter—about her being here and not being here we can solve it by having a spirited mind-body conversation.

But that would be boring.

Let me just say that John and Gottfried Leibniz agree that the mind and the body run parallel to one another, and only seem to influence one another. They function (mostly) in harmony, even though there are distinctions between what are mental and what are physical causes. By the way, this is how many people who believe in God think about the mind and the body, if they think about the mind, and the body, at all. Not too many people do though.

If you don't know who Leibniz is, don't worry about it. Don't worry about him (he is okay). Once upon a time he was a giant; now upon a time he is a footnote that describes him as an important, mistaken, thinker. His mistake was to think that God is the arbiter between mind and body. To what extent God arbitrates between (weaves in and out of) mind and body is another whole argument about free will. Apparently John Calvin figured that one out—but John isn't sure that he did. But who knows? After all, both Calvin and Leibniz were (are?) serious guys.

The reason I am nattering on about time is that John will go back and forth in time in some of the upcoming chapters. Some other people (most of them dead writers) will also go back and forth. The Holy Ghost will also appear, by and by, which may discomfort you a bit if you are unfamiliar with or disbelieve in appearances by the HG.

Not to worry: Leibniz described an active, arbitrating God, but he surely would have scoffed at the Actuality of the I AM engaged in arbitration, especially in so unpresupposing a place as Berryville, Arkansas. You are welcome to scoff; it is the nature of Big Thinkers.

John wants to be a Big Thinker, but he is stuck: he can't decide if he should be serious, or if he should be silly, and he only has ten years left (at the most) so he can't spend too much time choosing. Procrastination is the name of a town that no one ever leaves.

Because John is a Norwegian, he is inherently, characteristically, hopelessly serious. What this means, for example, is that he is constitutionally incapable of dancing the tango, that sublime and silliest of all dances. John, as a matter of fact, cannot dance at all, unless he is wearing wooden shoes and then thumps them with feigned enthusiasm on a sheet of plywood. (That is how Norwegians dance: they are a people so lacking in rhythm that it was abandoned as a method of birth control in Norway long before other nations pitched it over board.)

You would think that this means John ought to opt for seriousness, but his innate seriousness, sadly, does not mean that John is smart. He lacks and knows he lacks the brain power to be a serious thinker; John won't be asked to plan our next lunar landing … Mrs. Heartbreak won't even ask John to plan a trip to the post office.

Serious? Or silly?

Let's read the rest of this book and find out.

Chapter 7:

Hooking Up with Clara Jane and Etc.

I am about to advance the John slash Clara Jane dialectic, but first let us consider the Unitarians (again). This morning, John read in the Carroll County News that the Unitarian Universalist Church in Eureka Springs was about to commence a series of lectures on "Life After Death" with the probable—no, undoubted—conclusion of "one never knows, do one."

For sundry reasons the Unitarians always put John in mind of Dr. Jim Young. John does not know if Dr. Young is a Unitarian or not, but as the second nicest man in the universe, Dr. Young is as charming and well behaved as any of the Unitarians John enjoys knowing. Certainly, Dr. Young finds a receptive audience among the Unitarians for the many metaphysical books that he writes and publishes.

The whole notion of metaphysics makes Mrs. Heartbreak uncomfortable. She shares with John the underlying bias that most of what passes for metaphysical thought in this the early 21st century is claptrap and the past time of late-middle-aged hobbyists and angry divorcees. But unlike Mrs. Heartbreak, John gets "sucked in" when conversations or arguments take a metaphysical bent and happily spends hours confabbing with his fellow wizards when he ought to be shelving books or washing his Really Dreadful Coffee (RDC) coffee cups. When this happens the veins in Mrs. Heartbreak's neck throb and stand out.

You can skip the next three paragraphs: they are all gibberish.

Loosely defined (well, in the way one defines a "loose" woman. In some cases a loose woman is immoral; in other cases, merely but wonderfully generous. You decide.), metaphysics is a theory about how the universe is fundamentally organized. Metaphysics is supposed to answer the question, "What is the nature of reality?" It doesn't, of course, because metaphysics must be subdivided into ontology about the theory of being itself, and various cosmologies about the origins and structures of the universe. It's a mess trying to keep it all straight.

For John, the organization of the universe begins with God, and he has stopped thinking about what is the organizing principle for God Himself (or, as some of the more tiresome metaphysicians might say, "Herself). Simply put, John understands that God is the Essential Author of a process or series of actions involving static objects, particles, energy, and ideas that organize creation in ways that are not simply deterministic but involve some level of freedom. Teilhard de Chardin and Whitehead nattered on about this at some length and Kant and Schopenhauer nattered quite a lot more, but in a perversely complicated manner.

These birds led the way to the spontaneous emergence of even more complex organizational flowcharts involving evolutionary theory: from space-time and elementary particles to atoms, particles, molecules, crystals, DNA, cells, plants, animals, humans, and to human society, culture and, at the top of the heap, Sophia Loren.

Anyhoo, John is always willing to talk about these matters, especially to Dr. Young, but not before an initial feeling of impatience—here we go again—founders in an infinite well of enthusiasm for the sheer manic fun of such conversations. Mrs. Heartbreak wants to stick her fingers down her throat at the prospect. And, she believes that Dr. Young encourages such misbehavior in John.

Dr. Young may or may not be writing a book that may or may not be entitled "Jim Young talks to the Devil." If he is, or has, I will seek permission to excerpt some of it for this book

More about this later.

But for now, back to Clara Jane:

John stops shelving books and walks out the front door. Mrs. Heartbreak is aware that someone is either coming or going (it is John going) because the door is a famous squeaker. But her back is toward the door and she hasn't turned around yet. When she does she will smile broadly and say, "Welcome to Heartbreak's! May I help you?"

Mrs. Heartbreak has a beautiful smile and if she casts one in your direction it will make you feel good. I feel good when she smiles at me, and I know that John enjoys the occasional smile that comes his way. Not that it is happening at the moment. Mrs. Heartbreak has turned around to greet an entrant and what she sees instead is that John has left the building. And without as much as an adios or word of explanation. She hates it when she doesn't know where John is, or where John is going. Mrs. Heartbreak likes to know what's what, one hundred percent of the time. She is not smiling. She now has a grim expression on her otherwise pretty face.

When John gets back (rest assured, he will get back) she will quiz him. With some heat. If she knew that he was going out to find Clara Jane she would be puzzled. If she knew that Clara Jane was Clara Rinker the infamous serial killer she would be very worried. If she knew that John was going to speak to Clara Jane about the matter of Iowans, she would be appalled.

You, on the other hand—if you are still here ... you are still here, aren't you?—are probably delighted that something is about to happen. What should it be? Help me out:

John and Clara Jane meet and cook up a plan to snipe Iowans when they cross the Missouri-Arkansas State line?

John begins to dimly recognize that he is stepping on and off the lines of a parallel Universe called Real Life and the Novel?

Mrs. Heartbreak actually does know what is going on and has called the medics who will take John away and lock him in the local bin?

Dr. Jim Young intercepts John on his way to Clara Jane's and they have a long and discursive conversation about the mind-body problem. John never gets to Clara Jane's?

Which one do you pick?

Chapter 8:

I Lose Control

John shambles down Church Street on his way to Clara Jane Smith's house. John does not walk: he is a bit sloth-like, a bit koala bear in his engagement of pedestrianism. He operates similarly in his engagements with pre-determination, but that's another story. For the moment, let us keep focused on getting down the Church Street and into Clara Jane's yard.

John passes three vacant storefronts. They are freshly painted because John was sick of looking at them peeling away onto the sidewalk and got up one morning and painted them. Trace Ellen Kelly, a fine, nice looking woman who operates a vintage toy store called Childhood Memories, helped him.

John had thought about soliciting Mrs. Kelly's views on her running for Mayor, but could not come up with a way to introduce the idea. Consequently, he gave up the notion, but he did change a flat tire for her. No doubt she appreciated the labor more than lame, political requests.

John is another hundred feet closer to Clara Jane than he was when he passed the freshly painted but vacant storefronts. I mention this to keep you keyed to the fact that John, and this book, is progressing toward a dramatic moment, thereby and deftly hooking you in and causing within you a compelling desire to read on.

Yet, (yes, yet again!), we also know that John cannot pass by abandoned, distressed property without commenting on 1) the barefaced criminal audacity of property owners who don't maintain their property, and 2) the blind, contemptible, and wholly irresponsible neglect of Berryville by its governing masters.

How can these people let their town appear to the outside world—a world occupied by contempt-filled Yankees and retired Iowans with burrs of self-satisfaction tucked up their butts—in such disarray?

Okay, fine. Never mind.

John turns the corner at Pritchard Street and walks past his house and down a slow incline toward Clara Jane's home. Needless to say, John's house and yard are as neat as pins in a cushion. Juan Guzman and Mary Margaret, neighbors who live to the right and left of John, keep similarly tidy places. On the whole, Pritchard Street has spruced up a bit lately, a fact that John takes note of as he shambles along. A well-known Metaphysician has made noises about moving in across the street. Metaphysicians are not known for keeping tidy yards, the thought of said possibility causing John to frown. But there is Clara Jane, within line of sight. John has bigger fish to fry now than the mere worry of lawns neglected by semi-skilled intellectual neighbors.

Clara knows that John is coming to see her. She knew John had recognized her the first time their eyes met, she in the checkout line at Wal-Mart and John, in conversation with Catherine Henry near the exit door, he then seemingly willed to look up and away from a serious point Catherine was making about Joseph Campbell's explorations into the mythological dimensions of fairy tales, legends, and symbols, and into Clara Jane's stone cold blue eyes. Two ships, not passing in the night but colliding in recollection of a bond not comfortable but strong and enduring, that between character and reader.

Clara Jane leans on a rake—she is responsibly cleaning leaves from her yard—and smiles at John as he stops before her.

"Just look at the paragraph two up from this one," she says derisively. "'Two ships not passing in the night … ' What rubbish! That fool friend of yours has written a bunch of sentences at the 12th grade level on the Flesch-Kincaid scale and with a reading ease score of 40.4. Nobody is going understand a word he's written about how we met."

John scratches his head. Head scratching, by the way, is the common, not to say ubiquitous activity authors—such as myself— use to signify confusion in the scratcher who, in this case, is John. John has no idea what Clara Jane has just said, or what she means by it.

"You're in for a treat, John," she continues. "I'm about to introduce you to the wonderful world of parallel universes—since your pal the Authorial I is too cowardly to do it himself."

"I don't think we've been formally introduced," John says, ignoring her Flesch-Kincaid (whatever that is!) and "Authorial I" comments. "We've just waved at each other 'across the crowded room' so to speak. But I've long admired your work," John finishes up, lamely.

"You mean John Sanford's work," Clara Jane retorts. "I haven't worked at all. Sanford's the one who does the heavy lifting. I just go where I'm told and do what I'm told ...

"Until I got to Berryville, that is," Clara Jane says. "Since I arrived in town I've done nothing but rake leaves and clean this dump up."

She gestures to the tidy little house and yard behind her. "I wish your friend had given me a more exciting life ... and a more exciting place to live it in."

"Pardon me?"

"You don't have a clue do you? I mean, that you're in a book."

John nods thoughtfully, looks smart, a typical activity among the dumber than a post variety of human kind. He nods some more. Then says ...

" ...what?"

"You're in a book John," Clara Jane explains impatiently. "The "Authorial I," apparently your best pal, is writing a book about us. And about Mrs. Heartbreak, I might add."

"Mrs. Heartbreak will certainly object to being in a book. I'm sure she'll think it is my fault."

"Mrs. Heartbreak is the least of your problems, John."

John sighs. "You don't know Mrs. Heartbreak, do you?"

"Not yet. But I will. I'll be going to church with her, and you, by and by."

"Church?"

"I know. Unlikely, isn't it? One minute I'm blowing heads off with cell phone bombs, and the next I'm in Berryville, Arkansas, raking leaves and going to church with Billy Bob Book Boy."

John is offended. He loves Berryville, and he will be buried in Berryville, though he is not from Berryville—as every graduate of Berryville High School reminds him—constantly.

"I may be a "book boy" as you so alliteratively point out," he says, "But I am no more a "Billy Bob" than you are the governor of Alaska."

Clara Jane shrugs. "I can be the governor of Alaska," she says. "It makes no difference to me. I can be Margaret Thatcher if you want. Up to a few days ago my life was designed by John Sanford. Now it's being designed—written—by the Authorial I. Who is, incidentally, hiding over by that tree. He's the Manager of the Parallel Universe you have entered. "

Clara Jane points at a small pin oak about 15 feet away. I am, not incidentally, standing behind it: I have followed John in order to observe first hand his meeting with Clara Jane. John looks in my direction and scowls, looks more perplexed.

"He can make me into a chicken nugget if he wants too," Clara Jane continues. "I have very little control in the matter, or over the subject matter. That is, strictly speaking, the nature of being a character in a book."

"That's an awfully Calvinist point of view," John says.

"I don't know Calvin, but you better look to yourself. How do you like being in a book?"

"I still don't know what you're talking about."

She sighs. John may not be a Billy Bob Book Boy, but obviously, he hasn't had his lights switched on in a long time. "Tell me this," she begins. "What do you know about me?"

"I know that you are a serial killer," he says. "However, you seem to focus on Bad Apples whom no one will miss, once you have "offed" them, so to speak. Consequently, I don't think you are much of a danger to ordinary citizenry. And you appear to have good yard habits."

"And ...," she prompts ...

"...and ... up until now ... you're right ... I've only known you as a character in John Sanford's books."

"That's right, John. I'm a book character, a literary device written to create some suspense and excitement in the dull lives of middle class twits such as you. You may also recall that Sanford killed me off in his last book, *Mortal Prey*, so I don't even exist as a literary device any more. Or, at least, I won't in future books.

"Aren't you curious about how I happen to be in Berryville?"

John hadn't given it a thought, actually. He shook his head. "No, I haven't thought about it. Mrs. Heartbreak will tell you that I mostly exist in books myself—I read a bit, you see—so I admittedly draw less solid lines between what people say is real and what is and isn't real. Take the Town Square fountains, for example. The ..."

"No, no!" Clara Jane says firmly. "Don't go there! The fountains are real, whether people see them or not, and whether or not they appear in a book. But they are really booooooorrringgg! Quit talking about them. No one cares!"

"The fountains are in this book—which you say is being written, and where we both appear," John protests. "And yet, there"—he points to a car passing by—"goes Betty Rotramel. Betty is as real as a person can get. She is not a character in a book. So what is she doing in a book?

"You might ask yourself the same questions," John continues. "For example, isn't it possible that you are not in a book? That you really are in Berryville, Arkansas?"

No, it hadn't occurred to her. "I have been experiencing ... things ... feeling feelings ... talking with people who are not in the book ...

"...and I've been raking this yard ... which I resent, by the way."

"Maintenance of property is a sign of functional government and love of culture."

"If you're responsible for turning me into day labor," she says, "I hope I get the chance to kill you. Is that a potential plot line?"

"Let's not get off on the wrong foot, Clara," John says. "I'm no more responsible for what "my pal" writes—if he is writing--or for what he says, than I am for you being here in Berryville."

Clara laughs.

"John, you're not responsible for me at all! I'm not even sure I'm here! Maybe I'm not in Berryville, and I'm not standing in my yard raking leaves. Mrs. Heartbreak is back at the store shelving your books while you're out stalking an imaginary person. For which you ought to be ashamed."

"I am ashamed of myself," John said. "But not for reasons that will be disclosed in this so-called book.

"Besides," he continues, "I am NOT stalking you. I have walked down the street where I live—which I have every right to do—to make you a friendly offer I think you'll find interesting."

"John, I ain't going to kill no Iowans for you and no politicians neither. I kill for money, as well you know from reading Mr. Sanford's accounts of my life, and you have no money whatsoever."

For a reason to be disclosed later (maybe not), Clara Jane has begun to talk in a regional accent. John ignores this unexpected linguistic turn of events, but his eyes pop open at the mention of killing Iowans.

"Don't you go lookin' 'sprized on me," Clara Jane intones. "I know what is in yer black heart 'for you even to think it."

"Reading my mind, heh? I feel like I'm in Roswell, New Mexico."

"Nope, yer in Berryville."

John turns away from Clara and points in my direction. I am standing behind a large pin oak—the one responsible for all the leaves in Clara Jane's yard—taking note of these events. John is certainly in for a surprise, isn't he?

"You!" John shouts at me. "You've got a lot of explaining to do. What's with this "Authorial I" business?"

I smile—sheepishly. (By the way, what does that mean? How does a sheep smile? If you wrote "The sheep smiled" would anyone have a clue what that might look like? They'd think you were crazy, right?) (Okay. Sorry.) I shrug and look innocent.

"Let me test your theory," John says to Clara Jane. "How about if I give you fifty thousand dollars to banish Iowans from Berryville? Will fifty Gs do it?"

Clara Jane nods slowly. She smiles: work she understands for money she wants. Perhaps this will get her out of the leafy yard and back on the road to Hot Springs.

John looks over his shoulder at the pin oak. "Fifty thousand dollars!' he shouts at me. "Hand it over."

I no more have fifty thousand dollars than Hillary Rodham Clinton has charity in her heart or Sarah Palin has brains in her head. But, simply for the sake of moving the story along, let's pretend that I do. With a show of reluctance I come out from behind the pin oak and dig into an old satchel. I pull out a big wad of green and hand it over.

John is stunned. He knows I have no money, yet here I am, handing over a stack of Franklins as thick as one of Mrs. Heartbreak's gourmet pot roasts.

"You having money is an entirely fictional enterprise," he says in a quiet voice.

"Gosh. I probably am in a novel. Mrs. Heartbreak is in for a nasty surprise."

John hands the money over to Clara Jane, who takes it greedily.

"Fine," she says. "That 'ill git me started."

She pauses and looks at John and me. "But first, a ree-quest. How 'bout I stop talkin' like a dang hillbilly and start soundin' as educated as you two fellers?"

John turns and looks at me. He shrugs, making a face.

"How about it?" he says. "I hate reading dialect and, frankly, you're really lousy at writing it."

What do you think?

As the author of this mess it is certainly within my power to have Clara Jane sound like James Earl Jones, or to speak in Old Norse, for that matter. But, what of the ethical dilemma? After all, Clara Jane Smith is really Clara Rinker, a character belonging wholly and entirely to John Sanford nee Camp. Will Sanford allow such an infraction? Or, without regard to what Sanford allows or disallows, does changing how Clara Jane speaks intrinsically change who she is?

"Listen, Bozo," Clara says, stabbing me—the Authorial I—in the chest with a thin but steely finger.

"Try and get with the facts of this fandango. I am not real. John is not real. No one is reading your dang book just because you happen to be writing it. Therefore, "your" readers are not real. We are all simply figments of your imagination. Only Mrs. Heartbreak is real, but only because you have stolen the identity of a person much finer than yourself for such purposes as necessary to put John and me into some sort of social context."

I notice that Clara Jane no longer sounds like an Appalachian American. She sounds, instead, like James Earl Jones, only like James Earl Jones would if he was a short white woman of about forty years of age. Oh well.

I protest. "There are lots of real folks in this book. Gail DeWeese, for example. I also mentioned Betty Rotramel, Fred Mayer, Linda Jones, and Judy Turner and her husband John. They are all real. There is a LOT about this book that is real."

"Look at fountains on the Public Square," I say. I'm afraid that I am speaking loudly.

"Case in point," Clara Jane says. "The fountains on the Town Square can't be real. No one sees them."

"Besides," she continues. "You have bigger problems."

I am annoyed at this woman, but John is nodding his head in agreement.

"You do have bigger problems," he says. "But those are of a personal nature, and are not related to this book … necessarily."

John turns toward Clara Jane, and asks, "Exactly what would be the "bigger" problems?"

"For starters," Clara Jane says, "There is no sex, violence, or strong language allowed in this book.

"How then," she continues, "will it be possible for me to murder a bunch of Iowans, or local politicians? I suppose there could be some kind of metaphysical solution … but …" her voice trails off. She knows how boring that would be. Truth be told, Clara Jane was a lot happier in John Sanford's book.

Hmmm.

"I suppose," Clara Jane says pensively, "that John and I could engineer a solution—perhaps a chemical or pharmaceutical solution—that would turn Iowans into decent, more open minded people, and your local political masters into better problem solvers? Then you can advance the story a bit (good luck!) without resorting to SVSL. What do you think?"

I think that things are spinning out of control. And I am entirely unhappy that Clara Jane has seized control of my book. How like a woman!

"Decent, open minded Iowans?" I sneer. "Problem solving politicians?" I bark. "No thank you, my dear. This book is literature! Not fantasy!"

Chapter 9:

How About *Almost* Killing Them?

Clara Jane and John watched as I hump back up Pritchard Street, and away from the not small (infinite) well of annoyance from which they now seem to spring. When I reach the corner of Pritchard and Church Streets I look down and see John and Clara Jane still in conversation. I wonder what they are talking about, and I am filled with a bit of apprehension about the direction of this book: Clara Jane seems to have her own ideas and john is unreliable enough to come up with almost anything.

Mr. David Bell, the CEO of Braswell Printing, drives past on his motorcycle and waves in a friendly way. David is the music director at the First Christian Church in Berryville, and John and Mrs. Heartbreak enjoy the occasional solo from Brother Bell.

Mr. Bell appears to be singing now, a pleasant thing after my contretemps with Ms. Kill You Now-Kill You Later and the Infamous Mass Reader, John Heartbreak. But I feel more relaxed: it is enjoyable to hear a tune now and then from a cheerful, handsome man on motorcycle back, especially as he goes about his appointed and no doubt important rounds. I'm sure I don't need to worry about John, or Clara Jane.

"I have fifty thousand dollars of your money in my pocket," Clara Jane is saying. "But I don't see the Authorial I approving a use for it. Got any ideas?"

"I was intrigued by your suggestion of a pharmaceutical solution," said John, obligingly.

"It was a reach," Clara Jane replied. "Guns, knives, and exploding cell phones are more in my line of business. Though, now that I think of it, poisoning fits into the acceptable range of options available to the competent serial killer.

"I could almost kill some Iowans. Make 'em sick as dogs, so to speak, and send them back to Davenport in a big hurry. That, at least would get them out of your hair."

John shrugged, considering. "I kind of like the idea," John says. "God knows they have made me sick enough over the years. We'd have to get You Know Who to go along with it, though."

"I don't like your chances much," she said. "By all appearances the Authorial I is only a semi-skilled intellectual. They tend as a lot to be pretty stiff necked, and sure of themselves."

(Semi-skilled? Geeze.)

"Well, let me work on it," says John. "Why don't we get together a bit later? Maybe I'll have some progress to report."

John turns to walk away, then pauses and turns back. "How would you like to go to church with Mrs. Heartbreak and me on Sunday? I'm sure you'd enjoy yourself," he continues, hopefully.

"And since it is 'already written' so to speak, we might as well find you a church home, sooner than later."

"You're kidding, right?" she says. "I'll be glad to bump someone off for you, but I'm not exactly the church home type.

"To tell you the truth—all though I don't know why I should start now— I wouldn't even consider this church biz, no matter what "is writ", except that I had a weird encounter with some kind of thing when I was driving through Blue Eye."

"Thing?"

"Yeah. It was like a ..." Clara Jane pauses, uncertain whether to go on or not. "It was a voice that kind of yelled at me."

"What did it yell?"

"I was listening to George Jones on the radio when I drove through Blue Eye and I started thinking what a god forsaken place it is. Then a voice yelled, "God does not forsake towns! People forsake towns! It scared the pants off me.

"At first, I thought what I heard came out of the radio, but the voice didn't sound at all like George Jones. I mean, George has such a distinctive, lovely, voice."

"Yes, he does." For John, the hearing of George Jones necessitates a hurried vomit bag search, followed by water and two aspirin. "He has a very distinctive voice."

"Then, I thought, maybe Jim Bakker—Tammie Faye's Ex, you know?—is bombarding car radios with subliminal messages when they go through Blue Eye. I saw a sign advertising his new Christian Community, which is located there. 'Buy Here Pay Here' the sign said.

"But the voice wasn't like Bakker's voice either. It wasn't whiny, and it wasn't trying to sell anything. So, it wasn't Jimmy either, was it?"

"Doubtful. What did the voice sound like?"

"Like the wind."

The wind does not sound like anything, and John knows precisely how it sounds. Story follows … but for now:

"What you're reporting is not an unheard of phenomenon. Not common, but certainly not unheard of. Are you using drugs, or under the care of a psychiatrist?"

"For crying out loud," Clara Jane says, flatly. "I think I'm offended. If you've read Sanford you know I'm straight. And you know that I'm not seeing a shrink."

"Well, it is a fair question. When people start hearing voices its worth checking out their consumption of magic mushrooms."

"It gets a bit weirder," she confesses. "By the time I got out of Blue Eye—it takes what, two minutes?—I had already blown off the "Voice" and forgotten about it. But when I got to Berryville …"

"Yes?"

" …when I got to Berryville, the voice wind whatever, came back and told me to stop, rent a house on Pritchard Street, and look you up. That's why I knew who you were when we saw each other at Wal-Mart.

"This voice thingy is the reason I'm willing to consider your invitation to church, and why I've decided to let the Authorial I write that I've gone to church—which is totally out of character and the last thing anyone who's read about me would expect me to do.

"By the way," she continued. "Doesn't all that typing and waiting drive you nuts? Sanford was just relentless, and your pal here doesn't seem to be any better. I mean, there I would be, holding a gun to somebody's head and Sanford would stop and answer the telephone, or go out for a sandwich. And there I would be, waiting, to get on with it."

"I'm not aware of typing or waiting," John says. "I only wait for Mrs. Heartbreak, or for myself to catch up with myself."

"Can't you hear that god-awful typing sound?"

"Nope. But then, I believe that I'm real. I don't think somebody is in the background, typing out my life as I act it out. And I'm still not sure about this 'being in a book' business.

"Although," he says, pausing, "It is fairly remarkable that you, up to now only an imaginary figment of literature, happen to be in Berryville, Arkansas, living in a house on Pritchard Street.

It isn't something that happens every day."

(Maybe. Maybe not.)

"Anyway, if you come to church with me, maybe we can sort it all out. Lots of people there hear voices all the time and, as far as I know, they don't habitually abuse drugs or spend time and money on psychiatrists."

"Let me get back to you."

"Okee doakee," John replies. "In the mean time, I'm going to consult G.K. Chesterton about you. His character, Father Brown, has good luck with murderers of all types, and he too—actually, both Chesterton and Father Brown—heard voices all the time."

Chapter 10:

The Holy Spirit, Commentary on Church as Night Club, and a Dreadful Funk

The Heartbreak's have gotten through the week, and it is Sunday:

When John was a boy one of the priests who served in his parish for a short while was a schizophrenic. The priest also had a drinking problem. Consequently, parishioners never knew what to expect at Sunday services. It always depended on whether the priest had taken his medications or not, was or was not hung over, and so on.

John came to understand and accept—although much after the fact—that his fellow congregates had decided that its main corporate purpose was to pray for the priest. The irony or the paradox of the laity gathering expressively for the purpose of helping to keep their minister afloat was not lost on John. And, in fact, but of course much later, it made him rather glad that he was a Roman Catholic. It seemed like a decent thing to do then, and especially now.

It had been many years since John had been a practicing Roman Catholic, and Mrs. Heartbreak had been nothing but a pagan for nearly all of her life. Thus, when they decided to join the First Christian Church of Berryville it had been a momentous decision and something of a miracle. There were both glad of their decision.

Not that it was an unmixed blessing. Mrs. Heartbreak took to the First Christian Church like a duck to an old geezer tossing bread crust, but John often struggled with his Roman Catholic Culture. He recognized that you could take the boy out of the Church, but that it is a much tougher job to take the Church out of the boy. John managed his "cultural issues" with a fair amount of grace (he thought) but with a bit of acknowledged backsliding now and then

Similarly, while John had spent much of his professional life working with Protestant ministers and overseas with Protestant missionaries (John had not always been a bookseller) and liked them, he remained perplexed by a lot of Protestant clergy behavior. Catholic priests behaved, even the schizophrenics among them, with a certain amount of decorum. It is not always so with Protestants or Protestant clergy.

One of the things that most perplexed John about them was (is) their tendency to beat a dead horse, customarily employing the whip of exhortation or the ball bat of Sincerity. This happened most often during a "call to the altar" at Sunday Services. "Won't you love Jesus?" they might soulfully inquire, or, "Look in your heart for Jesus. If you feel Jesus within you, then do ... such and such a thing." In all cases the such and such a thing involves a walk down to the front of the church and much touching and hugging and whispering with a Pastor or trusted non-clerical designee. Add a cup of smaltz and you can see the holy ghost of Billy Sunday soft shoeing in the corner.

John is mostly a Matthew 6:6 guy, an Isaiah 26:20 guy: "But you, when you pray, enter into the closet and shut the door and pray in secret." That is what John does. John feels uncomfortably like a Dallas Texas Chamber of Commerce Membership Salesman when he is asked to pray in public. In a nutshell (why not use a cliché when it is fine and just?), altar calls and etc. give John the willies.

John is thinking about this now because the service he and Mrs. Heartbreak attended this morning clattered against his sensibilities like an umbrella stand tumbling down a staircase.

The service started off in the natural, relaxing, and peaceful way that John enjoys and finds comforting. That's one of the things he likes best about the First Christian Church: it is peaceful and John often feels a week's worth of stress recede and dissipate during its short services. John anticipated that good feeling today too, despite seeing in the front pews a contingent of hairy men in T-shirts printed with Sincere ball bat slogans exhorting YA'LL CHOOSE JESUS INSTEAD OF METHAMPHETAMINES and thus and consequently knowing that he was in for "testimony" today instead of one of John or Judy Turner's intelligent and helpful sermons.

John is okay with testimony (once in a while). And to the credit of the day's testifiers, they were a dignified and humble couple that dwelt on the saving grace of Christ's love and the redemption therein, and who provided little account of their sins or sinfulness, which John always finds boring and bathetic. There is no sin in the world that John is unaware of and he has met some of the world's fiercest sinners. So: he was thankful they skipped the usual litany of how bad I was and, say again, John was impressed by their dignified and graceful manner.

John was also of the mind that giving such testimony is good for the giver. The schizophrenic priest of his boyhood was not harmed by his, the priest's schizophrenic riffing, nor did the prayers of his congregants harm him. The priest was aware of his mental illness and would, from time to time, interrupt a particularly weird monologue on say, the characteristics of a fish dinner he had in 1956 in Belfast while visiting the Shrine of Saint Basil the Great with an abrupt "Oh. So sorry!" and a temporary winging back to the subject at hand which might be the turning of wine into blood and or etc.

At the end of services Father So and So would take his place by the door, shake hands and say, "Thanks so much! We got through another one, didn't we!" in acknowledgement that it was the power of prayer that had gotten them and especially him through another fine mass.

And so it was on this splendid Sunday morning—just a few hours ago—that the now doleful souls comprising the bulk of the First Christian Church's regular family sat scattered about prepared to hear whatever the testifier had in store for them. John prayed for the couple and prayed that they would be brief.

What tipped John over the edge then was not testimony but singing, and specifically the singing of Country Western ballads imbued with lyrics of a religious nature. These tunes were sung against (with) the help of VERY LOUD recorded background music, which, conjoined, failed to be either musical or religious.

John believed that under the very best of circumstances, and only under the influence of alcohol, that people should listen to Country Western music. He also believed that only Johnny Cash and Willie Nelson should be allowed to sing Country Western music, and then only when they were under the influence of alcohol or dope and then say, once a year on the anniversary of Robert E. Lee's Birthday, or better, only in Leap Years.

Mrs. Heartbreak thought John was a snob. She enjoyed an occasional C&W moment, a recidivist moment if you will, and resented John's cultural rigidity. "A dull world it would be, John, if it was all madrigals and Mozart."

John wouldn't buy the snob argument. The problem wasn't a world filled with Madrigals and Mozart but its out-and-out shortage of madrigals and Mozart. Just try and find a radio station in Berryville that didn't play Country and Western music night and day, day and night, try and find a café or restaurant that didn't serve Garth Brooks with the bacon. You'd have better luck finding the Lost Dutchman's Goldmine on Berryville's Public Square than you would have finding a madrigal. Was it necessary to dumb down the single hour a week where John relaxed and had the chance to feel peaceful?

"Dumb down?" I admonished. [NOTE: I apologize for inserting the Big "I" here, but I remind everyone that a writer—okay, a transcriber—is necessary to these proceedings. Let me also admit that I think John needs a clout on the noggin once in a while. What is this madrigal horse hockey about? Listen to madrigals for twenty minutes straight and you'll end up drooling into your farina. Pardon me while I administer said clout.

"John," I said, "You're not a Quaker. No one is required to sit and wait for the moment. The Disciples of Christ are not Papists and they are certainly not Calvinists. A little hoe down now and then might be good for the soul. Consider it, please," I said. "After all, there are other people in the pews besides WHY OH YOU. They might have enjoyed it and been edified as well."

"Butt out, Bud," John retorted. "If I want to go night clubbing I will. But I am hopeful of finding the eye of the storm on Sunday mornings, where I sit quietly and am glad that I am not in the storm. I am not there to be entertained. If I wanted song and dance, I'd stay home and watch Robert Schuller milk the sheep. He's good at it, and the Crystal Cathedral's production values are far higher than the First Christian Church's."

"This is an old argument, John." I said. "I think the Disciples broke away the mainstream so they could make a joyful noise, sing a few tunes, and tap their toes. I believe you're on the wrong side of the argument."

John's face turned red. When that happens I always feel a little surge of power and think about pole axing him with a stroke or heart attack. Ah, such is the majesty of the writer (sorry, transcriber). But I chose (for the moment) not to smite John out of consideration for Mrs. Heartbreak who, truth be known, would make a poor nurse.

He with the red face turned away and pulled a copy of *Elmer Gantry* off the shelf. "Let's talk to Sinclair Lewis," John said, opening the book. "He had quite a lot to say about small town churches."

"That old hack?" I exclaimed. "He was a notorious atheist."

"If you had married Dorothy Thompson you'd be an atheist too," John said. "By the way, "that old hack" won the Nobel Prize for literature."

"Nevertheless," I said. Never at a loss for words or a seasoned riposte am I.

John looked into the tired and barely intact copy of *Elmer Gantry*. "Mr. Lewis," he said, "Let me introduce myself. I'm John Heartbreak, Bookseller."

"I know who you are," Lewis said. "You're the last American who voluntarily reads my books." Lewis' voice, a high sour Midwestern twang, blatted words out like rifle shots through thin schoolmarm lips. "You wouldn't happen to have a drink around here, would you?" he asked.

"No, Sir, you're in Berryville, Arkansas, where yesterday, today and tomorrow converge. Berryville is in a dry county. You can't buy a drink here."

"@#$%&," Lewis said.

I have never been comfortable with the fact that John does not actually read books so much as he talks to them. Frankly, it makes a lot of people uncomfortable. Jim Bulman, who often stopped by to pick up Larry McMurtry or James Michener, is always unnerved when he hears John yelling "Swine!" or "What about the Gulf of Tonkin Resolution, you, you useful idiot!" and etc., to no observable person and while he, John, is sitting, seemingly alone, at his desk. It drives Mrs. Heartbreak to beyond uncomfortable and certainly to the brink of distraction. Consequently, she is always prepared to reassure customers. "No, dear," she'll explain, "He didn't call you an ignorant warthog. He's writing a letter to the President and sounding out various phrases and aphorisms."

But my comfort is unimportant. Therefore, or subsequently, or consequently—you decide—I interrupted them. "Mr. Lewis," I said, "Drinking is not the only no-no. No sir, there is no sex, violence or strong language in this book. So watch the adjectives, the adverbials, please."

Lewis jumped, looked around fearfully and then grabbed John's arm. "I'm hearing voices," he whispered. "I'm not having the D.T.s' am I?"

John cast an annoyed look in my direction, and then reassured Lewis. "No, you're fine," he said. "The guy writing this book keeps interrupting. He's standing behind Mrs. Heartbreak's fern. Just ignore him."

Lewis glanced suspiciously toward the fern. He didn't look reassured at all. "Buster," he said, "I could sure use a drink."

"Forget about it," John said. "Let me tell you why you're here. I'd like your permission to quote some stuff from Elmer Gantry in the next several paragraphs of this book. How about it?"

"Give me a shot of Mother Courage," Lewis replied, "and I'll trade you *Elmer Gantry* and throw in *Arrowsmith* to boot."

I could see that John was tempted. But if this book were left up to John there would be dead Iowans strewn about and even more nattering on about Unitarians. I firmly wagged my head from side to side. No SVSL. And NO DRINKING ALLOWED!

John looked exasperated, looked sorrowful. He turned to Lewis and said, "I'm sorry. The Boy Dunder here ..." he jerked his thumb in the direction of Mrs. Heartbreak's fern ... "won't allow it."

Lewis snorted. "Listen Bubba, a little wine gladdens the heart. Don't they teach you anything in this hick town?"

I stepped out from behind the fern and tapped Lewis on the shoulder. It was fun to see him jump out of his skin. John had to help him put it back on. But I'd also had enough of this Nobel Prize winning Bozo. "They teach us plenty here, Pal," I said, "including manners."

"That's why I'm NOT going to have you do something really stupid," I continued, "like have you bark like a dog, or break into song. But I'm tempted. What do you think your friend H. L. Mencken would say if I had you sing a chorus or two of "*What a Friend We Have in Jesus*" right here, right now?"

"You wouldn't dare!"

"Watch me, Mr. Nobel Prize Guy. You of all people should know what a writer is capable of."

"Assassination by preposition, no doubt," Lewis scoffed.

John laughed. "That reminds me of what Chesterton had to say about prepositions. A ..."

"Shut up!" Lewis and I said.

"Here's the deal, Lewis," I said sternly. "I've devoted 772 words exclusively on behalf of the   apparently famous Sinclair Lewis. John says that you have something to say about small town churches. Say it in 250 words, or less, or you'll be singing hymns. Now. Start talking ... or start singing."

"Small towns are mostly cultural wastelands," said Lewis, rapidly. "Small town churches are then, and by default, repositories of what constitutes not only higher culture, but culture itself. Within the walls of these churches people hear what rhetoric of an elevated nature there is to hear, see what fine art there is to see, experience what inspirational architecture there is to experience, and are given what pathways to philosophy and higher ideas that may exist in their otherwise unbearable, commerce driven lives.

Churches recommend by example what is worthwhile in culture. Without such cultural stewardship and guidance smalls towns will sink beneath the weight of Victorian parlor art, sentimental imprecations, and the popular kitsch of the moment.

"That, by the way," Lewis said after a pause, "is the critical message and most missed point in Gantry." He cleared his throat. "Enough?" Lewis asked. His hands were shaking badly and I made a mental note to provide alcohol in my next novel.

"I haven't a clue," I said. "You did it in 118 words, however, and that impressed me. "Still," I continued, "it is Mr. Heartbreak here who summoned you up and he is the guy who decides when enough is enough."

John was nodding. "Thank you Mr. Lewis. I think that was helpful. And," he said, after a beat, "I'm sorry we were unable to provide you with a beverage. I appreciate the fact that there is no beer in hell."

"I don't know about hell," Lewis snarled. "But there certainly isn't any beer in heaven." With that, John closed the book and Lewis was gone.

John turned to me, eyebrows raised. "I think Lewis made the case against popular culture in the pulpit," he said. "Don't you think so too?"

I hesitated. "A point of information first," I said. "Was that the Holy Spirit? Lewis, I mean."

John looked baffled. "Of course not. That was Sinclair Lewis. How could you possibly mistake him for the Holy Spirit? Lewis is an atheist."

I admit to being miffed. "Lewis is a "was" and not an "is". In any case, I don't see either one on a daily basis. It hardly seems an awkward question."

"The Holy Spirit requires no human medium by which to deliver a message," John said. "He appears unannounced and without invitation. He goes where he goes. And it is highly unlikely that he'll appear requesting a shot of whiskey."

"One never knows, do one," I said, archly.

"You used that line in Chapter 8," John reminded me. "Twice. Fats Waller will resent it."

"Mr. Waller notwithstanding," I said, "Mrs. Heartbreak and I observe more than occasionally that you talk to dead writers while you read their books. That inspires little confidence in your ability to distinguish the Holy Spirit from among the many voices you apparently hear. Did you hear, for example, from the Holy Spirit during services this morning?"

"I did not," John said emphatically. "I refuse to believe that a general piling on of wheedling and sincerity mixed in with a program of sentimental crooning results in any sort of spiritual intercourse with the Holy Spirit."

"And certainly not with the better angels of your nature," I said. "But some people seemed to be moved by the experience."

Okay. Enough. Let us revert to the third person singular and finish this chapter off:

John briefly discussed the dreadful funk that morning services had put him in with Mrs. Heartbreak. She was not sympathetic. "It was close to being over the top," she said. "But I felt okay with it all. We just have to get with the program, John."

"But what's the program?" John exclaimed. "We are not evangelicals. We are certainly not Charismatics!"

"Oh, John," Mrs. Heartbreak said, sympathetically. "Why don't you talk to Pastor John Turner about it?"

John sipped coffee and thought about it. There was one thing for sure, though. He was glad Clara Jane hadn't taken him up on his invitation.

Chapter 11:

Whither Charo?

John was concerned about how the day was shaping up. He had agreed to meet with Clara Jane sometime today—no time had been set—and he had sixteen boxes of books to go through that had been more or less dumped on him by a flea market operator from up in Missouri. A casual glance into a few of the boxes had been discouraging.

John knew immediately that the "valuable" books so entombed would be nearly impossible to sell. He was mildly depressed at the pending chore of sorting through the boxes and delayed action by pouring a cup of RDC black, no cream, no sugar. He stared out the window. Judge Kent Crow briskly stepped out of his office, out to his truck, and rushed off to the courthouse to spin the Wheels of Justice. Judge Crow is a decorated veteran from a not recent war. Probably the same war John had been in. John had received no decorations and deserved none.

John had received and read an e-mail from Mrs. Heartbreak's sister, Mikella A. Lowe, early this morning. Mickey corresponded more with John than with me—a fact that I resent—but my resentment has to do only with another fact, which is that she has more in common with John than with me. They are both strict adherents of Chaos Theory although Mickey, as a superintendent of schools, is in a Social Order Theory business... This is what Mickey wrote to John:

"John here is a game for you to complete during those long dreary hours when no one comes in to buy any of those books you try and palm off on people by the way you would do better if you had some better books anyway what you do is answer the 17 questions below with a word that begins with the first letter of your name which is John which starts with a J so all the words have to start with a J why don't you pass this along to your bookseller friends since I know all you guys are going bankrupt due to the economy and all the people who are on the internet instead of reading books so you all have time on your hands don't you guys know that print is dead HAHA love Mickey."

John had no interest in completing this game and he certainly had no dreary hours. Let it be known that, at least in his own mind, John might be a shy bookseller by day, but at night he is a fabulous street corner tap dancer who receives $100 tips from happy drunks on a frequent basis. (This is not true. John is a shy bookseller day and night and thinks of himself as such. I just liked the imagery of the line and so choose to use it here. Hey, remember, it's my book.)

On the other hand, and as you know from what I am sure is your close reading of previous chapters, John is a Partner in the firm of Spade and Archer Investigations Strictly Confidential. Would it be possible, John thought, to use the game as a forensic device to understand Clara Jane on a psychological basis? To "profile" her, so to speak? By substituting "Clara" for "John"—that would be a "C" instead of a "J" thank you very much Mickey, John might learn something useful about Clara Jane. John sat down at his desk and put pencil to paper. Let's see how it works:

1. What is your name? Clara Jane
2. Four Letter word: Cold (remember, no SL!)
3. Vehicle: Cadillac
4. City: Chicago
5. Boy name: Clark
6. Girl name: Carol
7. Alcohol drink: Coors
8. Occupation: Cut Throat
9. Something you wear: Culottes

10. Celebrity: Charo
11. Something found in a bathroom: Cuticle Remover
12. Reason for being late: Casualness
13. Cartoon Character: Charlie Brown
14. Something you shout: Crap!
15. Animal: Cat
16: Body part: Crotch
17. Word to describe you: Chilling

John was flummoxed by the list. Actually, he was nonplussed by the list but flummoxed is a flutier word so lets go with it, okay? In any case, what did the list mean, at least in forensic terms? What, John speculated, did he now know about Clara Jane that he hadn't known before?

Clara Jane was certainly a "Cold" person, but John already knew that. And, true enough, she had driven a Cadillac through Chicago on one of her prior escapes, had she not? But so what? She now drove a Ford Taurus. Was it also possible that Clara Jane had used "Carol Clark" as an alias in one of Sanford's books? Or, perhaps, Clara Jane PLANNED to use the Carol Clark alias in a not past nor present but future Berryville, Arkansas based crime! John was warming to the forensic utility of Mrs. Lowe's game. He knew that Clara drank beer—perhaps it was Coors?—and, when she cleaned up, she bore an uncanny resemblance to the youthful Charo, minus the ChuCheeChuChee. This made it easy for her to distract men (here's where the Crotch word comes in), and caused them to let down their guard so that she could slip a cuticle remover into their livers and PUT THEM ON ICE! Needless to say, Clara Jane/Charo looked as innocent as Charlie Brown with Crap in his mouth so, of course, she got away with it—or would get away with it pending a future event—as easily as a Cat in Culottes could slip into a crowd and be remembered only as a passing if cute novelty. What a Chilling turn of events!

John quickly drained the RDC black and leaned into in his chair. Things, he thought, were getting too complex. Although his analysis of the Clara Jane forensic evidence contained no passive sentences and was written at the 8th grade level on the Flesch-Kincaid Scale he had to necessarily confront a basic plot development barrier which is that he knows—as you should know—that although and while Clara Jane has Fifty Big Ones in her back pocket for the purpose of eradicating an Iowan or two, and that she certainly has a history of manic serial killing behind her, there would be NO VIOLENCE in THIS book.

John slipped even deeper into depression. Unless he could convince moi to lighten up on the SVSL restriction, he seemed destined to spend the rest of his life thinking about Unitarians. Just as he fell ever deeper into the Slough of Despond, Elaine West came into the shop. Elaine is the sweetest, kindest woman in Berryville. Mrs. West always made John feel peaceful and talking with her made him feel happy.

Chapter 12:

God Does Not Play Dice with the Universe ...?

After Mrs. West left the shop John returned to the window and stared out onto the Square. It is a busy morning: a crew of Iowans waggled into the Ozark Café; Barb Evans walks by with an arm load of clothes for the Senior Center Thrift Shop; Linda Mayer, wife of the Musical Farmer Dr. Fred Mayer, attempts to park her car between two pick-up trucks (ha ha ha); Ray the Barber switches his barber pole on: watch it revolve!

John puts all this excitement out of his mind and tries to hear me writing what is going to happen next. While Clara Jane can hear John Sanford scratch scratch scratch her unfolding life, or me type type type her next move, John only hears the dull collective whispers of dead writers arguing among the stacks behind him. He thinks that being in a book and out of a book is hardly different, is no big deal. He plans to discuss the matter with Douglas Adams at the earliest possible moment. If anyone knows it is Mr. Adams.

Ah: Mrs. Mayer was successful.

Mrs. Heartbreak approaches John and thumps him on the shoulder. Her thump is not unkindly intended. She is only trying to get John to look at her while she speaks to him.

"Do you intend to do any work today?" she inquires. "Rex Stout and Bret Harte need shelving, you know."

John nods.

"Straightaway," he amiably says. And: "It looks like there are a lot of people in town today. Maybe we'll have a little business. Make a nickel, so to speak."

"A nickel?" Mrs. Heartbreak archly replies (can't you just see it!).

"Yes, a nickel is possible. Yet, with the value of the dollar at its lowest point in forty years, unemployment arcing toward 8%, overnight markets collapsing in advance of our own declining markets, and an aggressive movement among younger workers to abolish Social Security, a nickel may not be enough."

John nods.

Mrs. Heartbreak returns to her counter.

John tries to remember who said, "God does not play dice with the universe." He thought it was Einstein, but he isn't sure. He is pretty sure that Einstein—who ever—had got it wrong. Minutes after God introduced free will Eve tossed the ivories and human kind crapped out.

On the other hand, Creation occurred before Eve's misadventure. Maybe Creation was not a gamble in origin but became so only after Man loused everything up? Perhaps Pastor Paul Andresen could help John figure this out. In John's opinion Presbyterians were good at that sort of speculative bifurcating (Ha Ha! You have to go to the dictionary, don't you) despite their reputation for avoiding whimsy.

John was wondering about dice and the Universe because he spied Clara Jane out on the Square. She was pulling a Stanley Steel tape measure across the width of the public fountain and marking down the feet and inches on a pad of paper. She also and carefully measured the depth of the fountain, which John knew to be 20 inches. It was deep enough to drown a cat, but good for nothing else, certainly not deep enough for the survival or maintenance of even the most tentative of La Dolce Vita fantasies.

The last time Clara Jane was concerned with careful measurement was when she shot Nanny Dichter once in the forehead and once more in each of his ears. (That would be three shots total). Nanny had it coming but, mindful of the no violence rule, I will not describe those reasons and John will not think about them. We do, however, have to think about Clara Jane and what she is up to now. Is she about to roll the dice and thereby weave another thread of chaos into the fabric of the Universe?

John ambled out of the shop and across to the (crab) grassy Square. Mrs. Heartbreak stared after John as he ambled—which Mrs. Heartbreak would describe as an indolent shuffle rather than an amble—and she watched him as he nodded to Linda Mayer who was on her way to the Post Office. John appeared to Mrs. Heartbreak to be in a sort of lizard-like trance.

Mrs. Heartbreak observed John talking to the public fountain, or talking to himself, if you were among the many citizens of Berryville who never saw the fountain. Obviously Mrs. Heartbreak did not see Clara Jane, the person to whom John was "actually" speaking, and therefore she naturally assumed that he was self-engaged in a mumbled conversation with himself.

The word "actually" is the interesting word here. Mrs. Heartbreak "actually" saw the public fountain, and saw it dispiritedly spit dribs and drabs of water hither and yon in imitation of a "real" fountain that might be in Rome or Boston or in front of the State Capitol in Little Rock. But Mrs. Heartbreak only "saw" the Berryville public fountain because of John's preoccupation with it, and his many comments about its, to him, deficiencies.

Without benefit of John's preoccupation and comments it is doubtful that Mrs. Heartbreak would be able to see the fountains, even though she is able to bring up memories of "real" fountains she had seen, or to recall images or ideas about fountains from books and movies. In this matter she is like all other Berryvillians: the Town Square Fountain was so much wallpaper, there certainly, but not really there. Only John saw these watery tubs of flatulence for what they "actually" are.

Mrs. Heartbreak did not "see" Clara Jane either because she is only "actually" in John's mind and in my mind too. Yet, you are reading this, and you see Clara Jane now, don't you. She is standing by the fountain—which you now see for the first time-- with a Stanley Steel tape measure in her hand, talking to John as he mumbles back in response. Let us assume, again, and because the SHOW MUST GO ON, that Clara Jane is "actual."

"What's happening, John?" Clara Jane asked.

"I am disquieted by what you are doing," he replied. "I recall Nanny Dichter and the bad end he came to as a result of your use of measurement."

"Disquieted, John?" she said. "Who uses a word like "disquieted" anymore? When I asked not to talk like a hillbilly (Chapter 10?) I didn't think that people would talk back to me like fops in Edith Wharton novels."

(I resist the urge to introduce Mrs. Wharton, who would deny ever having put a "fop" into one of her novels. Just so you know. What a narrow miss you have just had.)

"Okay, you are making me NERVOUS. What are you doing? What's with the tape measure?"

Clara Jane smiled. "I'm figuring out your Iowan problem," she said. "Since I'm not allowed to kill them off in the usual, efficient, and business-like fashion allowed in ALL other, and need I say, MUCH MORE SUCCESSFUL novels, I am thinking about a way to transform these peckerwoods from tubby, self-satisfied, cheapskate, know-it-alls into cheerful, open-minded, and generous human beings. Without the use of pistols, knives, or other instruments of bodily harm."

John was interested.

"What I intend to do," she said, "Is invite every visitor from Iowa to attend a big revival held here on the Town Square. And then I'm going to baptize them in that fountain, right there." She pointed at the fountain.

John was not interested.

"Clara Jane, Iowans believe they invented God. They're not going to show up for a revival sponsored by a bunch of hicks in Berryville, Arkansas. Besides, they're all Lutherans. They've already been baptized."

She smiled. "John," she said. "I'm going to offer free, all you can eat pork barbeque with every baptism. They'll line up from here to Wal-Mart."

John returned her smile. He understood again the value of working with a professional: Iowans would dance on the head of a pin for free lunch.

But first, a meddling question. "Once you get them into the fountain and baptized, how are they transformed into the better human beings we know them capable of becoming?"

Clara Jane stared off into the distance. This made the distance anxious and it turned around to stare back. "I'm still working on the SHAZAAM! part John. Let's roll the dice and see what happens. I'll get back to you momentarily."

As a frequent flyer, John knew that "momentarily" was a precise unit of time of between twelve minutes and twelve days. He nodded. He could wait twelve days.

When John got back to the store he looked at his e-mails. One of them was from Pastor John Turner.

"Dear John," Pastor Turner had written, "I have just finished reading Chapter 11 of this book and would like to respond if I may."

This is what John Turner wrote ...

Chapter 13:

John Turner
Sets John Heartbreak Straight(er)

"Dear John," Pastor Turner wrote, "I have just finished reading online the 11th chapter of a book about you. I wish to respond if I may."

John felt a rush of bemusement. Actually, he felt disquieted, and since Clara Jane isn't around to admonish him for sounding like a fop, let's go with that feeling and with that word. In any case, how and why does Pastor Turner know about "the book?" And, "Chapter 11?" How could anyone write a single chapter about him, let alone eleven chapters, let alone an entire book about his meager life? John, amazed as well as disquieted, reads on.

"First," Pastor Turner wrote, "let me say it is an unnerving thing to begin what I believe is a five-way conversation composed of you, John Heartbreak, the "Authorial I" who is writing about you, the Fabulous Mrs. Heartbreak—the three of you I will refer to from now on as "the Heartbreak Trio"—the author Sinclair Lewis and, of course me, John Turner who, along with Judy Turner, provide the ministerial leadership for our common church.

"The unnerving part consists of three matters: (1) Sinclair Lewis, whom I hardly know, (2) The Heartbreak Trio, whom I know in a confusing sort of way, and (3) the "Authorial I" who represents himself as your "best friend." Let me take these matters in hand:

"There is the matter of Sinclair Lewis: I admit to having read only a few books of any writer with either the given name or the family name of Sinclair, whether paired with Upton or Lewis. I am confused at the moment about what I actually read but have been more willing lately to read things by a Lewis when the name is paired with C. S.

"I admit that I am not much interested in Sinclair Lewis' notion of the church as a purveyor of culture. So far as I am concerned, purveying culture, either popular or classical culture, is an incidental that may be either a side benefit or a side curse of the church's worship and mission, but is not centrally defining. So perhaps, we should leave the Nobel Prize winner aside?"

John's disquiet turned to alarm. How was it that Pastor Turner knew he had been talking with Sinclair Lewis? John looked over toward Mrs. Heartbreak's fern, my habitual resting place. He was sure that the "Authorial I" Turner spoke of could only be me. But I was not behind the fern: "I" have sensibly absented myself from the exchange between these two Protestants. "I" will have a cup of tea with Mrs. Heartbreak while these two Johns duke it out.

Pastor Turner continued:

"The Heartbreak Trio's internal dialogue is a bit like watching a three-sided Ping Pong match. The nets transect a round table. What happens if I join in? Which part of the table is mine? To which volleys do I respond? Where should I hit them? What is my goal in this game?

"Then there is the big question, "Which two of the three do I know?" This is complicated by the fact that I suspect John Heartbreak's Authorial I is also Mrs. Heartbreak's Authorial I, so far unrevealed. The moral and legal implications alone are staggering, if not paralyzing."

"Good Lord," John exclaimed. "Implications?"

Sherry French, browsing in the mystery section, glanced toward John, but chose to ignore him. She was used to hearing him mutter and wheeze, used to observing him converse into the ether. She felt a twinge of sympathy for Mrs. Heartbreak and went back to Agatha Christie.

"John," Pastor Turner continued, "let me give you my take on last Sunday's service. Your friend "the author" is not the Single Seer in the Universe. This is what I think:

"Poor you. On Sunday, you were put in a funk by an overdose of personal testimony, country gospel music sung by a "Singing Testifier," and an altar call, which are all foreign to your religious upbringing. You were understandably culturally and emotionally disoriented; your background is Roman Catholic and your personality is private. You have read the history and fiction and viewed the movies and documentaries that set forth the many ways that evangelical and charismatic forms can be—and sometimes are—abused.

"This put you on guard in a way that you did not feel you should feel, especially in the laid-back, slightly liturgical, small town Protestant church where we worship. Billy Sunday and Elmer Gantry came into your mind. All this was exacerbated by the fact that the Authorial I, and Mrs. Heartbreak, although sympathizing on some points, gave you a hard time.

"Poor, self-pitying John and Judy Turner—Me and the Missus, so to speak—ministry leaders of the Heartbreak Trio's church, were on this particular Sunday, dealing not only with several people who share your concerns, but also with several others who, even at that relatively loose service, find their church stiff, formal, and, to put it crudely, "Catholic," not something that helps one survive in small-town Bible-belt settings unless, of course, the church actually is Roman Catholic, which our church—the Heartbreak Trio's church—is not.

"We all know from watching the news that there are real dangers to be found among evangelicals and Charismatics—and among Roman Catholics. In my experience, the staid middle of the road is not safer. Judy and I have seen enough of the weaknesses and strengths of each variety of Christianity to be a bit wary about all of them, but not completely rejecting of many of them. We put a bit of high church and a bit of low church together, a bit of tradition and a bit of the contemporary, and sometimes we forget what our combinations of styles might look like from other perspectives. Sometimes we are caught off guard by what we should have recognized in advance.

"But back to what most disturbed you: the loud country music of the Singing Testifier, and altar calls. We'll start with the music and eventually get around to the altar call (ahem).

"I have no developed musical taste," Turner continued. "And so am utterly unqualified to speak of such matters. That has never stopped me before. Personally, I really like the Singing Testifier's country voice when it is rendering contemporary Christian music such as "Let the River Flow." That song is certainly not Mozart, Bach, or Beethoven, but it is a warm and rich song celebrating the work of God in our lives, and it is not, Sir, a country song. Of course, this does not end your right to differ; taste is personal and is generally not to be argued.

"But now a confession: I personally like country music no better than you. If I had to lead a church that offered a steady diet of contemporary country music, it would be an experience of cultural hell or, at least, of learning Paul's meaning when he wrote in Galatians 2:20, "I have been crucified with Christ. It is no longer I who live, but Christ who lives in me. And the life I now live in the flesh I live by faith in the Son of God, who loved me and gave himself for me."

"Merely imagining that imagined calling, my flesh and soul scream out the words of Psalm 22:1, "My God, my God, why have you forsaken me? Why are you so far from saving me, from the words of my groaning?" I am a bit afraid to admit this because I happen to know that God is not above putting his servants in positions where they cry out things like this. I simply pray that God will choose a servant who likes country music a lot better than I do for that assignment.

"That's enough about me. It is more to the point to say that God appears to be more flexible in musical taste than I am. The meth world is a place from which, once in, it is extremely hard to get out. Some say that it just doesn't happen. Yet, God acted through a country song to deliver the Singing Testifier so far as I know instantly and completely. That kind of deliverance from meth abuse is almost unheard of outside the work of the Holy Spirit through the Christian gospel.

"Since coming to northern Arkansas, I have met an amazing number of people who claim to have received supernatural deliverance from destructive chemical dependencies. I think that the people in the "Sincere ball bat t-shirts" were trying to say that there is a way out of meth addiction, and that some of them have found that way. That is not just moral exhortation, but is potentially good news.

"There are people attending our church for which such dependency is either a personal issue or an issue within their close family. There are also people who, for other reasons, need to know that God still works miracles. They need to see the evidence in order to build their faith. They need hope. They need a living, reigning God. I'll swallow quite a bit of bitter medicine in the form of things that aren't to my taste or personality inclinations if I can help bring that hope.

"We need," Pastor Turner continued, "to find our church's place in the scheme of things. One person's bitter medicine is another person's sweet elixir. With our present members and people to whom we might reach out, we are bridging denominational heritages that run from high church (Roman Catholic, Anglican, Lutheran) through small town mainline Protestant (Methodist, Presbyterian, Disciples) to evangelical (Baptist, Fellowship Bible), holiness (Nazarene), Pentecostal (Assembly of God), and charismatic (Vineyard, Soul Purpose).

"We are also bridging generational, educational, and regional gaps that are every bit as big. Probably all of us feel stretched like a rubber band. You, John, are far from alone in being uncomfortably stretched.

"We will probably always have significant cultural diversity in what we do, but we cannot be all things for all people all the time. We must find what holds it all together, and we must find our distinctive voice, the voice that will be dominant in the midst of our diversity ... or is it schizophrenia? Having started with a schizophrenic priest, John H., do you now have a schizophrenic church?

"The church's mission," Turner wrote, "always involves some variety of holding forth the reigning power, holy righteousness, and redeeming love of God and challenging people to respond faithfully in every corner of their lives. Amidst all the issues of worship styles, that is the glue that holds us together across difference preferences. And that is what guides our selection of styles.

"So, we ask questions about how particular styles do or do not help us accomplish our mission. For instance, what would enable Clara Jane to find God, to commit to God, to serve God? Moving Clara Jane into a Christ-centered fellowship of faith and mission would give angels in heaven justification to party.

"That, John," Turner wrote, "may be the point of everything I am talking about. How will you and I, and all our dear neighbors, will bring Clara Jane to Christ?"

John stopped reading and thought for a moment. He realized the irony of contracting with Clara Jane to eradicate Iowans— or at least to dramatically, convincingly reform them—while simultaneously considering whether or not to invite her to church. Now, he found John Turner coming down on at least one side of how John considered Clara Jane.

He had no doubt that Clara Jane and Mrs. Heartbreak would hit it off since both were of a practical nature, both Social Theory theorists in their own way. No doubt they would enjoy discussing means to an end over coffee after services. Perhaps he should discuss the matter with Mrs. Heartbreak, and leave the question of a church invitation up to her?

John began reading again:

"What goes into the search for our distinctive voice?" Pastor Turner asked. "We must pay attention to our particular community and to what God is doing here. Our worship voice must aid our mission of connecting particular people to God. One thing that God is doing here in Carroll County is building neighborly relationships. Then, if we succeed in drawing together Carroll County natives and interlopers in mutually supportive relationships, how does that affect the worship language for our church?

"Music will play a part. Currently, we sing a blend of mainline Protestant hymns, evangelical gospel songs, and 1970's-1980's praise choruses. We need to update and find a distinctive intergenerational music language that ties it all together in a way suited to our setting. Perhaps Celtic instrumentation (with its American mountain offspring) played with classical skill and a contemporary feel is the approach. Spiritually, we would seek an ordered, Spirit-led vitality, grounded in scripture, centered on the Trinity, and connected to mission.

"My dream is that our church will find ways in its musical language to combine rich traditions, classical skills, folk roots, contemporary feel, theological authenticity, and spiritual vitality.

"I can only say that we are at best experimentally floundering toward the dream. We have to recognize that God may have another plan to be revealed by and by.

"And now, John, the altar call. Let me admit that I share your religious introversion. It goes against my personal nature to reveal my inner spirituality. And I am—rightly, I think—concerned about the integrity issue of not posturing as something I am not.

"You claim to be a Matthew 6:6 kind of guy where the point is to avoid practicing our piety for the sake of impressing people when the goal is to please and glorify God. Perfectly true, Sir. But that private passage must be balanced by the more public Matthew 5:14-16 and 10:26-33 and 28:18-20.

"For the past 300 years or so, the public and small group confessions, professions, and prayers that have characterized evangelical pietism have probably done more to change the world for the better than any other spiritual or secular practices.

"Let's get one thing out in the open immediately. There have been abuses. The gross, crude, chauvinistic, self-righteous, ignorant, and arrogant Billy Sunday comes to mind, but even he probably did some good along with the harm. The existence of abusers requires that we be careful and discerning, but the existence of counterfeit money does not end the utility of legitimate currency, and evangelical pietism at its best has been legitimate spiritual currency.

"Consider the eighteenth century England's George Whitefield, John Wesley, and John Newton, not to mention their protégé William Wilberforce: from them flow more changed lives and social practices than can be calculated. My favorite American history professor at the University of Chicago claimed that the two most influential shapers of America were Jonathan Edwards and Charles Finney, two quite different practitioners of evangelical pietism.

"Perhaps the most widespread revival, that began in Wales in 1904-1905, impacted much of the world. Major revivals seem to occur about once per generation; they are generally followed by waves of social reform. Perhaps the next revival will light the fire for freeing us from the corporate market economy and for rebuilding small, sustainable communities. Stranger things have happened, Mr. Heartbreak.

"In any case, the great revival movements have utilized various forms of altar calls. Public prayer and public commitment have been important to spreading the spiritual renewal. It is easy to see potential dangers in altar calls, but it is hard to imagine what would replace them. You, John, may not need an altar call and social reinforcement of your prayers in order to make tangible commitments to God, but experience says that some of your neighbors do.

"Finally, John, let me directly answer your question about why we "beat dead horses" with our altar calls and invitations. We are not so sure that the horses are dead, and we aren't sure when they might revive. We don't want to miss it when it happens. Perhaps it will start in Berryville, Arkansas. Perhaps it will happen sometime soon at The Heartbreak Trio's church.

"Stranger things have happened. Some of the stranger things, to my great surprise and consternation, have happened to the private, very rational me under the leadership of a Roman Catholic revivalist. I was an apparently dead horse, well killed at Vanderbilt Divinity School, resistant in every way to everything that happened to me at that prayer revival, but it woke me up to the personal reality of God, and it changed my life. You never know."

Chapter 14:

Let's Regroup, Shall We?

Things, events, appear to be getting out of hand. Are you confused? Don't worry, all will be revealed? Sort of. Well, maybe not. To be honest, not at all. Consider please, what we are dealing with, or as Mrs. Pearl Edlund, my High School English teacher would insist, with what we are dealing.

First, you are reading a "novel" that is full of people you know. Yodi, the Artist Formerly Known as Catherine Yoder (AFKCY), for example, who John sees just now, is having a spirited conversation with Clara Jane out on the Town Square. Yodi, a "real" person, is having a conversation with the "non-real" person Clara Jane. Yodi and Clara Jane appear to be discussing the Town Square Fountain. John deduces (surmises?) this fact because each of them is pointing at and otherwise gesturing toward the fountains. They are both laughing.

We know that the fountains are "real" because Clara Jane and Yodi are laughing at them—or, at least we know they are real because Yodi—a real person, is laughing at them. But virtually no one else really sees the fountains. The Square is full of people in addition to Yodi and Clara Jane. But John knows that if he asks them about the fountains they wouldn't know what he was talking about or, it would take them a minute to remember "the thing" he was talking about, even if they were sitting on the "thing's" edge. And since we know that seeing is believing we can sincerely believe that the fountains are not really there because they are unseen.

At the same time, Yodi "sees" the fountains: they are now "real" to her. But she sees them only because a "real" person, John Heartbreak, has pointed them out to her. Yet again, John is a dual existence John Heartbreak—a character in a book and a character (maybe) in real life who you, a real person, should know well by now if you've been reading along from the beginning.

We are mindful also that John is married to the Fabulous Mrs. Heartbreak, who is entirely real and thus and consequently exists in this book, outside this book, and in your minds and memory, both as a character in this book and as Majordomo of Heartbreak's Books and Really Dreadful Coffee. That—count them—is at least three, and perhaps four dimensions of reality: in the book, outside the book, in your conscious mind, and in the recesses of your memory.

If you have hung in here so far, congratulate yourself. This is complex stuff; only a really smart person would get it. On the other hand, the preceding paragraphs and all those before may be a pile of indescribable dribble. In which case, you must be an idiot for having put up with it so long. Are you a really smart person? Or an idiot? You decide. I'm sure you'll make the right choice.

Let's regroup, shall we?

We started out with five plot lines. Those plot lines are:

1. Social Order Theory versus Chaos Theory
2. Clara Rinker AKA Jane Smith
3. The Fountains on the Town Square
4. The Problem with Iowans
5. Unitarians

A few of these plot lines have thinned out. Unitarians, for example, have been neglected for the last several chapters. The battle between Social Order Theory and Chaos Theory theorists has also lost ascendancy.

Clara Rinker AKA Jane Smith now Clara Jane, has ascended and been woven into the Problem with Iowans plot line. You should also see by now that John's tiresome reoccupation with the

Town Square's fountains is in fact an elementary and therefore necessary ingredient to the excellence of the literary cake we prepare to bake or half-bake.

So here it is: Iowans, due to their general and truculent air of superiority and their ham fisted closeness with a dollar, will be "taken care of" by the Serial Killer Clara Jane Smith, who is hiding out on Pritchard Street in Berryville, Arkansas. Clara Jane may or may not use the Town Square's fountains as the means to take the Iowans "out."

As we review the summary above we see that the Problem with Unitarians is the only thread left unbound. Perhaps we'll have a group of them cheer Clara Jane on? Or, more likely, should we have them publish stern Op Ed rebukes in the Lovely County Citizen about the pestilence of free barbeque and why Clara Jane should not be allowed to use it as Iowan bait? If you happen to be a Unitarian—and believe you have a dog in this fight—please advise.

John continued to watch Yodi and Clara Jane converse. Herman Melville had stepped out of the Ms' and now stood next to John and sipped coffee and watched too. "Those gals appear to be having a time," he drawled. "Not that I know anything about gals," he added.

John nodded.

"One thing you should know is that they don't like to be called gals anymore," he said. "They prefer to be called "women or "Miz."

Melville grunted. "That's a reason there are never any "women" in my novels. They have so many preferences that I am never able to keep up with them.

"Let me tell you," he continues. "It's easier to kill a whale then to figure out all the preferences you modern people have. Half the time you sound like that fool Ralph Waldo Emerson."

John nodded again and says, "Sir, we are called to keep up."

Melville snorted, walked back to the Ms' and climbed into *Billy Budd*.

John remains at the window and watches life unfold on the Square. He has a lot on his mind. In the last little while he has discovered that he is a character in a book, even though his reality is that he "is" a character in real life. Similarly, but also entirely the other way around, Pastor John Turner, a character in real life, is now a character in a book.

John Heartbreak is not upset about being a character in a book. In his experience, life in books and life in reality is much the same. You were a good guy or a bad guy in real time or book time because of the way you behave. If John had had to depend on real people in real life to know how to conduct himself, he'd be a pretty poor specimen. Happily, he knew Woodrow Call, Father Brown, Ulysses, and Sam Spade, guys like that. John knew if he was good or bad, when he was good, and when he was bad.

What did upset John was the way I, now dubbed the Authorial I, seem to meddle in his life. Since there is no sex or violence or strong language in this book, John is not upset about how I the Authorial I (eye?) am conducting myself with Mrs. Heartbreak. In any case, Mrs. Heartbreak can take care of herself. Let me tell you.

But how embarrassing, John thinks. To have his views on religion! Exposed to "everyone" who reads this book! (I refer to "everyone" henceforth as Roy and Dale or Chip and Dale or, Howdy, you two.) John was not sure that he wanted Roy and Dale or Howdy, you two, to know that Mrs. Heartbreak observed him in "lizard-like" trances. John means to speak with me, to serve notice, as soon as he can find me.

In the mean time, John Turner has interjected another possible plot line. That is, how to bring Clara Jane to Jesus?

What that might mean, or how that might come about, John does not know. The only thing he is certain of is his hope that it does not involve personal testimony, altar calls, or the singing of hymns written between 1848 and 1990.

Chapter 15:

Après Moi Le Deluge Ha Ha Ho Ho

As you know, John Heartbreak gets up early every morning. If the newspaper has arrived, he might read it. *The Arkansas Democrat Gazette* gives proof to the old saw that given enough time and typewriters a tribe of monkeys will eventually turn out a Shakespearian sonnet. Without question the second worst newspaper in North America, the *ADG* may in fact do injustice to the monkeys in the Monkey-Shakespeare story. If you doubt the continued existence of Flat Worlders and Cross Burners, please peruse the *ADG's* opinions page.

That aside, Mrs. Heartbreak rises an hour or two later and, sitting in a small leather chair next to John's slightly larger chair, anxiously reads, out loud, excerpts from the paper. That John has just read. Mrs. Heartbreak knows that John has already gotten the "news," but she is concerned that he may not have fully grasped its implications. This happens every morning, as sure as day follows night.

This morning the ADG reports the imminent bankruptcy of Medicare, as well as the sheering off of an iceberg or glacier or, in any case, a very large piece of ice—whatever—from an even bigger piece of ice which may or may not be the North Pole or Greenland: some very cold place.

This immense chunk of ice, the size of Connecticut, is floating south towards New Jersey. John, having once spent eleven hours in the Newark, New Jersey Airport waiting for a delayed flight, is grimly satisfied: he hopes that every bozo living in the "Garden State" gets his butt frozen off. This paragraph represents the entirety of John's interest in science and nature.

Mrs. Heartbreak, on the other hand, anxiously predicts the end of the world and the possibility that she and John, impoverished because of the high cost of health care insurance and no more Medicare, will be eating grass on the Town Square. John assumes that the NO MORE MEDICARE disaster occurs before the END OF THE WORLD disaster. The order of disaster is important since the real problem, if the NO MORE MEDICARE disaster happens before the END OF THE WORLD disaster will be finding any grass to eat on the Town Square. Doggy dooly and chickweed are in plentiful supply, but grass? Ha.

John keeps these thoughts to himself and nods along as Mrs. Heartbreak sings the morning blues. John does not dismiss Mrs. Heartbreak's end of the world predictions. He knows that the world will end, that it constantly ends, one. person. at. a. time. So John nods along and loves Mrs. Heartbreak even more for how reliably she keeps up with current events.

What John is most aware of is that Mrs. Heartbreak's anxiety is not so much about the world ending as it is that such end will be uncomfortable. John also understands that French people, the root of All Evil, are the source of her anxiety.

It is well known that France affords its entirely undeserving citizens with 51 weeks of paid vacation every year and all the free wine and gravy they can drink and eat (French people call gravy "sauce"). As a consequence, Social Order Theorists compare the rest of the world to France. Obviously, the rest of the world comes up short.

Comparative analysis of this type leads governments into sloppy policy making, sloppy legislation and, more broadly speaking, to generalized states of anxiety among nations and people who worry about not being keeping up with the Jones', or in this case, France—and all of its very comfortable, Nazi collaborating citizens. For John, the causes of Mrs. Heartbreak's anxiety (French people) quite naturally leads him to the State of

Iowa, and therefore to Iowans themselves, which was the whole point of the preceding 577 words.

And you thought John and I had forgotten about Chaos Theory, didn't you? Let us connect the dots:

John had attended LaSalle High School in Minneapolis, which is just a block off Marquette Avenue. LaSalle and Marquette are the names of two early French explorers. They traveled up and down the Mississippi River between Minnesota, and as far south as the Gulf of Mexico. As a result, many Place Names in Minnesota and along the Mississippi are French in origination. However, the early French explorers did not settle in Minnesota. They stayed only long enough to be terrified by the snow and the sight of a few Ojibwas ice fishing on Mille Lacs.

On the other hand, both LaSalle and Marquette stopped in Iowa for considerable periods of time and Marquette's journals reflect a favorable impression of the area. In fact, so favorable was Marquette's report of the yet to be State of Iowa that another Frenchman, Julian Dubuque, went there in 1788 and spent the rest of his life sitting by the river, cheating Indians—and everyone else—who was unlucky enough to pass by.

When John left Vietnam and his part of the war, he chose to be discharged in Tokyo. He enrolled at Sophia University (Jochi Daigaku) near the center of Tokyo for the purposes of studying the Japanese language and chasing Asian girls. For some reason, French students were in plentiful supply among Sophia's student body.

John had more luck with his language studies than with the girls. The thing that most stuck in his mind from that time, however, was how rudely and frequently the students from France called him "an imperialist baby killer". They did this every time John wore his old Army field jacket to school, which was every day, because John was poor and couldn't afford less military attire.

If John had had a kettle handy he would beat those potheads to within an inch of their lives. But being called an "imperialist" by a Frenchman left John both speechless and inert. The example of Vietnam, a country and people the French had looted and enslaved for more than 200 years—and then duped the United States into adopting—hardly seemed to register in their minds. Let alone

Algeria, let alone Equatorial Africa, let alone … the French always left destitution and revolution in their wake.

Sometimes, now years later, John would survey the books in the shop and look into de Maupassant, Voltaire, Flaubert, Camus, Sartre, Rousseau, and wonder what all the fuss was about. Voltaire may have written a few interesting pages, but good lord, the bulk of his stuff was utter and contemptible rubbish. Existentialism? John would take the honest Dane Kierkegaard, any day. While it is true that the French had turned out a couple of fair to middling mathematicians—d'Allonville and Denjoy come to mind—what was all the hubbub about French "culture?" For John, French culture represented 500 years of failed diplomacy and Perfection of the Art of Rudeness.

In John's mind, the Problem of Iowans began with Julian Dubuque. He, in the French manner, enslaved 200 Indians and forced them to work in his coal mine. Dubuque had 45 children with several of the Indian women, upon whom he had forced his garlicky attentions and abused in the usual French manner. Since he was not married to any of the Indian women, he was unable to commit adultery—in the usual French manner. Therefore, he cheated on himself with himself, fell into a state of despair, and wrote *Extension du domaine de la lutte*, or *Whatever*, if you prefer English. Which, I do. John is just showing off.

Extension du domaine de la lutte was not a big hit. There is no record of even a single copy being sold. In hopes of creating word of mouth appeal for the book Dubuque began to read several chapters out of it each night to the Indian women and children. This so filled the Indian women with Whatever, that they, along with Dubuque's children, fled into the dark and stormy night. They hid out in what has become, in modern times, downtown Waterloo, where they stayed for a long, long time. As an entirely irrelevant fact, Waterloo is the second worst city in the world.

"And it came to pass …" much as Joseph Smith began 905 sentences in the Book of Mormon … that a band of Lutherans happened upon the women and, all in God's Good Time, properly married them and began raising little Lutherans. Much as Adam and Eve propagated the human race, every Iowan today springs from French and Lutheran loins.

79

Such an unlikely—not to put too fine a point on it, perhaps—so unnatural a pairing boggles the mind if you wish to boggle, wish to put your mind, to the task of sorting through the implications. To the left, we have French arrogance, nationalism, pride fullness, self-satisfaction, rudeness, and over-whelming self-regard; to the right is Lutheran humorlessness, miserliness, avarice and suspiciousness, stoicism and silence, Lawrence Welk. Surely, (verily?) these Iowans are the Spawn of Satan.

Okee doakee. Enough Chaos Theory for one day.

Chapter 16:

Seeing is Believing

John is racing to the post office to mail books he has sold on-line. He is not racing to make a delivery deadline. A new stamp featuring Marjorie Rawlings goes on sale this morning and John will kill two birds with one stone. He wants to make sure that he gets a sheet of the stamps before they sell out.

Fat chance, huh? John is one of two people in Berryville who cares who Marjorie Rawlings is—you are the other one, right?—and you and he will be able to buy Rawlings' stamps for the next several months.

From time to time John talks with Mrs. Rawlings, the author of *The Yearling*. He doesn't enjoy their conversations much. Truth be told, Mrs. Rawlings has a drinking problem and she can be unpleasant after a few bumps. She whines a bit. But John talks with her because she is lonely and not very popular any more.

My recollection of *The Yearling* is only the Walt Disney movie with Gregory Peck and a very blond, very pneumatic starlet whose name no one remembers any more. I recall the starlet as an unconvincing "Ma" who whined quite a bit about living in a Florida swamp (and wouldn't we all?). John has no recollection of the movie. Of course, he prefers the book anyway. I hazard that John would not remember the blond starlet under any circumstances since he has always had a jones for bony redheads. Did I mention that Mrs. Rawlings is a scrawny redhead? Did I mention that Mrs. Heartbreak is a redhead?

It gives me the creeps when Marjorie is in the store. I am usually unable to see her, but I can always hear her, and I can hear John's quiet murmurs of comfort. "Marjorie, I'm sure a copy will sell any day now," he lies. "We just have to be patient. Perhaps Disney will film a re-make."

Marjorie certainly gives customers the creeps. They also hear her hiccupping weepiness. But they dismiss the idea that dead authors haunt the shop, and assume that what they hear is John talking to himself, or John practicing ventriloquism. Mrs. Heartbreak is quick to reassure anyone who looks alarmed. "John is trying out for a part in Billy Bob Thornton's new film," she says (she lies). "John is hopeful about playing the part of the Village Idiot. That accounts for the expression on his face."

Not everyone is reassured. A large percentage of the population is fearful of Village Idiots; they are also afraid of people who are just trying out for the Idiot's part in Hollywood movies. Interestingly, the large percentage that is fearful of Village Idiots includes a substantial percentage that is themselves Village Idiots.

There are also substantial numbers of people who are uncomfortable being around people who talk to themselves. And many people feel uncomfortable being around eccentric people. Consequently, Mrs. Heartbreak has a hard lot; she must explain that her husband is: *a)* trying out for a part in a movie that does not exist; *b)* only sounding out phrases and aphorisms for a letter of stern rebuke to the President of the United States, *c)* a ventriloquist, *d)* perhaps eccentric, but in an entirely harmless, middleclass, and thoroughly Republican way.

John Heartbreak is unaware of Mrs. Heartbreak's hard lot (typical!). He is still rushing about and nearly knocks David Buttgen down as he hurtles out of the PO: John knows that Marjorie will be cheered when she sees her picture on the new stamp and, so intent is John on his purpose, he does not hear David's muttered howdy. John is unaware of so much.

Yodi, the Artist Formerly Known As Catherine Yoder, is once again on the Town Square and once again in deep conversation with Clara Jane. They are not laughing during this conversation.

Yodi explains to Clara Jane her plan for the improvement of the fountains, a plan that she has made up on the spot. The plan involves something celestial and something borrowed from the deep blue sea. Yodi, who owns a shop around the corner, is an artist and so can see things before they become. That is why she can see Clara Jane and converse with her.

Because of his state of hurry, John does not see Yodi and Clara Jane, nor does he know that he now has at least one, and perhaps two allies who see the fountains in the same light as he. I say "perhaps two" because it is not clear yet that Clara Jane cares much about Berryville, or its malignant Town Square fountains.

For Clara Jane, Berryville is just a good place to hide out. It is a town that sees what it wishes to see. Consequently, much of Berryville is invisible to its residents, and what is invisible to them is unseen, or taken on faith. Berryville does not wish to see serial killers, and Berryvillians take it on faith that there is no sex, violence, or strong language in Berryville—unless the SVSL involves Mexicans, methamphetamines addicts, or Yankees living in Eureka Springs—so these things are not seen. Clara Jane is not a Mexican, a methamphetamines addict, or a Yankee—so she is not seen.

This is not entirely bad, John thinks. A few, maybe many, Berryvillians are able to see Christ for example, and they say with certainty that they observe Christ walking about, talking about, and moving in and out of the their lives and the lives of their families and neighbors. They take it on faith that Christ is among them: believing is seeing. They may not be able to see serial killers or the visible litter and cancerous smear of abandoned downtown properties, but there are other and invisible things that they can see.

What does this mean?

One thing it means is that you're reading at the 7.7th grade level on the Flesch-Kincaid Grade Level Scale. Six percent of the sentences in this chapter are passive sentences. If you understand what you've read so far—whether it makes any sense or not—you are doing better than I am. Six percent is at least 1% over the acceptable passive sentence limit. I'm mortified. Or would be, if anyone was reading this.

Skipper French, the pastor of the Methodists, says that life cannot make sense and cannot be fair, unless one believes in the resurrection of Christ. The "book" you are reading right now—which exists in your life since you are reading it—makes sense or does not make sense depending entirely on your judgment of the matter and, perhaps on the conventional wisdom of a mass of readers and critics who might or might not offer opinions about its sense or lack of sense. Whether or not it makes sense is entirely independent of anyone's belief in the resurrection of Christ.

John believes in the resurrection, yet also believes that his belief or disbelief is not important. The sun also rises whether John believes it will, or does not believe it will. So it is with Christ; he is risen without consideration of our belief or disbelief.

So it is with the fountains: they are ugly whether we believe in them or do not believe in them. And they will always be ugly unless we can see them. Believing is seeing, but it is only by seeing that the absence of Good can be made Good.

The next chapter will contain some jokes. Hang in there.

Chapter 17:

Slouching Toward SHAZAAM

In moments of sorrow or confusion John sometimes dips into Carney's *The Boy's Book of Complete Knowledge: Everything a boy should know in preparation for manhood.* The BBCK has served John well over the years, but it is far from complete. In the matter of gender, for example, the BBCK simply says, "Women and girls are different than men and boys and they see the world differently than does the male species. Baseball is a healthy, safer, and acceptable alternative to relations between the sexes."

What the BBCK lacks in coherence it more than makes up in the brevity of its conclusions and the grain of Truth in each. It subscribes to William Occam's principle that "entities are not to be multiplied beyond necessity" or, more economically phrased, "please cut the crap." Judged in these terms, the BBCK amply demonstrates how most ideas, books, sermons, cultures, etc., can benefit from a close shave.

Clara Jane is encouraging John to advocate for more economical ways to solve his Problem with Iowans. Over coffee, over which she winces, Clara Jane tells John that she is having difficulty coming up with the SHAZAAM part of the plan to transform Iowans into better, more loving, and more generous human beings through the ruse of free barbeque and the rite of baptism.

"What I have figured out so far," Clara Jane says, "is how to get those suckers into the Town Square fountain, and how to hold their corn-stuffed carcasses under water until they are dead, dead, dead. What I haven't been able to figure out is how to pull them out of the water alive and reformed."

"Perhaps the Holy Ghost will assist," John suggests. "It is possible that He is the one who instructed you to park here in Berryville. I doubt that he will leave you adrift without some assistance. By and by ... maybe."

"I'm not exactly up on the Holy Ghost business. I admit to hearing a "voice" instructing me to stay put for a while. But it's possible that the voice I heard was just a plotting device by the Authorial I. And a pretty lame one let me tell you."

John reaches over and pats Clara Jane on the hand. He knows instantly that his gesture of comfort is a mistake. Fortunately for John, I am writing this book instead of John Sanford, in which case his hand would be stuck to the table with a railroad spike.

"Don't do that again, Bub," Clara Jane says, drawing her hand back. "I'm not one of your ditsy has-been lady writers."

A muffled squeak pops out of the Rs' from Mrs. Rawlings. "You despicable, low rent witch! How dare you!"

"Pipe down, Tootsie," says Clara Jane, "or I'll burn your sorry books on the City Hall lawn by the light of the moon."

Marjorie Rawlings begins to moan. Clara Jane narrows her eyes and hisses. Mrs. Heartbreak, startled, looks over from the sales counter, her head swiveling from left to right in time with the faint sounds originating on either side of John, who seems stuck in the middle of it all. She is unable to "see" Clara Jane yet, but she does observe a mirage like haze that is somewhat human in shape. Mrs. Heartbreak gives no credence to the rumor that bookshops in general, and her bookshop in particular, are haunted, but there does seem to be an abundance of "psychic" energy about the place, especially lately.

Mrs. Mary Trimble, who has been looking at dictionaries, decides to forego a purchase until another day. Mrs. Heartbreak watches her as she goes out the door and worries that business may not survive her husband's peculiar behaviors.

If John is unaware of Mrs. Heartbreak's worries, it is because he thinks he has bigger fish to fry. This little hissy fit between Clara Jane and Marjorie is small potatoes in the scheme of things. Because John organizes his books in alphabetical order by author, small and large crimes of taste are committed on a regular basis. When he filed Jimmy Baker within an inch or two of the good Jew, Martin Buber, Buber screamed and cried out, "My God, My God, why have you forsaken me!"

Buber's point was well taken. But John, despite Mrs. Heartbreak's opinions on the matter, is a fairly canny bookseller and knows that Reverend Baker will leave soon and will soon leave Buber splendidly alone once again.

In the interests of authorial harmony John had thought about organizing authors based on his assumptions about their compatibility with one another. Instead of sticking Jane Austin alongside Jean Auel, for example, perhaps Jane would enjoy spending time with John Cheever, a mannerly and interesting fellow. Similarly, maybe Mrs. Auel would appreciate the conviviality and company of John Jakes or Olivia Goldsmith.

You can see the problem with the compatibility scheme, though. Unless John is on the spot all the time "interfacing" with customers, no one would be able to find anything. John is pretty much a failure at interfacing; John is almost never on the spot. Strike one for the compatibility scheme.

Strike two is that the really good writers are lousy company and get along with no one; they ALL want their own shelf and they all HATE TO SHARE. They are poor at conversation. What a collection of drunks, snobs, and rascals. Strike three is Henry Miller and Anais Nin. Put them together and suddenly Heartbreak's Really Dreadful Coffee and Pretty Good Books is a Porn Store. Berryville will put up with an infinite amount of literal dirt, but God forbid that figurative dirt is available. John is sticking to the alphabet for the foreseeable future.

John has calmed Marjorie and turns his attention back to Clara Jane, who has stopped hissing. Mrs. Heartbreak has turned her attention to a gaggle of Red Hat Ladies who always spend a bundle. John and Clara Jane are ostensibly alone.

"Clara Jane," John begins, "I was so impressed with the way you used a cell phone to decapitate Eddie Francine. Imagine: an explosive device that an unwitting victim holds to his head and triggers himself by pushing the "send" button. It was truly, magnificently, creative. I know you'll come up with something."

A happy memory, surely. Clara Jane smiled fondly at its recollection; but only for a moment. "Johnny boy, there was no resurrection involved." Clara Jane jabbed her finger in John's direction. "As you well know, Eddie isn't walking around today. He isn't a better, more loving, more generous human being. Eddie was buried and his head was scraped off the headliner of his Buick. He didn't come back from the dead."

See John. See John sip coffee. See John nod pensively. "The author of this mess has certainly got us into a pickle," he says.

See Clara agree. See Clara brighten. "You know, John, this isn't really our problem. Your Pal the writer (that would be me moi, the Authorial I—just so you know I am paying attention) is the one to figure it out. You and I are just the means to his sorry end."

John wants to disagree. He does not object to investing some responsibility in the Authorial I; he does object to being a means to an end.

"You and I may only be characters in a book," John says. "But we are becoming real and, real or not, we both have the potential to be greater than mere reality. That is the true beauty of literature— it is to be greater than reality."

Clara Jane snorts.

"Seriously" John says. "Look at it this way. You and I may be experiments in literature. Now, literature is a bit like the physics of virtual reality. Just as physics is about revealing the laws that govern the physical realm, literature is about revealing the laws that govern the mental or imaginary realm."

John pauses, and then says, "We are being revealed. When we are fully revealed we will be not only virtually but fully real."

Clara Jane—and you, perhaps (no doubt?)—are perplexed. On the other hand, so far I've written only 2% passive sentences and have kept everything at 7.2 on the Flesch-Kincaid Grade Level scale. I think we're fine.

Let's see where John goes with this virtual stuff:

And John says: "The world described in Genesis was a volatile and dangerous place. It molded human life through incomprehensible caprice. Natural benefice tempered by natural disaster defined reality. For centuries the goal of human effort was to tap Nature's terrible power."

Clara Jane is about to snort again, perhaps derisively. Knowing, however, that you are keenly observing her every move (you are, aren't you?), she chooses a more lady-like, derisive eye roll.

"Remember Occam, Bud," she says. "Cut the crap. Cut to the chase."

"Here's the chase scene," John says. "Our success in tapping Nature's power has been so complete, that a new world has emerged, a world created by human ingenuity. In many respects the modern world is a world of artificial reality."

"Are you telling me that what is artificial is real?" Clara Jane asks. "That I'm as real as anyone walking the streets of Berryville?"

"Why not? You walking about is not an oddity, or unusual in even the strictest sense. Our world is full of fat-free food; television is mostly "reality" programs and news about people whose lives are unquestionably meaningless if not artificial.

"Religious leaders operate businesses out of immense tin buildings that have fiberglass crosses nailed to molded plastic steeples sitting way on top of all that tin. These leaders have television programs and warn us that sexual intercourse will lead to dancing.

"We have peeled mathematics away from physical reality," John continues. "$X + Y = Y + X$ can mean the sum of anything and its opposite, and the sum may be utterly independent of space and time.

"Philosophy is now a game for linguists, and the greatest challenge facing business is how to build machines dumb enough for human beings to use. We hire millionaires to play games on plastic grass that we used to play ourselves on real grass.

"It goes on and on," he finishes, looking a bit frantic. (He has depressed himself.)

"Watch me yawn, John," Clara says, and YAWNS. "What has this got to do with the price of gas, or how we reform Iowans?

"Now" she continues, "is definitely not the time for another tiresome rant about modernism."

Watch the reader yawn, I might add. Lord knows how this stuff gets into John's head, or how it leaks out of my fingers onto the keyboard. But John is impossible to restrain.

"We've gone way beyond modernism, Clara Jane," John said. "We live in a world where anything is possible as long as we're willing to trade culture, and literacy, for the next new thing."

Pick one: *a)* a light bulb goes on, *b)* see the dawning of an idea, *c)* awareness abounds. Then, watch Clara Jane ask:

"John, am I an Avatar? Am I becoming real? Is that right?"

"Why not, Honey Bunch? All is Virtual; it is a New World, no Bravery required."

If Clara Jane was your run of the mill Berryvillian, that is to say, polite, anxious to please, and precisely average on any known computational scale, she might have a dreamy, perhaps bittersweet expression on her face. But Clara Jane is a serial killer (you haven't forgotten that, have you?). Instead, she begins to calculate the change in odds, the change in circumstances. She smiles.

"Alls ya'lls had me worried for a minute," she says, lapsing into her Tisdale, Missouri accent. "Fixin' them dullards from Des Moines is gonna be a piece of cake. I mean, now that Virtual is Actual, the Authorial I can make Hillary Clinton a Stigmata, show her crying tears of blood. Heck, he could help George W. Bush pass an IQ test, or find a problem Barack Obama couldn't spend a billion on."

"Wrong," John says. Firmly says.

"Reformation and resurrection should not be tricks of the mind or exercises in logic. We should stop trifling with reality here and now."

"But artificial, virtual, is so much easier," protests Clara Jane. She stretches her arm across the table and grabs John by the wrist. Squeezed. "Come on, John," she rasps. "Make me real!"

John pulls his arm away. "You have to make yourself real. This book is just helping you figure that out.

"And these Iowans," he continues, "As sorry as they are, most of them are real. We are going to reform them for real. You are going to reform them for real."

Clara Jane, exasperated, says, "Why bother? It is SO MUCH TROUBLE. Why can't we just apply a little Wittgenstein, a little French-derived mathematics, a soupcon of Hollywood, and call it real?"

"Because it would be joyless."

Chapter 18:

Venus on the Half Shell

In a way that is quite alarming to John, it appears that other Berryvillians are coming to know that this "novel" is being written. It is becoming common knowledge that John, the drudge-like bookseller and dimly adequate spouse of the Fabulous Mrs. Heartbreak, is also a character in a book. For example, Pastor Paul Andresen just e-mailed John:

"Dear John," he wrote,

"I have been thinking about the "authorial I" compared to the "narrative I" and the "I for an I" offered by the "editorial him" in the book about you—Coffee with John Heartbreak—that I have been reading on the Internet. It confuses me too much to keep all that straight. I'm just glad that the Authorial I stayed away from Jay McInerney's "narrative you" from *Bright Lights, Big City.* How irritating was that to read?"

John sips from a cup of RDC and shudders (not over the coffee which really was dreadful, but) over the havoc that I am sowing in his otherwise quiet and humdrum life. Good Grief! He thinks. What if Mrs. Heartbreak gets wind of what he has been thinking! Serial Killers! Pig jokes! Iowans! Dead writers whispering sour nothings in her husband's ear! Yikes!

"As for the reality of the characters in the book," Pastor Andresen continued, "I like what John Irving said in *The World According to Garp* when he wrote that the most important characters to keep alive are the ones you are going to kill. That is so interesting an idea—and maybe biblical too, considering my line of work. (Darn whimsy!).

"Do characters know they are characters?" Andresen wrote. "I say the person to ask is Kilgore Trout!"

John pushed back from the keyboard. Paul Andresen is the second wittiest man John knows and he reads Andresen's sermons every week on-line. He laughs and laughs at how well—and gently—Andresen is able to invest popular culture with scriptural purpose. In John's view, that is the equivalent of turning water into wine.

John also likes knowing that at least one other person in Berryville knows who John Irving and Kilgore Trout are. (I initially wrote ..." who are John Irving and Kilgore Trout ..." in an ineffectual but sincere engagement with the rules of grammar. But let us allow John his own manner of sentence construction.)

John Irving is real, of course. Irving was, in tandem with John Heartbreak, once new and bright as a penny, but is now an Old Warhorse. Nevertheless, John Irving still writes books and John Heartbreak still enjoys his books and wishes that people would still read them. (He also and simply wishes that people still read).

Kilgore Trout is not real. But only in a manner of speaking, of course. Kilgore Trout is a character in novels by Kurt Vonnegut. The character Kilgore Trout is the "author" of a novel titled *Venus on the Half Shell*, that was actually written by Jose Farmer—which is the nom de plume of Kenneth Baker. So here it is: Kurt Vonnegut invented a character named Kilgore Trout who later wrote a book that was really written by Philip Jose Farmer.

(By the way, the "character" Kilgore Trout is based on the Science fiction author Theodore Sturgeon, a colleague of the late Mr. Vonnegut, and Salman Rushdie mentions Trout as "a famous Science Fiction writer" in his novel, *The Ground Beneath Her Feet*. And so it goes. (Sorry).

Insofar as John is concerned, characters know they are characters. John knows Kilgore Trout as well as he knows John Irving, or Kurt Vonnegut, for that matter. He knows them very well. And Vonnegut himself seems to get it. When presented with a copy of Venus on the Half Shell he wrote, over his signature,

"I did not write this book!" He didn't write "Kilgore Trout is not real!"

John turns back to Pastor Andresen's email. "I'm sure this e-mail could use a triple close prose shave," Andresen wrote. "Then again, write about 2,000 words each week about God in Three Persons and you'll better understand the hazards of my occupation."

How interesting, John thinks. Andresen alludes to Occam's Razor. "I wonder where that came from?" he says aloud.

John steps away from the keyboard and walks over to the windows at the front of the shop. He peers down the sidewalk and spies a group of Iowans exiting the Ozark Café. They are obviously in a hotcakes and sausage induced stupor and are trying to decide in which direction to go.

The puzzling but intriguing e-mail from Pastor Andresen recedes from John's consciousness as Iowans gutter-ball their way toward the Heartbreak's shop. They peer suspiciously right and left out of little red eyes as they roll, each clutching a fat wallet stuffed with welfare checks from the United States Department of Agriculture. John feels the hair stand up on the back of his neck.

Chapter 19:

Waiting for Joe

As you know by now, Clara Jane is not an introspective person. Like most Social Order Theorists she sees herself at the top of the human heap, supervising or shaping the lives of those less fortunate or informed than she. She does not spend time thinking about whether this is fair, or even if it makes sense. It is the way her mind works. Top to down is the vantage point.

Clara Jane's profession is murder, of course. That does not discourage her from believing that the world is a more rational place because of her professional pursuits. Clara Jane engages her work in a systematic way, knows victims as mothers know the child at breast, and has sussed out the ways in and the ways out of rooms, buildings, streets, towns, cities, highways, states, and countries. Her getaways are masterful; she practices death methodically; her world is planned, zoned; outcomes are projected with a reasonable certainty. Such are the advantages of Social Order Theory, even for Serial Killers.

The disadvantages of, or the hazards to, the foundations of Social Order Theory are acts of God, the habit of Marxism to bankrupt any economy it manages, senses of humor, and the mulish resistance of some peoples to supervision. Serial killers, as a general rule, are at least a half step off conventional career pathways. They work only sporadically and rarely consistently. Consequently, they experience Social Order Theory hazards and disadvantages only on a part time basis, but benefit from the advantages on a full time basis. That accounts for their relative success (viz. "serial") ... and for the occupational success of members of public service unions and foundation and arts council executives.

Clara Jane, however, has started to wonder if time has begun to run out on her. John Sanford had killed her off in his last novel. As a fictional character her death was of minor, no, truthfully, of no interest to her. But Clara Jane was now resurrected, not by her creator John Sanford ne John Camp, but by a complete stranger who thinks of her as real, or at least virtually real. And she herself, Clara Jane, has begun to wonder about her new life, not as only a character in a novel, but as a person with whom real people, living people, like Catryn Yoder and the Authorial I, relate to as a real and actual person.

A measure of success for serial killers depends on their ability to blend into the wallpaper of their surroundings. It was for this reason that Clara Jane selected Berryville—most of the town is wallpaper to its citizens—and the reasons why she adopted the Jane Smith moniker and drives an old Ford Taurus station wagon rather than her usual Porsche Boxster.

Many people in Berryville also believe that the Devil saunters about the town and tempts the weak and foolish. They name these Devils environmentalists, Scientologists, and vegetarians (and sometimes Unitarians) and they are so busy naming these Devils and praying against them that they overlook the run of the mill serial killer in their midst. Clara Jane had counted on that, and until John Heartbreak got wise to her act, everything had been honky dory.

John Heartbreak also believes in the Devil. But John believes that the Devil is so busy collecting sales taxes out on Highway 62 West—on behalf of the City of Berryville—that he can't be bothered with the general run of sinners our small town affords the Great Mandela. Anyway, there are enough Landlords in Berryville who won't repair tenant's leaky roofs, and enough switch-sleeping politicians around town, to allow Old Nick to take several days off every week.

In any case, the Devil does not bother John. The Devil is not God and he is not the Anti-God. Lucifer is merely a fallen angel who manages to get by with a little help from his friend, Human Kind. What is Lucifer compared to God except a spectacular failure? More to the point, John was able to see Clara Jane, not because he was looking for Evil, but because he was looking for Good.

That bothers Clara Jane a lot, too, along with John's being able to see her at all. For all of her fictional existence (now that's worth ciphering!) she operated solely as a machine and as efficiently and productively as one wants a machine to operate. But now Clara is thinking about things she has never thought about before. For example:

Resurrection—of any kind, would be defined by Social Theorists—and by Clara Jane—as one of those acts of God that, like Marxist Theory, can derail the best laid plans. Suddenly, startled, she realizes that she has used the word "resurrection" to describe her own circumstances such as her appearance in this book. And this is the first time (right now) that she has ever thought of God. At no time in her prior existence as a character in John Sanford's novels, or in this "novel" up to this moment, has she had a thought about a god of any sort or of God in particular. Acts of God are extremely unsettling to Social Order Theorists. It is just so to Clara Jane, and she does not like it much.

What has further complicated Clara Jane's life is John's persistence in involving her now in a serial non-killing or, if you will, the reform of Iowa derived tourists. Clara Jane's business has always been destructive acts rationalized away by the arguable fact that the Universe has been a better place for the absence of the scum she took out by means of garroting, electrocution, stabbing, shooting, poisoning, bombing, suffocation, defenestration, and arrangement of "accidental" and deadly misadventures by automobile, animal attack, aviation crash, and forest fire. But John Heartbreak insists not on destruction but reconstruction. This requires Clara Jane to think differently about her work.

"Thinking differently" is hard for Social Order Theorists. Mrs. Heartbreak, for example, has informed John that he always hits the curb with the right back wheel of their car while making right-hand turns onto Springfield Road because he has not been "thinking mathematically."

"It is clear for all to see, John," said Mrs. Heartbreak, "that you have not considered the spatial relationship between our vehicle and the basic right-angle, 90 degree functionality of our byways and junctions. Please," she said, sweetly, "apply a bit of basic geometry when you turn onto Springfield Road. If you do, you won't drag the back wheel over the curb. Think mathematically, dear."

John had nodded agreeably. He knows that it will do no good to explain to Mrs. Heartbreak that the Engineering Giants who planned Berryville's streets built them two and a half feet narrower than standard sized-streets. Consequently, John, who drives methodically and ON HIS OWN SIDE OF THE ROAD always clips the curb when dancing the Springfield Locomotion.

What Mrs. Heartbreak means by "thinking mathematically" is to take over both left and right lanes, thereby preventing traffic on Springfield Road from making a turn onto the street Mrs. Heartbreak possesses. Part two of the "thinking mathematically" formula is to hurl the Heartbreak vehicle into the far left lane in front of on-coming traffic with the prayerful expectancy that everyone's brakes work well enough to give Mrs. Heartbreak time to shift into the proper (right) lane before all and sundry crash and die. John prefers to clip the curb.

And, of course, John says nothing. If Mrs. Heartbreak would say, for example, "let us have mice for dinner," John would nod and smile. "Okay," he would say. John knows that circles and squares are identical, that bending one into the shape of the other is a trifle, that the shape of the moment can change in a moment, but that the basic inherency of the square and the circle are immutable. What are a few mice, a bit of "mathematical thinking," in the face of that!

But Clara Jane, like Mrs. Heartbreak, like Social Order Theorists everywhere, thinks of circles as circles and squares as squares. The observable potential of a butterfly to shift the course of a hurricane from Miami Beach to Savannah is not factored into their plans; they believe that entropy is the end of times, things, and disbelieve that it is the beginning of new times and things, that there is such a thing as organized (reorganized) chaos.

Clara Jane's life is being reorganized. Her career as a fictional character and as a serial killer had reached an advanced state of entropy when, SHAZAMM, she now appears as a vital if not leading character in a non-plot to not-kill people (Iowans) who—by virtually any definition that John Heartbreak can come up with—need killing. Clara Jane's life has been reorganized, and she feels lost and directionless. If she is no longer a serial killer but rather a serial non-killer, what is the meaning of her life? What are its organizing principles?

Both God and the devil are details in an organizing principle's play by play. There is deep structure (please forgive the linguistic borrowing) in chaos's apparently random, chaotic behavior, behaviors that also characterize all of nature's and most of social phenomena's organizing principles. And within that deep structure—and some details, if you will—is the strange attractor toward which all systems are drawn. That strange attractor is the author of ceaseless creation, evolution, and the destruction of forms. John Heartbreak will argue that within that deep structure is God, the strangest of Strange Attractors.

But enough parsing. Here it is:

Clara Jane's Self—fictional, virtual, or real—is in a state of chaos. I, the Authorial I, am reorganizing it. Or, perhaps, he (that would be me) is merely reporting on her Self-reorganization. Either way, Clara Jane has suddenly realized that her reason for being has radically altered; but into what, or for what purpose, she does not know.

Her one directional pointer is through John Heartbreak and his desire to rid the earth—or at the very least, Berryville—of Iowans or, also at the very least twice, of the less attractive qualities inherent in the characteristic make-up of Iowans. That is her task.

The one organizing principle she is privy to is the non-violence principle: she is not allowed to kill these sap sucking Hawkeyes. Her task is to be accomplished through the uses of free barbeque, baptism, and SHAZAMM.

Her task will be accomplished in the Town Square fountains on the Town Square in Berryville, Arkansas. The fountains are important: perhaps Berryville's citizens will gather about, observe the Miracle of Decent Iowans emerging from the fountain's waters and, as Christ removed the scales from the eyes of the blind man, see for the first time the demoralizing state of the fountains and vote on the spot for their improvement. Decent Iowans, Decent Fountains: a parable for modern times.

Her analysis of the SHAZAMM part is becoming clearer, but also more complex. She is still clueless about how SHAZAMM will change the Iowans, but she now knows that a bit of SHAZAMM has been worked on her: she has recognized resurrection (of a sort); she has started to think about gods, or God; she has become more Self-aware. She is beginning to wonder about how she will spend the rest of her life—or at least the rest of her life as allotted to her by this book.

Clara Jane is also nervous. Her prior existence was all about hiding, getting away, blending into the wallpaper. Now, she is a topic of conversation and speculation: she is no longer wallpaper, and it is not clear that she will get away with anything.

Will the readers (will you) of this "novel" report Clara Jane to the authorities? Clara Jane knows that John will not report her (it says so in Chapter 3) because she keeps a tidy yard: John will accept any number of serial killer-neighbors over a neighbor who doesn't cut his grass. But what of the ministerial types who are reading along with you? Will they view Clara Jane's voluntary surrender to authorities and a cheerful walk to the gas chamber as the only genuine signs of repentance? Or, will a good cry and voluntary membership in a local church suffice? Let bygones be bygones and so on?

There is also the matter of choice. If caught between the rock of say, Baptist Church affiliation and the hard place of the gas chamber, which will Clara Jane prefer? Either is a life sentence. Where does resurrection, thinking, wondering, and Self-awareness lead? Poor Clara Jane.

Poor John Heartbreak. The covey of Iowans who emerged from the Ozark Café at the end of Chapter 19 are now entering the shop. They refuse to make eye-contact with John, and they

100

do not respond to Mrs. Heartbreak's cheery "Hello!" Outside, the sun moves behind a cloud and a dog begins to howl. Shadows lengthen out on the Square and cash registers in the stores begin to rust. Global warming gets worse. Unaccountably, bats fill the half-lit sky.

Finally, one of the Iowans speaks. "Got any paperback westerns?"

"Sorry," John replies. "We don't carry paperbacks."

"And you call yourself a bookstore!" sneered the Iowan. He tapped the harridan standing next to him on the forehead. "Let's go, Hazel," he said. "There ain't a thing in this dump we want."

John and Mrs. Heartbreak smile at one another. "That wasn't so bad," she said. "They didn't stay long, and there was only the one insult."

"Only the one," John agreed. He walked back to his desk. "What are you going to do for the rest of the day?" he asked.

"I think I'll just spend it, waiting for Joe," she replied.

Chapter 20:

John has received a flurry of e-mails this morning. Think of the word "flurry." It's okay for you to take a moment of your busy day to think about a word. You deserve at least a minute for trivial pursuits.

Flurry connotes a windy day, doesn't it, bitter in character, the bitter air filled with bits of fluff, the fluff kicked by the wind; the wind and the fluff strikes one in the face, sticks to the eyebrows, nestles in the hair, melts, and trickles down your neck.

But: what a lot of bother. Look at how using nouns as adverbs and adjectives wastes time. Would it not have been better if John had simply received e-mails this morning, and I had skipped the whole "flurry" business?

Besides, Berryville is hot today. Flurries are not in evidence except in John's mind, which is buffeted by e-mailed threats, insults, wounded feelings, the needs of people from distant lands, inquiries about his mental health and, most of all, advice about Clara Jane. Enough flurries; here's the mail:

The Monsignor

Monsignor Jerry Bachxner, an Auxiliary Pooh Bah in the Archdiocese of St. Paul and Minneapolis, writes, "In theological, and in practical terms as well, nobody should give a rat's patootie what form Clara Jane's repentance takes, as long as it is genuine and that she is truly sorry for her sins.

"The problem you pose is ironic: you want to bring her into the arms of the Lord and simultaneously wonder if you must turn her over to the long arm of the law. Let me tell you that Clara Jane's salvation isn't your business; it is business for Clara Jane and God to work out. Your role is to suggest to her that she think about it. All those Protestants you're hanging around will give you plenty of advice about how to make the suggestion.

"As far as turning her over to the law, don't worry about it. If your town is like any other small town, some busybody will put the screws to her before you can say goodnight nurse. In my humble opinion, it will be far more likely that the people of your town will send Clara Jane to the gas chamber before they cut their grass like civilized people who live in self-respecting communities. Look at what George Bush did to Carla Fay Tucker. He couldn't wait to send her to Jesus.

"Personally, I don't spend much time thinking about hell anymore. First of all, no one in the pews wants to hear about it and, secondly, who knows how to keep score anymore? And I'm old. Old people don't have to worry about hell if they've lived right. There it is: I don't have a dog in the fight.

"Let me remind you that both of us were taught that Martin Luther, unless he made a perfect Act of Contrition at the end of his arrogant life, IS BURNING IN HELL. Today, people are taught that Luther isn't the grand heretic I know him to be but merely a Protesting Brother in Christ or some other such modern claptrap. So, who's to say that your serial killer isn't actually an Angel of Mercy on a mission from God to rid the earth of underworld scum?

"PS," the Monsignor finished, "I want you to know, John," he finished, "that you have certainly fallen into Bad Company."

Jerry had never been big on Ecumenism.

The Boss

Charles Roland Staley, President of the Board of Directors of the Institute (Rooty toot toot) for Social and Economic Despair, which is headquartered in Des Moines and which employs John from time to time, wrote, "Heartbreak, the opinions expressed in that so-called novel about Iowa and its citizens are reprehensible.

If your intention is humor let me tell you that you have FAILED. Be assured that ISED and its employees will not trouble you again!"

Charles (Chuckles to John) is one of the rat's patooties Monsignor Boxleitner wouldn't give. John clicked the DELETE button.

The Artist

Yodi, the AFKA Catherine Yoder's e-mail was interesting in a complicated way. "For a while," she wrote, "I thought I was Clara Jane, that she was based on me. I was waiting to be revealed! But I guess I am only a character, and minor at that.

"Don't you think you should reconsider? I would LOVE to knock off some people! I could dispose of the bodies in my kiln!"

The Animist

"John," wrote a Hmong man from Laos named Blong Vue, "there are too many ghosts in your story. When Mrs. Rawlings was speaking it was very scary because it put an old belief back in my head. Hmong people don't like story books very much because they are full of ghosts. That is the idea I have to deal with now.

"You should have left Clara Jane in the book where you discovered her. Now she is out of the book and walking around your town. I don't think she will become a Christian and a better person. It is not the nature of ghosts to be good."

The Saint

Daniel Berrigan wrote, "You must pray for Clara Jane, and thank her for making you a better person. Maybe she will save you.

"By the way," he closed, "Don't forget my birthday! I'll be 87! Can you believe it?"

The Muslim

"May you be safe with all the bad things happening in your town," wrote Vjosa Mullahatari. "But why are you talking so much with this murderous woman? And why do you want her to kill Iowans? If you think about it, all you Americans are like people from Iowa: you are all too fat (not you, John—I mean the other Americans), and you think you know everything. Americans are cheap too: what is your dollar worth now? Nothing! I think you should forget about killing the Iowa people. You might as well kill yourself (not you, John—I mean the other Americans) if you think your reasons to kill them are the right reasons.

"The woman is not resurrected, John," Vjosa continued. "Christ was not resurrected by our belief—so this woman could not be resurrected either. Christ was in a swoon and revived later with the help of his Disciples and his Dearest Mother, Mary. If Clara Jane was here in Gjakova, I would cut her down myself. Your plan to change the Iowa people is foolish and she has only taken your money.

"I am also having trouble understanding why you hate the fountains in your town. Why do you stare out your window and poison your mind with grim thoughts? The fountains will be improved or not improved, inshallah, and not because of your hard thoughts.

"By the way," she concluded, "Berryville sounds like a very rural place. Do the peasants have any need of your books? Why aren't they out working instead of putting noses in books?"

The Pastor

Paul Andresen, our Presbyterian Don, wrote, "What should a ministerial type say about Clara Jane?

"I will give my opinion, and even more I will try to make sense; the latter infinitely more difficult than the former. But before I get started, I must let you know I am answering the questions posed in Chapter 20 in reverse order … not out of whimsy, but because I am a minister and we tend to redefine questions before we answer them.

Should we let bygones be bygones and so on?

"No. I don't think we can. I am a strong believer in forgiveness, but we can never forget. Whether it's just because we forget how others wrong us or because we should never forget the lessons being wronged taught us; people don't forget.

"Clara Jane's actions have consequences--whether she is forgiven or not. Sometimes the bygones come back very quickly, to use an expression outside of my tradition: instant karma. And sometimes, not so much.

"However, the nature of sin (JOHN CALVIN ALERT!) permeates all we are and all we do and doesn't allow us to forgive perfectly as we are forgiven in Christ. There is no way bygones will ever truly be bygones.

Will a good cry and voluntary membership in a local church suffice?

"For Clara Jane" Pastor Paul wrote, "—a grace filled if not truly repentant human being—membership in a part of the Body of Christ is an important part of living.

"Of course I'd say that. I believe it too! No pastor in their right mind would say "Stay home and watch the NFL Draft on ESPN. But if she is going just for show, who is she showing? She can fool me all she wants; I'm human, I'm mortal, and in the end I'm very small potatoes. Fooling me is nothing. Fooling her creator is another matter.

"In the Godfather III, there is a scene where Michael meets the Cardinal who will become Pope John Paul I. Michael talks of hypocrisy within the church. The Cardinal takes a stone from the water of a bird bath and says that the church is filled with such people, constantly immersed in the water but because of their hard shell, the water is unable to penetrate. Clara Jane can sit in church forever and cry as the banshee wails, but if the Holy Spirit does not penetrate her shell, it is all for loss.

Are Clara Jane's voluntary surrender to authorities and a cheerful walk to the gas chamber the only genuine sign of repentance?

"Wow. Gary Gilmore, call on line one, Gary Gilmore, call on line one! I once heard that Utah is the only state in the union that still allows firing squad as a capital punishment option. Mormons strongly believe that atonement for sin comes through blood and the only means of capital punishment that draws blood is firing squad. Gary Gilmore, call on line one, Gary Gilmore, call on line one ...

"Really, the answer to this question is no because there is more to repentance than the "cheerful acceptance of consequence." I don't even think you have to be cheerful about accepting consequence as long as we acknowledge the plain fact that a higher power exists (whether earthly or divine) and that there are consequences to actions. Being cheerful about it is just plain masochistic.

"The joy is that we are given forgiveness, prevenient grace (ACK! MORE CALVIN!), grace which was given long before we could ever think to ask for it. We are called to respond to grace in repentance.

"In the Old Testament, to repent meant to turn around, to go back, or to change belief, or to change your course of conduct. In the New Testament, to repent meant to change your mind, feel regret, be converted. If Clara Jane's response is all for show without changing her mind, feeling regret, or being converted; then there is no repentance.

"In Mario Puzo's *The Sicilian*, bandits under the direction of Tori Giuliano kidnap a Cardinal on Easter Sunday. Some of the bandits took the Sacrament of Holy Communion because they had made confession the night before and the kidnapping was not to take place until after the mass. Confession, perhaps; repentance, I don't think so.

"Now, Clara Jane may talk a good game, but again, who's getting fooled here? Not you—not even her.

"But now, the first question—the one I think is the toughest of all, at least for me:

Will I report Clara Jane to the authorities?

"The worst part of answering this question is that because of mandatory reporting laws that are in effect for service professionals in Arkansas, there might be an obligation to report. As a Pastor and a person with training in counseling (even beyond my seminary education) I am obligated to report Clara Jane to the authorities if I believe she is a threat to herself or others.

"Is there true citizenship when the government has to legislate the duties of a citizen?

"What do I report? And to whom do I report it? Do I tell the County Extension Agent that she has wonderful herbal and lawn and garden hygiene?

"In my personal contact, I do not have direct knowledge of Clara Jane doing anything which requires my reporting her to "the authorities." Unfortunately this opens the Pandora's Box of second guessing and guilt if a short stack of Iowans are found resting at the bottom of the city fountains much in the same way as pancakes are found at the Ozark Café.

"Of course, you are the ultimate authority in this universe; and since you all ready know, there is no need for me to tell you (less than) what you all ready know. (Now that's whimsy!)

"And, anyway, since Clara Jane thinks she is on the top of the heap, there is no higher power and this whole thing is moot.

"Did you know moot is the Hebrew word for dead?"

John did not know that.

Chapter 21:

Mrs. Heartbreak

John spies Carol Ann Engskov crossing the Square. Is she going toward Dirt Poor to buy something fun? Little puffs of dust kick up behind Carol Ann's heels as she passes by the old courthouse, and then past two or three wickedly disreputable store fronts that molt and sag like exhausted hens sitting on the last eggs they will ever lay.

Loretta Tanner is also in town, standing on the corner by Carr's, and waiting for the light to change. She sees John's shadow behind his window and waves at him. Her manner of waving is friendly and open, not at all like the chilling little wave that Clara Jane sent his way so many days ago. Loretta is a serious student of the Bible and John is always interested in hearing her opinion about what is being discussed at Bible Study on Sunday nights.

Loretta, like Elaine West, fills John with feelings of calmness and a sense that the world is not bad. John waves back.

John has, so far this morning, enjoyed looking out his window. Yesterday's flurry of e-mails (okay, e-mails, no flurry) had left him bilious and distracted last night during Mrs. Heartbreak's gourmet dinner, and she said something about casting pearls before swine. Or, maybe John had simply misheard her, so deep was his distraction, and so advanced is his deafness. Today, however, the sun is shining, John is not thinking about Clara Jane, and he is making plans to take John Cheever or Jack London to lunch over at Royal Sundae.

Ah. Carol Ann has gone into D's.

Carol Ann was John's first friend in Berryville. He met her when he applied for a library card and Carol Ann, who is our town's librarian, helped him fill out the application and asked him if she could help him find a book. John thought that was a generous thing to do and he appreciated the kindness of her attention.

When John moved to Berryville, I had nothing better to do than tag along. I am fond of John and of Mrs. Heartbreak for that matter, and Mrs. Heartbreak's plan to run an antiques store seemed like fun. John was gone most of the time and I could make myself useful running errands for her and toting furniture around the place and out to automobiles if someone happened to buy a chair or lamp.

When John retired from his day job shortly after the Heartbreaks moved to Berryville, Mrs. Heartbreak suggested that he open a bookstore. John had thousands of books lying about and Mrs. Heartbreak was hopeful that having a bookstore would aid her in her efforts to clean out the house. She also hoped that it would keep John occupied and in her line of sight. Mrs. Heartbreak likes to know what John is doing, all the time. Every minute. Every second. Every ... okay, okay.

It has all worked out. Mrs. Heartbreak is able to supervise John and keep an eye on him to her hearts content. Her engrossment with his whereabouts does not involve suspicion, or concern that John may have a loose-limbed chippie stashed away somewhere. Mrs. Heartbreak simply lusts for supervision. It is her nature. She cannot help it. "Chippie," by the way, is Mrs. Heartbreak's word for any woman younger than she. A wholly sensitive, new-age male such as is John would never—I certainly wouldn't—use the word "chippie."

John is not oblivious to Mrs. Heartbreak's various non-marital lusts, nor does he mind them. He is her private Light Brigade. Into any number of valleys he has charged and thundered, his not to reason why, his but to do or die, at her explicit direction or preconscious whim. John can no longer imagine drawing breath independent of her than he can imagine vaulting up the wall and crawling across the ceiling on his hands and knees. It is all fine. John loves Mrs. Heartbreak.

Mrs. Heartbreak is entirely aware of John's devotion. But like so many naturally fabulous women she takes devotion as her due. This probably has something to do with the way Betty Davis Kaiser, Mrs. Heartbreak's mother, raised her back on the farm in Indiana. Personally, I believe that there will be some penalty imposed in the great beyond for this rearing. What do you think? (John does not think about this and he would not offer an opinion).

One of John's favorite bible verses is "Blessed are they who expect nothing, for they shall not be disappointed" (perhaps he hasn't gotten the wording exactly right). This is not cynicism on John's part but the belief that God has already given him everything he needs, and that he has no right to ask for more. John does not ask God for anything except for a grateful heart; his prayers are all prayers of thanks. Mrs. Heartbreak, on the other hand, views herself as the object of ALL the blessings in the Sermon on the Mount and is optimistically certain she is deserving of them all.

John is not disturbed by what Mrs. Heartbreak grants or by what she takes for granted. Unlike so many other dim, semi-skilled, and marginally capable men, John is aware of who he is and is awfully grateful for his luck in being chosen by Mrs. Heartbreak. He would have it no other way.

Devotion and loyalty aside, John is also not oblivious to the fact that Mrs. Heartbreak has more ticks than Old Roy. She could have, may have, served as the archetype for the Princess and the Pea. Yet, another favorite verse of John's, not biblical, is a line from a poem by Winfield Townley Scott: "We love each other because our ailments are the same."

John and Mrs. Heartbreak's ailments are not the same, but Mrs. Heartbreak puts up with plenty. John is deaf, stoical, and duller than lettuce. And bless his heart he doesn't even know how to try to be different. Conjoined, Mr. and Mrs. Heartbreak's ailments form the perfect marriage.

John can't decide whom to take to lunch. If he takes John Cheever he knows the conversation will get around to Berryville's dissimilarity to Shady Hill, that lovely suburban East Coast enclave of tennis whites, High Church wife swapping, and martinis on the train home. Then, John will spend the afternoon feeling homesick for New England, although it has never been his home.

If he takes Jack London he'll have to hear at least one dog story, and though it will be a great dog story, it is still a story about a dog. John gets plenty of dog stories from Mrs. Heartbreak, all about Jane, her Jack Russell Terrier. And, of course, London drinks, so you never know what kind of shape he'll be in.

On a whim, John turns his back on Cheever and London and pulls Ole Rolvaag off the shelf. Cheever and London mutter imprecations—they were looking forward to getting out of the shop for a while—and Skip French, who is browsing through the Modern Library editions, overhears them and looks up, startled. "What?" he asks, loudly. "What was that?"

"Never mind," Mrs. Heartbreak says, reassuring him. "It's John, practicing his ventriloquism.

"Your husband is stranger than a monkey grinder," Pastor French replies. "Among ducks he would be odd."

"Yes," says Mrs. Heartbreak.

John and Ole leave the building and shuffle toward Royal Sundae. John felt happy that he had invited Rolvaag along instead of Cheever or London, both of whom are unreliable company on many levels. During lunch, John intends to find out Ole's views on Einar Haugan and whether or not Haugan influenced him when he wrote *Laengselen Baat*.

Rolvaag … oh. Excuse me. You don't care about Ole Rolvaag, do you? Okay. Let's skip his biography. (But you should really read *Giants of the Earth*. It's the second best book written in America during the first half of the 20th century.)

As John stepped through the door of Royal Sundae, Alexander Virden automatically picks up the ice cream scoop and begins making John a pecan ice cream in a waffle cone. John, who we know to be a man of limited imagination, always orders the same thing. Meanwhile, Rolvaag stares out the window at traffic passing by on Highway 62. The grass alongside the highway—right in the middle of town—is 20 inches high. Rolvaag shakes his head in bewilderment. John, standing next to him, licking his ice cream cone, nods sympathetically.

"How hard would it be to make your town look presentable?" Rolvaag asks. "The simplest people in the rudest fishing villages back home in Norway know at least to keep their towns tidy looking."

"It is depressing," John agrees. "The people of Berryville don't seem to care that their town looks like a sink full of dirty dishes."

Alexander looked up from behind the cash register. "Did you say something, John?" he asks. "Were you talking to me?"

John half-way gestured toward Ole, and then stopped. Alexander can't see Rolvaag and there is no use explaining to whom he'd been talking.

He smiles nervously. "I'm just talking to myself, he says. "Pay no attention."

"I knew it," Alexander laughs. "So it's true! You are practicing to become a ventriloquist. For a while there," he says, "I thought Mrs. Heartbreak was pulling everybody's leg, but she isn't. You're pretty good. I really liked the Norwegian accent! "

Ventriloquist? This was the first that John had heard about becoming a ventriloquist. What on earth for? What had Mrs. Heartbreak been telling people?

Rolvaag tapped John on the shoulder. "Is this man saying that I am speaking with a Norwegian accent?" He sounds indignant, wounded. "I'll have you know that I speak perfectly good English."

What Rolvaag really said was "I-lah heffa yew knau I-lah speka purfuctly guuuda Engalush."

"That's great!" Alexander exclaims. "You didn't even move your lips!"

John began to nudge Rolvaag toward the door. Rolvaag pushed back. John pushed harder. Alexander laughed louder.

"You're a card, John," he says. "Now you're imitating a Norwegian stoke victim. Tasteless, certainly. But very funny!"

Out on the street, John propels Ole Rolvaag away from Royal Sundae and east toward the crosswalk in front of the post office. Bill DeWeese was walking down the street across from them, probably headed around the corner to Hanby's Lumber Company. John and Ole slipped over the cross walk and head back to the shop.

"I can't say that was much of a lunch, John," Rolvaag complains. "And I don't understand why you want to be a ventriloquist. It seems an undignified occupation for a bookseller," he adds.

"I don't!" John says heatedly. "I have no interest in ventriloquism!"

Fred Mayer, who was going into the Ozark Café, turned around at the sound of John's voice. "That's not what I hear, John," he says. "I hear you're pretty good at it, too."

When John got back to the shop and Rolvaag slipped back into the Rs, John approached Mrs. Heartbreak, who was just hanging up the phone. "That was some woman named Clara Jane Smith," she says. "She wants you to call her as soon as you come in. I could barely hear her. She speaks in the most ghostly whisper! What does she want?"

"Never mind," John says sharply. "Why are you telling people that I'm a ventriloquist?"

Mrs. Heartbreak crossed her eyes, looked at the end of her nose. "I'm doing no such thing," she says, mildly. "You certainly have some strange ideas, John.

Chapter 22:

Bring Me the
Head of Fuzzy Markowitz

For a while, angels were very popular. Maybe Oprah had said something about them on television, or perhaps there had been a suddenly popular angel themed movie. Whatever the cause, John couldn't keep an angel book on the shelf before it flew—sorry!—out the door. Books that turn into money quickly are certainly angels in John's eyes.

On the matter of angels, Unitarians are generally in favor of the idea and seem to believe in them, again generally, as a group. This strikes John as a serene pastime, but a curious one since Unitarians, once again (that would be again times two) generally, tap dance around the whole idea of a defined God yet will natter on all though the soup and be cracking nuts before concluding the thrilling story of their Spirit Guides—which are surely angels—and their mutual, sundry adventures.

Otherwise, though, John does not think about angels much, even though he believes in them. But why is it (how is it?) that people who don't believe in God will believe almost anything else? I suppose Chesterton would call that a paradox.

What John does think about is that Man and God are the two rails of a ladder that reach all the way to heaven. Between them is an arc of Spirit, blind electric power that pulses and shocks, infrequently a steady unencumbered hum traveling from the lips of God directly into Man's ear, more often a tripping, flummoxed, only half heard whisper that confusedly seems to emanate from anything, anywhere. Perhaps that is the cause of Unitarian ambivalence and the Buddhist's all is one fandango. Please write in and let me know. Anyway ...

The blind electric power between those rails, which by now must look to you like a sort of Jacob's ladder, is how John thinks of the Holy Spirit. The higher one climbs on the rails—the higher one ascends above the vanities and glories of the earth—the clearer and steadier becomes the unencumbered hum.

Oh, geez. *Mayday! Mayday!* Is there a metaphysician in the house? I'm really sorry ... but let's dig this hole a bit deeper anyway, shall we? You know I can't help myself, and it only goes on for a couple of more paragraphs. Hang in there.

Yes, certainly, the Holy Spirit is a questionable character, easily or uneasily acknowledged by the faithful, but whose existence is certainly and professionally ridiculed by Big Minds and Serious Thinkers everywhere. Can a spirit be real, they ask?

Man we know is real, never mind Descartes: dump a hot cup of John's RDC into your lap and that's the only proof you need of I am. Is God real, does God exist? That's such a boring question. Both John and I are tired of it. Everyone, on both sides of the stoop, is tired of it. You decide for yourself, okay?

Clara Jane has gotten into the deciding business, although she is deciding from a position very far back in the pack. Let's assume at least, that she is far back, and that she has a lot to figure out, since serial killers aren't usually in the front pew.

For example, Clara Jane is beginning to experience anxiety about her existence and to assume that she herself is real—I suppose we could dump a cup of coffee into her lap to see if she jumps—and she is beginning to wonder if God is real too. The two questions always seem to go together: Man sits by a banked fire under the stars and wonders about his place among the stars. Then he begins to wonder what, who, is beyond the stars. Unfortunately, we can't test God with a cup of hot joe. (And who would we get to run the test?)

John long ago decided that God is real; because he needs someone to thank, and because he needs someone to rage against: God is always johnny on the spot. Thank you, God.

Clara Jane is, as we said, less sure of God, and is still unsure about herself for that matter. But things are changing. Her call to John, intercepted by Mrs. Heartbreak at the end of the last chapter, was a call to discuss the matter. That Mrs. Heartbreak could hear Clara Jane, albeit as a ghostly whisper, was a sign to both Clara Jane and John that she was real or becoming real enough to be heard. There are no flies on Mrs. Heartbreak: she hears what she hears and if she heard Clara Jane, then Clara Jane is an audible fact. This is by way of saying that Mrs. Heartbreak is the final authority on such matters; if she says a tree has fallen its falling is definitely heard.

So here we are. John is shuffling down Prichard Street toward Clara Jane's house. He has been invited for tea. A neighbor on the corner, no doubt genus Appalachian Americanus, has strewn the body parts of an old pickup truck around his yard. John has called the City about the mess and the City has made sympathetic noises in response. But it has done nothing for the months and years that the truck has sat there, rusting into the ground, not three hundred yards from City Hall.

John wants to fly into a rage over it, but he doesn't have it in him today. His complaints to City Hall have no effect, never have effect, and have only served as a source of discouragement to John, and an annoyance to city officials. In the end, he supposes, cleaning up Berryville is only putting lipstick on a pig; it will still be a pig no matter how crimson its lips. At least, that seems to be the attitude of Berryville's legislators. Oh, maybe they just like pigs? Who knows?

Clara Jane's house and yard is the neat exception to the disconsolate Berryville rule; her grass is mowed and the house and yard are orderly. She has no chickens in her yard, unlike certain residences on Bobo Avenue, and her hedge is trimmed and stands decorously between her house and the ruinous flop next door.

If Clara Jane's intention had been to hide out unnoticed in Berryville the obvious upkeep she invests in her property makes her stand out like a sore thumb. John feels compelled to warn her, but then backs away from the idea. John is willing to forgive serial mayhem in light of her good housekeeping and he is hopeful that you will as well. Come; let us reason together, John will ask of you, will ask of CJ's neighbors. John feels sure that she will remain safe.

Clara Jane is waiting on the porch when John comes into the yard. Next to her is a small table with a pitcher of tea and two glasses filled with ice. She motions to John to sit down, and then pours tea into the glasses.

"I'm glad you came," she says. "Our Iowa deal is becoming complicated in ways that I never imagined. I'm not sure I want to do it anymore. I'm not sure I should do it. We need to talk."

"So Mrs. Heartbreak said," John replies.

"I wasn't sure your wife could hear me," Clara Jane says. "She kept telling me to speak up. By the end of the call I was screaming into the phone."

John nods. "She did say you were whispering. But the important thing is that she heard you. Mrs. Heartbreak trucks not with the fantastic. Ergo, you must be you."

"I'm beginning to believe that I am an I am," she agreed. "Which is not without its downside."

"Such as?"

"Such as, what is my place in the universe?" she answers. "How am I supposed to live? If I'm real, will your pal the Authorial I still pull fifty Gs out of his back pocket when I ask for it? Can I go on killing for money? Or, will I have to gut chickens at Tysons, or stock shelves at Wal-Mart?

"Will the peckerwood who lives in the excreting mound next door turn me over to the cops? Will the cops turn me over to Judge Kent Crow? Will the good Judge pull the trigger and sentence me to death?"

Clara Jane and John pick up their glasses of tea. The ice tinkles in the glasses on the way up, clink on the table on the way down. John has no trouble hearing Clara Jane. Each word is as clear as a gonging clock.

"Do I spend the rest of my days in Berryville," she continues, "assuming my neighbor doesn't out me to the cops? If I stay here and keep hanging out with you, do I need to thump the bible?

There are thirty-five churches in Berryville. To fit in, do I need to pick one? How do I pick one? Do I pick only one where I do my thumping? Why do I have to thump? Will all that thumping do me any good? Why do I suddenly feel like I need to thump?

"Let me tell you," she says. "I don't like having so many questions to answer."

"Answering questions is what being real means," John says. "There are lots of people in the world who never ask questions, or even think about asking them. Those people aren't real, you know. They just take up space. Like the fountains on the square. There they are, but there isn't any there there. You can see them if you remember to, but there isn't a compelling reason to remember them."

"Does asking questions about what makes things real make them real?" she asks.

"Asking questions is the first step. Living out the answers, or living with them, is the second step. Reality is a two step program."

"Reality is a two step program?" Clara Jane retorts. "You think I need a recovery program?" She sniffed. "I'm a serial killer, John, not a toss pot. I live a very quiet life."

It is true. Clara Jane is, aside from that one little thing, an orderly, disciplined person. John made a face, placating. "Kurt Vonnegut thought that Alcoholics Anonymous would be the religion of the future," he said, "The Big Book, of course, will be its bible."

"Sounds like horse hockey to me," Clara Jane says. "John Sanford gave me a boyfriend one time," she recalled. "The BF had an alcohol jones and his probation officer sentenced him to go to AA. What a loser. All three of them, if you get right down to it."

"I don't know. Vonnegut was prescient about many things. Some churches are more like self help groups than anything else. It looks like a trend, actually. That's probably what he was alluding to."

Clara Jane shakes her head, slowly. "The condition my condition is in (oh, get out!) is beyond self-help. I mean, look at the construction of this sentence. What a mess I'm in!"

John agrees. On the other hand, you have to dance with the one you brung.

"As I recall, Clara Jane," he says. "You have a passing acceptance of SHAZAAM and the constructs and concepts inherent in the whole SHAZAAM business. After all," he continues, "it was your idea to apply some sort of SHAZAAM as a solution to our Iowan plague. Am I right?"

"SHAZAAM is easy in novels," she retorts. "The writer claps his hands, summons up a little old Ozark folk wisdom, and SHAZAAM, there it is.

"This situation, on the other hand, is real. I haven't been able to come up with a single SHAZAAM source. Where do I find SHAZAAM in Berryville?" Clara Jane looks past John out onto her neatly coiffed lawn. She pours more tea.

Linda Jones drives past in her green Escort station wagon. She waves at John and wonders what he is doing, sitting all alone on the porch of a stranger's house. Curiously, though, maybe John isn't alone. Linda catches a glimpse, as she tootles up Pritchard, of a shadowy someone sitting across from John. Linda wonders if Mrs. Heartbreak knows what John is up to.

Of course Mrs. Heartbreak knows. You didn't expect her to take a call from a strange woman asking for John without first getting a satisfactory explanation of the hows and whys, did you?

"She's new in town," John had told Mrs. Heartbreak, honestly. "She's looking for a church home," he had lied. "I'm going over to invite her to our church this coming Sunday," he had said, inventively.

The opportune moment appears to have arrived. John clears his throat, takes a sip of tea.

"The only source of SHAZAAM I'm aware of," John begins, "is religious in nature. Although, I believe the technical term is "miracle" rather than SHAZAAM."

"I knew you were going to get churchy on me," she says flatly. "What's next, an invitation to services?"

"You are certainly welcome to come with me and Mrs. Heartbreak if you want.

"Or," John continues, "in recognition of the fact that Christians are a contentious and diverse lot, you can start with any one of

Berryville's thirty plus churches and work your way through the list. Take it alphabetically and identify your zone of comfort by trial and error."

"Frankly, John, I'm a little worried about fitting in. If you know what I mean. If you get my drift."

"Clara Jane, fitting in is the least of your problems. Many of the great villains of the world have "fit" quite comfortably into church communities. A few of them have even started churches. I know that at least one of them is in Eureka Springs, and another one is here in Berryville.

"No, your problem" John continues, "is not about whether you fit in or not, but about whether you love God, or even know who is God. A church is only a place to demonstrate love. You may or may not find God there, but it is often a good starting point.

"Of course," John finishes, "a church is also a place to test your love. We show God that we love Him by how well we love the bozos, nincompoops, misers, Pharisees, deadbeats, snobs, bible whackers, and serial killers sitting next to us."

"And a good time was had by all," says Clara Jane, dryly. "Who will I be sitting next to?"

"You'll be sitting next to me, if you like" says John. "My role at the First Christian Church of Berryville is to represent each of the human categories listed above. Minus the serial killer, of course. I have only murdered in my heart."

Clara Jane nods thoughtfully. "There is one thing," she says slowly. "I am probably carrying a little more baggage than your average Baptist."

"Than a Baptist? Don't be too sure about that," John replies.

"I mean baggage in the literal sense," She says. "Do you recall Fuzzy Markowitz?"

"Markowitz? The name escapes me. Who is he?"

"Fuzzy's a "was he" actually. Fuzzy had the bad idea to go after Felix Mendocino's Miami cocaine concession. So I helped Felix out. A little bit. Just a tad."

John gets the picture. "So … you helped Felix out? A little bit..? In the usual helpful way?"

Clara Jane nods. "Just a tad."

John nods back. A thoughtful guy, John.

"Well," he says. "I suppose one more or less won't make a difference to the job ahead ... as long as you aren't planning on adding any one else to the list? Are you?"

"No, sir. I am reformed."

"Okay. We'll deal with the past as soon as we are able. Let's concentrate on the here and now. For the moment. Which has already become the past, actually. Just a second ago. There it goes again. Wow."

"Slow down, John. Let's say we "look to the future" okay, and let the past handle itself for awhile."

"Right."

"But back to Fuzzy Markowitz."

"To the past?"

"John!"

"Ah. Sorry. Back to Fuzzy."

"The thing," says Clara Jane, "is that Fuzzy Markowitz is in the past, but he is sort of in the future too."

"Meaning?"

"I'm usually efficient at body disposal. But I made an error in judgment about Fuzzy.

"I whacked him at a fishing camp in the Everglades. Ever been there? Beautiful! Anyway, the spot was perfect, not a soul around, just me, Fuzzy, and a wood chipper. "

"Wood chipper?" John asks.

"Yeah, a wood chipper. A machine you toss trees into, branches and stuff."

"Limbs?" John inquires.

"Yeah, limbs. Branches and stuff ... and ... limbs."

John got it. "You mulched Fuzzy?"

"Yeah. Everything but the head. It wouldn't fit into the chipper thingy. So I packed it into a suitcase and carried it away with me."

John nods again, getting more of it. "So, Fuzzy's head is the baggage you're talking about. He's in a suitcase. In your house? Here in Berryville."

"Right on all counts. Except that I put the head into a nice box and wrapped it with brown paper. Neatly."

John swallows. He looked at Clara Jane's beautiful lawn. He had no doubt that she had made a professional job of wrapping the box.

"That is a problem," he says, after awhile. "Your hits have been pretty theoretical up to this point. A head on the closet, on the other hand, is in your face. Kind of right now, so to speak."

"So to speak," Clara Jane agrees. "Now you can see why I'm reluctant to jump into the whole church thing."

"Church thing? I don't understand."

"I feel bad about Fuzzy. I mean, about what happened to Fuzzy. What I did to Fuzzy, not to put too fine a point on it. I'd feel kind of funny if I went all Church Lady while I still had his head in my hall closet. What would the other Church Ladies think?"

"I believe your worries are bigger than whether or not the women of the congregation have a high opinion of you," John says. "What about the law? Surely they will have some questions about how and why you came to have a boxed head in your closet."

Clara Jane sniffs dismissively. "I've handled cops my whole life. I can handle your local bunch." She pauses, and then says, "Really ... I feel bad about doing Fuzzy. I'd be thinking about him in the closet the whole time I'm supposed to be singing hymns, whatever I'm supposed to be doing, during your church deal."

"So, John," she says, discouraged. "Thanks for the invite. But I'm going to have to pass."

"You can't come to church because you have Fuzzy's head in your closet?"

"I'd feel hypocritical. Fuzzy's head really weighs on my shoulders."

John makes a decision.

" Bring me the head of Fuzzy Markowitz," he says. "I'll take care of him. It."

Chapter 23:

The Answer is ... 42

John put Fuzzy's head on his desk where it nestled among a hodge podge of other brown paper wrapped boxes and packages containing books. There, it would be safe from Mrs. Heartbreak's attentions and, frankly speaking, could reside unmolested for quite a while. John was not particularly quick about getting inventory out of boxes and on to shelves.

John is not nervous about his new possession. Owning Fuzzy is simply a variation on a theme: John has often thought of his bookstore as sort of a graveyard. This is not a grim thought, by the way, and it is not a sour and doleful John thinking it. It simply means that John imagines that the rows of shelved books resemble headstones and within each book is a story about some fumbling soul. To his way of thinking a soul is a story that happens to go along with each grave. When someone buys a book John thinks of it as a resurrection; he is pleased well beyond the merely transactional nature of the purchase.

He is even happy when someone simply lifts a book off the shelf and leafs through its pages. Then, it seems to him that a bit of the book's spirit has been released as it is opened. The released soul-spirit of the book glides and soars among the stacks for a moment or two. John has actually imaged Willa Cather caught up in the currents of the ceiling fan; Cather laughs and swims along in the fan's steady wake.

Yes, of course. John is crazier than a hoot owl.

Conversely, Mrs. Heartbreak is quite sane, the second sanest woman that John and I know. She has certainly not imagined Willa Cather among the fan blades. As a sane person, Mrs. Heartbreak's interest in small details is vast—no, infinite—and questions about the Navigation of the Universe are fundamentally, merely, trifles and a possible sign that the questioner is showing off. The resurrection of dead writers isn't even on the table.

John, on the other hand, is the second craziest man I know and it is likely that John is himself aware that he is crazier than a bed bug. As an insane person he is fundamentally— vastly— interested in questions about the Navigation of the Universe. He is not particularly interested in the details, therein residing the devil.

So now you have it: a diagnostic tool to distinguish say, between someone who is just plain nuts and someone who is simply neurotic in, let us also say, a classical, spectacular sort of way. Ha ha ha ha!

John ambles to the front of the shop and stares out the window. It is Memorial Day. Dr Squires is putting flags up around the perimeter of the Public Square; they snap smartly in what is by now a fairly brisk wind: a thunderhead is welling up west of town near Christview Retreat Center and John expects a big rain pretty quick. Dr. Squires is moving smartly now; he surely does not want to get wet.

There isn't a soul in Berryville except John and Dr. Squires (unless you count Fuzzy). This is often the case. By 3:00 on Saturday afternoons Heartbreak's is often the only business still open. On Sundays no one is open unless John goes up to the shop to fool around with some books. Then, he may open the doors with unrequited hopefulness about snagging a passing Yankee with a book jones.

People in Berryville are sometimes resentful about Yankees and wonder why they have so much money. John knows the answer: Yankees work hard, figure out novel ways to skin cats (they call it innovation), and open their stores on Memorial Day. Work, save, and deny the flesh is the Yankee credo. What a dull bunch, huh?

Dr. Squires has finished putting up the flags and hustles over to his truck just before the rain hits. He slams the door with a Big Bang and buckets of water fall from the sky. The events are not related. Maybe. John steps out of the shop and stands under the awning; he remembers the rain in Vietnam which always fell in buckets, in oceans really.

John does not like Memorial Day very much. John went into the army because he knew he would be too embarrassed to run away to Canada, or to go to jail, which would have been the penalty for refusing induction. What would people think, he had wondered?

John did not wonder about how and why soldiers died. They did not die for their country. John had never met anyone who was interested in dying for their country. Everyone John met was interested in staying alive, including John. What John knew was that soldiers died because they were more afraid of being embarrassed than they were of the Viet Cong, or of the North Koreans, or of the Nazis, or of the Germans in World War I. Now, young people were being embarrassed to death by Muslims in the Middle East.

Last night at Bible study, John and Mrs. Heartbreak looked Amos and Hosea over. These are Minor Prophets according to John Turner, the pastor of the First Christian Church of Berryville. John heartbreak is not sure if this means minor leagues as opposed to the Big Show that Isaiah must certainly be, or if it means that the books the Minor Prophets appear in are just short books.

In any case, what John thinks he has learned is that the prophets, big league or minor league, are told by God to tell "the people" to shape up, get right, or they will suffer consequences. The people don't shape up; they suffer the consequences; they are sorry; God restores his favor; all is well: until the next time.

In a nut shell, here are the twelve prophets:
Prophet: "Shape up!"
People: "Ha Ha! Ha Ha!"
God: Whack!
People: "We're sorry! We're sorry!"
God: "Okay. Have a sandwich."

Stage Direction: Repeat 11 times and every other generation thereafter.

John is not indifferent to the Bible as literature, which is sublime, nor is he troubled by the oft told tale: all the novels in all the world share the same five or six stories. Wasn't it Leslie Fiedler who said that *Moby Dick* and *Billy Budd* are just a retelling of the Old and New Testament minus the repetition?

No, it is not the prophetic repetition that bothers John so much as it is that Human Kind must be so dull as to require all that repetition, like a cocker spaniel that won't housebreak. What is so hard about behaving well? Is behaving well the secret meaning of life?

Paul Andresen, Berryville's Manager of Presbyterian Mysteries, once quoted Douglas Adams, author of *The Hitch Hikers Guide to the Galaxy*: "the answer to questions about life, the universe, and everything else is ... 42."

"Obviously," Andresen noted, "answers are fine, but without decent questions, answers are worthless."

So here is John, standing under the awning on Memorial Day watching the rain belt down the chickweed on the Town Square's patchy lawn. He is trying to understand Amos, to understand the whoremaster Hosea, trying to figure out what questions he is supposed to ask.

Meanwhile, John has begun hearing me tap, tap, tapping on the key board. John has paused, ears cocked ... and so I have paused. What will John do next? We both wonder.

Chapter 24:

Ole and Lena

Humor is not supplied in Berryville, and it does no good to import jokes or ideas whose existence is to inspire fun since few souls in town get the punch lines. The no joke rule also rules out irony, sarcasm, understatement, overstatement, satire, lampoons, spoofs, mockery, paradoxes, parodies, send-ups, absurdities, farces, gags, stunts, caricatures, and stories about Ole and Lena as conversational ice breakers.

Mrs. Heartbreak is of no help in the humor department. As a Social Order theorist she is constitutionally incapable of grasping the underlying humor of say, well, anything at all. Like other Social Order theorists such as union officials, Marxists, Democrats in general, and Baptists and Unitarians specifically, Mrs. Heartbreak figures that legislation rather than laughter is the way to go. The only reason John voted for Bob Dole was because Dole could tell a joke, even if he was otherwise as mean and unreliable as a snake.

It is possible that a town as serious about the Bible as Berryville trades in its sense of humor for the good news in the Good Book—which is a good book but not humorous in any way that John can tell. There is certainly no fun in fundamentalism and, as far as anyone knows, no jokes in the bible either. But please write in if you know of any we have over looked.

Protestants are serious people and seem to tell few jokes. Maybe that's one reason why Berryville is pretty solemn: it has only one Catholic Church and it is a small one, mostly attended by Mexican people. These folks, incidentally, smile and tell jokes when they come out of mass. When John sees them he acutely misses Catholic joie de vivre, Of course, Mrs. Heartbreak will have none of it. "Too much bouncing around!" she says. "Up and down! Up and down! It's like gym class!"

Walker Percy, a writer John esteems above all others, wrote a book titled *Love in the Ruins; The Adventures of a Bad Catholic at a Time Near the End of the World.* That title really captures the problem of Protestant humorlessness: no devout Protestant would ever identify himself as a "bad" Protestant, while devout Catholics have no trouble at all recognizing their corporality.

Percy's second most known character, Dr. Thomas More, a small town psychiatrist, said "I believe in God and the whole business, but I love women best, science and music next, whiskey next, God fourth, and my fellow man hardly at all." Imagine a devout Protestant, as Percy was a devout Catholic, admitting that.

During the entire time that John has lived in the Berryville no one has ever told him a joke. Nor has he overheard anyone tell a joke to another person. Since he has not overheard a joke, John assumes that the lack of anyone telling him one isn't personal. At least, John hopes that it isn't personal since you only tell jokes to people you like, unless the joke is on him. Come to think of it … maybe all the jokes are on John.

John gets jokes over the internet in e-mail attachments, but he is usually afraid to open them because the jokes often contain cartoons of a salacious nature. He worries that a customer will peer over his shoulder and be shocked at the sight of a housewife in her skivvies saying goodbye to a milkman in an overly friendly manner. He also receives photographs of Muslim women—who always seem to have mustaches—with captions beneath explaining that the mustaches are why Muslim men are so willing to strap on loads of dynamite.

John grew up listening to Ole and Lena jokes. Ole and Lena are an old married Norwegian couple, in case you didn't know. Here is one of the funnier examples:

"Ole died and Lena, his wife, complained to Sonja the neighbor that Ole had left no life insurance. Sonja, noticing a big diamond ring on Lena's finger remarked, "It don't look like Ole left yew too bad off. That's quite a rock yer wearin'!"

"Ole left $500 for his burial," Lena explained. "$100 for the burial and $400 for a big stone. This is the big stone."

As you can see, humor does not come naturally to John, nor to Norwegians generally, which is why he is always on the lookout for it. John's father had belonged to the Sons of Norway and both parents spoke English as a second language, as did most of the older people in the South Minneapolis neighborhood where he grew up. Humor does not often translate well, and you might expect that their lack of English proficiency was the overall cause of Norwegian-American humorlessness. That is not the case, however: Norwegians find very little in life that is funny, and while Norway is a tidy nation it is no fun spot.

This presents a puzzle that you may be able to help John solve: Humorless people like Norwegians and the majority of Iowans— and Mrs. Heartbreak for that matter—tend to be orderly and tidy about their persons and property. Yet Berryvillians, a humorless bunch indeed, have let their whole town fall into wrack and ruin for want of care and self-respect. Do humorlessness and tidiness correlate? Obviously, not all the time.

Ole came home one day and found Lena packing her bags. "Vatcha doin'?" he asked.

"I hear dat girls in Las Wagus are gettin' $50 fer what yew ben gettin' fer free," she replied.

Ole scratched his head for a while, and then started packing too.

"Vat are yew doin'?" Lena asked.

"I vant to see how yew are goin' to live on $200 a year," he said.

I don't think this joke is a violation of the NO SEX NO VIOLENCE NO STRONG LANGUAGE rule. I prefer to think of it as an economic development joke rather than ribaldry. And, it is funny.

Isn't it?

Meanwhile, back at Heartbreak's Pretty Good Books and RDC, John is staring out the window at two squad cars and an ambulance parked in front of one of the Town Square's fountains. The lights on each of the vehicles are pinballing around and expressions on the officer's faces are grim and certainly humorless. A small crowd has begun to gather and one of the officers has begun to string up yellow crime scene tape and pushes the crowd back.

John pushes the door opens and walks over to join the crowd. "What's going on," he asks James Jones (the farmer, not the author), who is leaning over the crime scene tape. James points toward a large body floating in the fountain.

"That's what's going on," James answers.

Two officers take off their shoes and socks and sensibly roll up their pant legs. They get into the fountain and roll the body over, face up.

"Oh, my!" John exclaims. He recognizes the face as belonging to the Iowa tourist who came into the shop a few days ago looking for paperback westerns.

What has Clara Jane been up to?

Chapter 25:

Who is Sodjerberjer?

John is quite certain that when he is inconveniently old and dribbles even more than he does presently, Mrs. Heartbreak will set him adrift on an ice flow, drop him off by the side of a less traveled road, or install him in an old folks home where government welfare covers the fees. Mrs. Heartbreak does not like to be inconvenienced, thus the end chosen will be driven by the relative availability—to her—of ice floes, less travelled roads, and government resources.

John is not a convenient man to have around. A fact of which he, and everyone else in Berryville, is well aware. Shelly Buttgen, for example, has wracked her brain trying to find some way that John might help out at the First Christian Church's annual firework's sale. Finally, she came up with the idea of using John as "security" at the fireworks tent. Providing security requires that John sleep overnight among the Roman Candles and yell imprecations at errant Appalachian American ruffians who might creep into the tent for the purpose of thievery. Shelly assumes that John has experience as a sleeper and, consequently, can do no harm and requires no training. Mrs. Buttgen will not be inconvenienced in any way by John.

"To inconvenience or not inconvenience" is the question foremost in John's mind as Berryville's police hoist the dead Iowan out of the fountain. John is certain the cops will trace the body back to Clara Jane, who will refer them to John, who will in turn refer them to the Authorial I—that's me!—who is strictly a dead end. God like, writers can do anything they want and are completely unaccountable! I'll be standing behind Mrs. Heartbreak's fern when they cuff John and haul him off to the pokey.

John is not resentful of my abandonment. He knows that I am at best a weak vessel. No, John's mind is entirely focused on the inconvenience Mrs. Heartbreak will experience—and resent—at the prospects of raising his bail money, finding him an attorney, and explaining to her mother and the ladies at church why John is consorting with a floozy from out of town. That the floozy in question is not a floozy but is rather a serial killer will not matter much.

John mulls over strategies for preparing Mrs. Heartbreak for considerable inconvenience when he sees Clara Jane come out of Encore Clothing. She is carrying a small package and sporting a rueful grin. John is in no mood for rue; he huffs across the Square and braces Clara Jane directly.

"What have you done?" he asks, and with some heat.

"I have purchased a lime green sweater set and an A line skirt in a coordinated yellow that just hits the knee," she replied. "What have you done, since you are so nosey?"

"I don't care about your wardrobe!"

"I know," Clara Jane said. "I'm just responding to Colleen Shogren's request—you know Colleen, from Holiday Island?—who has written in to complain that no one in this book appears to be wearing any clothing. She says that in order for it to be a believable book there needs to be more verisimilitude, more character development, such as in "clothes make the man" if you get Coleen's drift.

"Which I have just supplied, at no cost to you, thank you very much," Clara Jane added.

John, who is wearing a blue oxford cloth button down shirt, size 17x32, khaki pants size 40x30, and topsider shoes—the same outfit he has sported without variation and daily since 1971—is in no mood for digression. Yet, he is reminded that he needs to pick up a charcoal grey Brooks Brothers suit 44R from the dry cleaners. The suit, with either a red or dark green Countess Mara tie and black Wingtip shoes, is the entirety of John's business attire and has been since 1984, which is about the time John had enough money to afford business attire. (Yes, John is aware that he is a large person. Please do not write and in and exclaim "Size 40 pants!")

Happy now, Colleen? For future reference, let me repeat that what John is wearing today is what John wears every day. Neither John nor I have a clue what other people in this book may wear tomorrow—and we have taken no notice of they have worn in the past, nor have we ever been interested in what they might wear—but I will try and pay attention going forward. Now then:

"Clara Jane, there's a dead man in the fountain!" John nearly shouts. He is hopping from one foot to another and gesturing.

"So I see," she replies, nodding toward the crowd. "By the way, you might want to keep it down. The cops are taking notice of you."

John whirls around and, indeed, the cops are staring at him. What they have seen is a fat man in a blue shirt and khakis hopping up and down and yelling at a shadow he has called "Clara Jane." Naturally, Clara Jane is not visible to the cops, although they do wonder at a mirage-like, trick of light perhaps, playing against Encore Clothing's plate glass window.

It is a job of work getting the Iowan out of the fountain. The cops have turned away from John and are hefting the market weight corpse out of the water; they roll it onto the ground next to an unpainted (of course!) park bench adjacent to the fountain and begin to rifle through its pockets for identification.

John, no longer the focus of attention, resumes conversation with Clara Jane. "You told me you had reformed," he whispers urgently. "For goodness sakes! I was going to introduce you to Mrs. Heartbreak!"

"Who are you worried about?" Clara Jane giggles. "The law or Mrs. Heartbreak?"

"Duh!"

"I thought so," she said. "If it helps any, I didn't have much to do with Mr. Sodjerberjer's demise."

"Mr. Sodjerberjer?" John asks.

"Yes, I know there are too many Js in his name," Clara Jane says. "But that's the way he spells it."

John's face is turning red. "What are you babbling about?" he yells. "Who is Sodjerberjer?"

The cops leaning over the body look back at John when they hear him yell the name Sodjerberjer, which is clearly heard by everyone on the Square since John is, of course, yelling. One of the cops, holding a dripping wallet, looks down at the wallet, looks at the body, and looks back at John. He repeats the cycle—wallet, body, John—twice more. He starts the short walk over to where John stands.

"Oh, oh," Clara Jane says. "Now you've done it."

John turns away from her and faces the crowd and the approaching cop, whose name we will pretend is Chester. Chester chews gum and nods slowly, as if in agreement. Since words have yet to be exchanged between Chester and John, it is apparent that the cop has agreed with himself that John is up to something.

"Who you talking to, John?" he asks.

"My peers!" John says heatedly. "It's a free country. I can talk to anyone I want."

"Ah," Chester says. "Them dead writers, huh? I thought maybe you were practicing your ventriloquism."

"I am not a ventriloquist!"

"That ain't what Mrs. Heartbreak says," the cop replies.

"Mrs. Heartbreak doesn't know everything," an exasperated John says.

"That ain't what I hear," replies Chester.

The crowd has shifted away from the body and slowly made its way over to where John and the cop are talking. Clara Jane has circled around the crowd and stands behind it, smiling. No one seems to notice her. James Jones has folded his arms and looks forward to more witty repartee. So too the crowd generally. Well. Maybe not. But it's something to do. More interesting than the dead guy. Well. Maybe not. Let's find out.

"So, John," Chester begins again. "How's it you know the dead guy's name? Sodajerker?"

"Sodjerberjer," John corrects. "It's an old Norwegian name, meaning "I am the man whose goose was slaughtered by the son of Olaf Rejrebrejsod, an imbecile."

"Interesting," Chester says. "So, how's it you know the dead guy's name?"

"He came into the shop the other day," John answers, thinking fast. "Looking for Max Brand or Zane Grey. In paperback. Wife's name is Hazel."

"Disappointed him, didn't you?" Chester says flatly. He knows that Heartbreak discriminates against writers of paperback westerns. Chester has never found a book in Heartbreak's.

"Disappointment is the middle name of every Iowan," John says.

"How'd you know he was from Iowa?" Chester asks.

"We had a spirited conversation," John answers. "About people and places, the never-ending cycle of Zionist-Palestinian conflict, the prophecies of Nostradamus, about the price of corn. Iowa came up in the conversation."

Chester nods through all of this. Then says, "Do you know where we can find Hazel?"

John shakes his head. "Nope. She has a small dent in her forehead though. Look for her in the buffet line at the KFC."

"Okay," Chester says. "Thanks for your help." He starts to walk away, then stops and turns around. "Don't leave town, though."

"Don't be ridiculous!"

"Sorry," Chester answers. He looks contrite, crestfallen. "It's what they say," he explains.

"Who are *they*?" John asks in an exasperated tone.

Chester does not answer. He resumes his walk back to the scene of the "crime". The crowd begins to disperse and, in a few seconds, John and Clara Jane are standing alone again.

"You handled that very well," Clara Jane says. "For a Christian, you lie real good."

"Never mind that," John says. "How did you know the man's name is Sodjerberjer? And what did you mean when you said you "didn't have much" to do with his demise?"

"It was a Holy Ghost thing, actually. As you know John, I am simply an intermediary. When I worked for John Sanford, I was the means to his creative end—but the creative aspects of his novels always involved my working on behalf of some mobster intent on wiping out some other baddie.

"In the case of Sodjerberjer I was simply working on behalf of the Holy Ghost." She smiles. "So there you have it, John. No harm, no foul."

"Clara Jane," John says in a harsh whisper, "I am doubtful that the Holy Ghost employs hit men!"

"Hit woman, actually," Clara Jane corrects. Then she twirls. "As you can see by my fetching blue skirt and matching sweater set, I am all girl.

"Do you like the pearls? Too much?"

Chapter 26:

The Angel of Death

But first, a bit of verisimilitude:

Clara Jane walked up Pritchard Street past four or five weedy yards, past the Heartbreak's tidy clapboard house and yard, and up to the corner where Pritchard meets Church Street. Mary Margaret's house is on Clara Jane's right and the bricked back of the Baptist Church is straight in front of her, marking the terminal end of Pritchard. Mary Margaret's yard is tidy, but she owns or at least takes care of five or six cats. These cats come over and sit on the Heartbreak's front porch early every morning for the purpose of driving Mrs. Heartbreak's Jack Russell, Jane, insane. All that barking you hear at six o'clock in the morning is Jane off her rocker.

Clara Jane is discovering herself as Human Being, is noticing things she never noticed before. As Clara Rinker, John Sanford's creation, what she noticed was cops and get-a-way routes, the ease or difficulty with which a knife slit a throat, and the mendacity of the bozos whose deserving throats she slit. Hiding out in Berryville as Jane Smith, she remains vigilant and in character, a serial killer taking time out in the sticks. Her existence as Clara Rinker hiding out as Jane Smith was of no importance to her; her life was of no interest to her: she was simply a machine invented by a paperback writer.

And then John came along with his odd theories and requests, and I had made her into Clara Jane Smith, prospective Church Lady and candidate-enrollee for the Pastors Turner's Five Finger Exercise class that commences, by and by. Shortly. Oeh.

John Heartbreak has complicated her life because he believes that people in books can be as real as people you might actually know or be related to. For example, John learned more about how to be alive and how to be a man from Woodrow Call, a character in Lonesome Dove, than he ever had from his father Jann Heartbreak, a man that John believed for the longest time was really a Robot Machine from the Planet Norway. Captain Call was certainly more real to John than Jann Heartbreak had ever been.

Without putting too fine a point on it, John is himself a character in a book, but I know him to be real and, if you are reading this book, you will suspect he is real as well. So, who is most real? John Heartbreak the suspiciously human presence you are reading about now, or So and So Next Door who watches television seven hours a day and doesn't know in what century the American Civil War was fought? Who would you prefer to know?

Clara Jane turns right onto Church Street and passes by Mary Margaret's long and tidy side yard until she reaches the corner of Church and Shaver Street. She pauses and looks north and up Shaver. What she sees is three mostly abandoned shacks owned by a Carroll County Public Official—and what a fine citizen and public servant he is. The yards of his properties are a tangled, weedy mess, windows are broken, and trash is strewn about. He certainly cares about the public good, doesn't he?

Clara Jane smiles at this insult. Before she became Clara Jane and was only Clara Rinker ne Jane Smith it never occurred to her that a place, that space, could be pleasant or ugly. As Jane Smith, she kept her Pritchard Street house and yard tidy the same way and with the same motivation that she keeps her Smith and Wesson .38 clean and well-oiled, out of professionalism, self-respect, and a sense of self-preservation.

Clara Jane had also mistakenly assumed that tidiness and maintenance is the expected norm in Berryville and that it is not tidy and maintained has become more and more evident to her, especially as she sees the legally sanctioned shambles the Public Servant makes of Shaver Avenue. She now understands that her anonymity would be more secured by piling dead tires and old sofas and defunct stoves on her porch than by mowing her grass.

Clara Jane has actually considered letting her tidy, well groomed property go to the dogs, but has not done so because she knows it would wound John if she did. Considering the feelings and wants of other people is something new in her life as well. Up until only a few days ago Clara Jane could have dropped a piano on John's head with no more thought than had she slammed a garden slug. Now, she feels protective of John in the way a mother might feel toward the particularly stupid, runty child that has entered her life quite late in the game after all its siblings are busy My Spacing and working part time at the Sonic Drive In out on Trimble Drive.

She crosses Shaver and passes by an old wrecked house on the corner and continues by the First Christian Church's parsonage. The parsonage has an acceptable but barely acceptable front yard that would be improved with four flower beds, and the planting of, say, a hedge of forsythias or snowball bushes. (Sorry. I can't help myself.) Clara Jane passes the parsonage and crosses in front of the First Christian Church where she stops and turns to look at its pretty red door.

The FFC is probably the oldest church in Berryville. Thanks to Robert and Elaine West, it is certainly the tidiest and best maintained. It should be no surprise that John chose it as the Heartbreak's church home since, after all, CLEANLINESS IS NEXT TO GODLINESS. That wasn't the only reason, of course, but it was a factor: John would no more join a disheveled congregation than he would send his children out into the world with dirty necks.

Clara Jane stares at the church and wonders what it will be like when she, inevitably, goes into it. She is not worried about fitting in. Her success as a serial killer is due in part to her chameleon ability to become her surroundings, although attending church will be a first. The only hymn she knows is "In Heaven There is

No Beer" and she is not certain that it is even a hymn. She'll find out.

The sun is beginning to set, a big nickel dropping into the slot of the horizon. Reluctantly, Clara Jane turns away from the church, heads west on Church Street and picks up the pace a bit. She has an appointment on the Town Square that may or may not involve SHAZAAM but it will certainly (as you know) involve the parting of a soul from its earthly vessel. Clara Jane will be there in—oh, say three minutes—to help it along.

Three minutes is about the length of time it will take Clara Jane to get from where she is, on the corner of Church Street and Springfield Road, to the fountain on the east side of the Square. Three minutes provides enough time for 450 words that could be devoted to more description of Berryville's maintenance "issues" along the balance of East Church Street. But you don't want to hear anymore about that particular subject. Do you?

Okay. Fine.

Clara Jane crosses Springfield Road and passes by Hanby's Lumber Yard, passes the Carroll County Literacy Council, passes Arts of Mud, and passes the bodega and Don's Country Consignments. All without comment on the tiredness of buildings. Until she reaches the Square. Where she smiles. Again. Her appointment is early.

"I am become death, the destroyer of worlds," quoted Robert Oppenheimer, thought Clara Jane Smith. Sixty feet away sat a lumping figure, its back to Wilson's TV and Appliance, its shoe clad feet stuck in the tepid water of the fountain. It, he, looked over his shoulder at the sound of Clara Jane's approach.

"Are you the one I'm supposed to meet?" he asked.

"Are you supposed to meet someone?"

He shook his head. "I don't know," he said. "I've just had a feeling all day long that I was supposed to come here and sit by the water and wait for someone. So I'm sitting here, waiting."

"Why didn't you take your shoes and socks off?" Clara Jane asked. "It is unusual to see a man of your age soaking his shoes along with his feet."

"I admit that it is unusual, but it feels good." The man lightly kicked his heels against the side of the fountain.

"I'm not myself today," he said, out of nowhere. "I feel as blue as I've ever been."

"Despondent even," Clara Jane said, nudging him gently, soothingly.

"That word works just as well. You're right. I am despondent."

"It started when you went in Heartbreak's Bookstore this morning, didn't it." It is not a question. Clara Jane is simply reporting.

The man agreed.

"Yup. I went in there with the wife to buy a book and came out feeling all wrecked up inside. Different, anyhow.

"All day, I walked around, following Hazel in and out of junk shops, trying my best to keep her from throwing money around. The whole time, my mind was unsettled. I was thinking about things I haven't thought about in fifty years."

Clara Jane slipped her shoes off and settled in next to him on the ledge of the fountain. She dangled her feet in the water alongside his and splashed a bit. "It does feel good, doesn't it?" she said. "The water, I mean."

"Yup. It's pretty good." The man offered his hand Clara Jane. "My name's Sodjerberjer. With two Js."

"That's a lot of Js for one name," Clara Jane said, shaking his hand.

"It's Norwegian. Norwegians have plenty of Js. That's about what we have as far as culture goes. Them, and Vikings, of course. We are a reserved, stoic, and formerly violent people."

"John Heartbreak is a Norwegian," Clara Jane said. "He takes some pride in it."

"I thought so," Sodjerberjer replied. "I could tell by the way he sniffed at my reading request for western literature. Down his big nose."

"John's a big sniffer. This whole book is full of sniffing."

"What book?" Sodjerberjer asked. He gave her a quizzical look, half smiling. "What book are you talking about?"

"This book," Clara Jane repeated. "You're in a book now. A man who lives with John is writing about what John sees through his bookstore's window. John saw you coming this morning, had thoughts about you coming, and his thoughts about you went into the book.

"Look," she said, pointing at cars on the road bisecting (gutting) the Town Square. "There goes Steve Hanna."

And there," she said, pointing at a red pickup speeding by, "goes Dickie Clark. Steve owns the liquor store and Dickie works for him. Now they're in the book too."

"I'll be darned," he said, wonderingly. "Maybe that's why I've been feeling so odd all day.

"What's this writer saying about me?" he asked. "Anything I got to worry about?"

Clara Jane smiled. "Not really. Your worries are over."

"What's that supposed to mean?"

"This is where it all ends, Mr. Sodjerberjer," Clara Jane said. "You don't have to worry about anything, anymore."

Sodjerberjer nodded. "That's the funny feeling I've been having all day. I've been feeling that it's all over."

He kicked his heels against the fountain's wall, splashing. "Maybe that's why I didn't take my shoes off," he said. "What would be the point, after all?"

Sodjerberjer turned to Clara Jane, an intent inquiring look on his face. "Who are you?" he asked.

"My name is Clara Rinker," Clara Jane Smith answered. "I'm the Angel of Death."

"Not someone you meet every day," Sodjerberjer replied.

"No, not every day. Just once."

Sodjerberjer nodded again. "So. What happens now?"

Clara Jane took Sodjerberjer's hand in hers and held it, gently. "Tell me all about it," she said. "Tell me all about Sodjerberjer."

Chapter 27:

The Death of Sodjerberjer

"I've been a farmer my whole life, "Sodjerberjer began. He is holding Clara Jane's hand and looking into the distance. "My father was a farmer before me, and his father farmed as well. I'm third generation on the same home place.

"When I was a boy, we raised a few hogs and a few chickens, and out back there was an apple orchard that smelled like heaven every spring and fall. Bees would congregate among the blossoms and fruit and buzz around, happy and busy. I'd climb among the branches and look at the sky and feel the way a boy should feel.

"Ma kept the hens in good shape and sold the eggs in town. The hogs Pa slaughtered for home eating and sold the rest to Einer Fulstad, who came around once or twice a year and hauled livestock off to the yard in Sioux City. Hog profits paid for Christmas, and Easter dresses for my sisters and Ma. Sometimes Christmas was slim but we always had Christmas, thank you Jesus.

"In the spring we'd bale hay and what a job that was. Baling was how boys learned to drive tractors and pull wagons. Pa had an old Minneapolis Moline tractor that I cut my teeth on, ten years old I was and King of the world, driving the tractor and pulling a wagon that Pa and a hired man stacked bails on as I went through the field. I felt so good, and so big on that big orange rig, helping the men folk. It was my ticket to being a man myself.

"Ma would feed the haying crew the biggest noon day dinners you ever saw: piles and piles of pork cops and fried chicken and potatoes and apple pies and plenty of vegetables, all you could possibly eat, every scrap of it grown or raised beneath our very feet. After, we'd dead fall into a thirty minute nap, and then back up on the Moline I'd go.

"When we were finished haying Pa would sit on the porch on an evening and look across the pasture at the cattle and smile and say, "Well, then, the livestock will all be fine this winter. Plenty of hay to see them through." It was a precious moment and we knew that Pa wasn't just talking about the cattle: he was telling us that we'd be fine too.

"Winter would come and I'd concentrate on the books. Learned all the stuff I needed, including love of my country and my state. One year I had to memorize every county in the state of Iowa and the county seats to boot. But it was fun! And I learned, and every kid in class learned, where they were from and why it mattered. We knew in our hearts that Iowa was about as close to Heaven on earth as we were ever going to get.

"Sunday's we'd go to church, Emanuel Lutheran, and we'd thank God for the bounty of the land and our good fortune to be Americans and to have had the luck to be Iowans as well, the best place and the darned best State in the Union. Oh, how my heart would soar when we sang "A Mighty Fortress is our God" and "Onward Christian Soldiers!" me, along with Ma and the girls and Pa in his good blue suit.

"After services we'd gather in the basement of the church and have a meal, or coffee and cake with our neighbors, catch up on the news and eyeball the girls all dolled-up in their Sunday duds. Oh, my, it was fine.

"That's where I met Hazel, and wasn't she as cute as a button? Sixteen years old and shy and a fine alto in the choir. Poured the coffee at many a wedding and funeral she did. Always helpful, always merry and bright. I had my eye on her from the time I was seventeen years old. Smitten I was. In love.

"Oh God. To be in love. To even remember being in love ...

"When I graduated from High School Pa and me had a talk. I could go to Ames and study and be a school book farmer or an Extension agent, or I could be partners, him and me. I could hardly believe my God blessed luck and we shook hands and I was on the farm for good. An hour later I drove over to Hazel's folks' house and proposed. The next June we married at Emanuel and this time it was her sister Margaret that poured the coffee. And the next June Walter was born and Hazel and me, we were as solid and set as Plymouth Rock, as steady as the Mississippi flowing through Dubuque and down to the Gulf of Mexico."

Sodjerberjer dropped Clara Jane's hand and continued to stare off into the middle distance. His smile, animated and joyful a moment ago, receded along with the daylight and seemed to break into pieces. To the west, the sun was nearly down, night nudging twilight off the horizon. Sodjerberjer sighed, a deep heave from his heart.

"That was a long time ago," he said slowly. He sighed again, another deep, retching heave. "I don't really know when things started to change. I suppose it was in the '70s, maybe. Land got high priced and fellas started walking around, millionaires on paper, and started to borrow and spend like millionaires too. Equipment got bigger and bigger; my old Moline is just a toy compared to the monsters we're using now. All financed, of course.

"Farms got bigger too. If I had to put my finger on the day everything turned I suppose it was the day I burned down the orchard and plowed it into soybeans. An acre that had been blossoms and fruit and daydreams and wishes became more goddamned beans ...

... but we hadn't picked the apples in a long time ... and we hadn't had a garden since a few years after Ma died. And we didn't hay any more so there was no need for the big dinners and the long naps under the elm trees. I didn't think about cattle the way Pa did because I'd gotten rid of them. I plowed up the pastures, burned more trees down and took out the fence rows and put in more beans and corn. That was the end of pheasant hunting and them long sweet walks through the corn stubble on cool autumn days with the sky above and blue as Betty Davis' eyes.

"Earl Butts says "Get Big or Get Out!" and we all got big, nothing but miles and miles of corn and beans. In a hurry we was, time is money we all said. No more screwing around at the coffee shop. It was drive, drive, them big financed machines. Farming became pouring chemicals onto the earth and driving over it, back and forth, 20 hours a day.

"And then prices went to hell. Next thing we know Willie Nelson is singing for Farm Aid and guys are blowing their brains out in their empty dairy barns. Hazel was pouring coffee again, at funerals mostly.

"But I made it through. And more than made it through. I bought more land and more machines and more diesel and grew more corn and more beans. Let them other guys blow their brains out, I said! I'm going to make it through. And I did."

Clara Jane took Sodjerberjer's hand in her hand and squeezed it gently. "And now you're in Berryville, Arkansas, with your shoes in the water."

"Yup," Sodjerberjer said. "I'm in this dumb little town with a big check in my pocket from the Government and wet feet.

"Do you know what people call us farmers now?" he asked.

"What?"

He grunted. "They call us Welfare Queens," he said. "And it's true. We pour petroleum products into the sacred heart of our Mother Earth and collect big welfare money for doing it." He paused and splashed his feet a little. A Tyson's chicken truck blew by the square and through the light on the corner. Feathers filtered through the dark.

"And now I'm in this hillbilly town," he said, "getting insulted by booksellers and talking to you … waiting for you to do what it is you're going to do."

"You are despondent," Clara Jane exclaimed. "And I'm not sure I know why. Your life seems like most other people's lives. I've known men who would do anything for money. And I mean anything. But that is not unusual. Most of the things I've done in my life I've done for money."

"What I did was worse," Sodjerberjer said. "What I did was what Adam did. I lived in Paradise and turned it into a commodities factory. I let Earl Butts whisper into my ear and I burned down the apple tree.

"I've been thinking about that all day," he said. "All day, I've been thinking, and keeping Hazel from spending money, money

147

that I earned by plowing Paradise into corn. Why couldn't I let Hazel have some trinket money? What's the matter with me!

"And what am I going to do with that money?" he asked. "Let me tell you. Nothing! I'm going to die and it will go to our boy Walter and he'll piss it away."

Sodjerberjer sighed again. It was nearly a sob. He said ...

"Walter, our boy, wouldn't go to Church with us once he got out of High School, not even to bury our dead neighbors. He said that Martin Luther was a notorious Anti-Semite and a drunkard to boot. Didn't believe in God no more, did Walter. Believed in a Movie Star religion and space ships and some maniac out in California named Hubbard who lived on a steamboat out in the ocean.

"It made me and Hazel sad beyond words, church being a big part of our lives. Our whole history was wrapped up in that little white building. Both me and Hazel baptized there, married there, and raised our children there. No doubt they'll be pouring coffee for us there soon enough. Or at least, pouring coffee for me.

"Walter didn't care to stay on the farm as you might have guessed by now. Never cared for farming. All thumbs that kid. It was kind of sad, really, to see him try to be an intellectual and scoffing at the very dirt that paid his way through life. He was always worried about his hair; did it look okay and so on?

"I remember when he told me he wanted to be an Art Historian—can you believe it—and off he went and studied that at school. Sells life insurance now, in Ankeny, just north of Des Moines. Married to a miserable cow of a woman. Two sullen, mean kids. Both of them have little round eyes and pointy noses. Look like the devil, both of them, and they haven't got an hour to spare for Grandpa or Grandma, no sir. Hazel and I hardly ever see them anymore.

"I guess that's where all my Secretary of the Devil Earl Butts money will go. To Walter and his mean kids and that nasty woman he married. I don't even like Walter, God forgive me."

Sodjerberjer put his hand over his chest. "I don't feel so good," he said. A dim sign of alarm etched his face. "Lord. Lord. What is happening? What am I feeling?"

Clara Jane put her arm around his shoulder and hugged him to her. "Your heart is breaking, Mr. Sodjerberjer. You are dying of a broken heart."

"Lord. Lord," he repeated. "Is this the end? Am I going to Jesus?

"It is the end," Clara Jane answered. "I don't about Jesus."

Sodjerberjer looked even more alarmed. "Aren't you the Angel of Death? Don't you know Jesus? Didn't he send you?"

"I am. I don't. No ... I don't think so."

"Am I really dying?"

"Yes."

"And you don't know Jesus? And you don't know where I am going? Am I going to heaven?"

"No. No. I don't know."

"Well, for crying out loud," Sodjerberjer yelled. "What damn good are you? What makes you the Angel of Death?"

"It's my job," said Clara Jane, simply. "I think it's up to you to know Jesus and to know if you are going to heaven or not."

"What!"

"It's up to you to know Jesus," Clara Jane said. And: "Do you know Jesus?"

"Of course I do," Sodjerberjer shouted. "Of course I know Jesus!"

"Then say "hello"," Clara Jane said.

Sodjerberjer stood straight up in the fountain and clasped his breast with both hands. Then he sat back down abruptly and looked, far-a-way, and smiled. "Hello," he said. Then he slumped against Clara Jane and died.

Clara Jane eased Sodjerberjer into the fountain and pulled out her cell phone. Since no one could really see the fountains, or wouldn't really take notice of them even if they glanced in their direction, she knew that Mr. Sodjerberjer might float about the town square indefinitely unless someone notified the authorities. She called the Berryville Police Department, hoping that she had become material enough for them to hear her.

Chapter 28:

Thanks, Metafizzies, for the Alibi

"And that's how Mr. Sodjerberjer died," Clara Jane said to John. "As you can see, I *didn't* have much to do with his death."

John and Clara Jane are still standing on the Square. The EMS personnel have loaded Sodjerberjer's body into the ambulance and the Berryville police are shooing the crowd away. James Jones is leaving the east side of the Square and is heading in the direction of La Cabana, over on the west side, for a lunch of beans and rice. The police pull away. One of the squad cars is headed to the KFC Buffet in search of Hazel Sodjerberjer. John would be gratified to know that at least one person follows his advice. But he is deep in conversation with Clara Jane and he does not see Chester the cop move out smartly in the direction of the KFC.

John is about to ask Clara Jane for more details about her "didn't have much" disclaimer, but she held her hand out in stop sign fashion, the palm up. "Before we get into that, I would like to have an editorial conference."

John was surprised. "Editorial conference? What the heck you talking about?"

"I think this book has some structural problems," she said. "You may also want to note that we are now averaging 5% passive sentences—which is close to unacceptable—and we are hovering around the 11th Grade level on the Fleisch-Kincaid ease of reading scale. No graduate of a State of Arkansas Public High School will be able to read it.

"Not that they would anyway," she finished.

"Thanks a bunch," John said. "You've just managed to insult 90% of the 57% of the people in town who graduated from High School. You've also sealed my reputation as a snooty boy wisenheimer. Everyone in town will hate me."

"They already hate you," she said. "Or they will, once they read your whining about unmowed lawns and what you've said about Baptists."

"I've said hardly a word about Baptists," John protested.

"Not yet," Clara Jane retorted. "But later in this book the Authorial I has you speaking several semi-coherent stream of consciousness paragraphs on the Southern Comfort Baptists and the True Value Baptists. It's sort of a James Joyce, Ulysses riff, only not as interesting or as well-written.

"I'm also not sure that my emerging transformation into a Christian and Church Lady is very convincing," she continued. "Does the Authorial I have a clue about such conversions?"

John rubs his chin. He is rubbing his chin to suggest deep thought, introspection, and the whole mind body fandango if you will. Personally, (that would be me, the Authorial I, who is observing this conversation from behind Mrs. Heartbreak's fern) I think most modifiers and nearly all adjectives, adverbs, yatta yatta, yatta—which Pastor Andresen says is Hebrew for "he knows, he knows, he knows"—are boring and time wasters. But, anyway, John rubs his chin, and says:

"Your experience as a literary character is really quite limited," he explains. "So. You may not be the best judge of what works and doesn't work in a book.

"Remember, this is book is only your second appearance," John said. "True, you have appeared in several of John Sanford's books, but frankly speaking, while Sanford can tell a good story, he isn't Donald Harington. He doesn't really resonate with readers of better books."

"Who is Donald Harington?"

"My point, exactly." John said.

"My goodness. You are a snooty boy wisenheimer."

151

"Every town needs one."

Clara Jane folded her arms, pausing thoughtfully before saying: "So ... you think my transformation from unrepentant serial killer to believing Christian and participating Church Lady is plausible?"

"The first person to enter Heaven with Christ was a crucified thief," John said.

"No kidding?"

"No kidding."

Colleen Shogren has just pulled onto the Square in her new car, a Honda. She is wondering what the fuss is all about. She will certainly quiz Mrs. Heartbreak all about it as soon as she goes into the shop. Colleen's husband, Steve Shogren, is the second best photographer in the Ozarks. Colleen and Steve have just moved to the area from Minnesota and are undergoing a predictable period of severe culture shock. They live in Holiday Island, a suburb of Wal-Mart.

Mrs. Heartbreak sees Colleen step out of her car and advance toward the store. Mrs. Heartbreak has been concentrating so hard on watching John talking to the rather shadowy female figure in front of Encore Clothing that she has been largely unaware of the transaction Sodjerberjer has recently effected with Death, nor of the current-moment entertainment he has provided Berryville's various rubberneckers, police, EMS personnel and, of course, the men from Public Works who are arguing about whether they need to drain the fountain or not. It looks clean enough but, after all, the guy *was* from out of town.

Colleen sends a cherry "Hello!" in John's direction, but she sees that he is talking to himself, loudly, and he does not hear her greeting. "What do you mean you're the Angel of Death?" she overhears John shout. "And how could you just leave his corpse in the water overnight?"

Colleen shakes her head and enters the shop. Not for the first time does she wonder how and why Mrs. Heartbreak has saddled herself with such a dullard. "Hello Dear," she says to Mrs. Heartbreak. "Are you aware of what John is doing out on the Square?"

"Not entirely," Mrs. Heartbreak replies. "Who is that woman he is talking to?"

"What woman?" Colleen says. "You know perfectly well that John is talking to himself. And loudly, I might add."

Mrs. Heartbreak doesn't bother with the ventriloquism subterfuge. Colleen is her oldest friend and knows where the bodies lie. Yet, she is certain that she saw a woman standing next to John.

As you can see, Mrs. Heartbreak is becoming aware of Clara Jane as well. She has heard Clara Jane's voice on the telephone, and now she is becoming aware of an emerging material presence that is Clara Jane the Human Being. Soon, John will introduce the two women. He is sure they will get along. Two peas in a pod so to speak, Mrs. Heartbreak and the Serial Killer. That is also to say, two Social Order Theorists of the first rank.

Meanwhile, Clara Jane is nearly finished talking with John. She has recounted Sodjerberjer's apparent or not apparent meet-up with Jesus, Sodjerberjer's passing, and she explained her decision to allow him to steep a while in the fountain before notifying the police.

"I admit to feeling a bit pressured about the whole Jesus-heaven thing," Clara Jane said. "He was *so* insistent that I facilitate the introduction. Yet, what could I do?" she added, somewhat plaintively. "I'm not exactly an authority—accept on the death part, of course."

"I think you handled it very well," John said. "I believe that you were inspired by the Holy Spirit," he added.

"When you said "Say hello" I think that came directly from God's lips to yours."

"Mr. Sodjerberjer did seem happy and sincere when he said hello," Clara Jane admitted.

John also had an admission to make. He admits to himself a sense of relief that he has an unshakeable alibi for the time of Sodjerberjer's death—which was described as "when twilight was nudged off the horizon by night" in the last chapter. That would be about 8 PM. (Geez!)

John and Mrs. Heartbreak had responded to an invitation to attend a lecture by Dr. Chuck McNeil on "Reincarnation" at the

Ozark Metaphysical Society in Eureka Springs on the previous evening. About eleven or twelve seconds into the Question and Answer period it was obvious to John that several members of the audience were running about a quart and a half low on lithium. Still, Dr. McNeil's lecture was cogent and intelligently informative.

John had no opinion on the truth of reincarnation. He believed in it to the extent that he got up each morning feeling reborn, ready to do the same thing, in the same way, all over again, but maybe with a little more grace and competence than on the day before.

John also believed that people who did not believe in God would believe anything. (I wonder who said that first. Maybe you could look it up for me?) In any case, John knows what he knows.

In the next chapter John will take up the matter of Town Square baptisms and SHAZAAM once more, more directly approach Clara Jane's engagement of the Five Finger Exercise, and say something really annoying about the utterly contemptible condition of the Public Toilets on the Public Square. In the mean time, THANK YOU! Metafizzies, from the Authorial I, for providing John with an alibi.

Chapter 29:

The Chains from Which God Saves Us

Clara Jane's exchange with Sodjerberjer had impressed John. Although she had not explicitly invoked a higher power—and in fact had disavowed any knowledge of Christ or Heaven—she had identified herself as an Angel and had, in the fashion of Angels, delivered a message of importance. Clara Jane had also acknowledged witness of some sort of SHAZAAM occurring between Sodjerberjer and a presence that was seen—but, of course—only by him.

John felt perplexed by several remaining questions. How was it that Clara Jane knew to keep an appointment on the Square with Sodjerberjer? How did she know that he expected her, and would be waiting? The Metaphysicians lurking about Eureka Springs would no doubt rack it up to karma, and they would certainly enjoy several hours of speculation about whether or not Clara Jane might really be Shiva, the God of Death. (Are you speculating about it?)

The manner in which Clara Jane had addressed Sodjerberjer and the language—okay, the words—she chose in answering him, was fascinating to John as well. Simply put, Clara Jane had been brutally factual ("Yes. No. I don't know.") in the midst of a lucid but frankly abstract conversation. The abstraction was not

155

Sodjerberjer's faith that he was about to meet Jesus—for John, as well as Sodjerberjer, faith is in fact a brute fact—but rather, it was Clara Jane's acknowledgement of the possibility of Sodjerberjer's faith being realized. If Clara Jane is realizing possibilities for others, she must be considering similar possibilities for herself.

John realized that it was probably time for him to refer Clara Jane to someone trained in theological matters. It was easy enough for him to invite Clara Jane to Sunday services. And, to introduce her to Mrs. Heartbreak, who would no doubt welcome another project, particularly one who's mode of interpreting the Universe was so in tune with her own. But John's agenda was two-fold now. First, to help Iowans throw off the shackles of their culture (thereby freeing them to spend some money at Heartbreak's) and second, to help Clara Jane come to Jesus. John knows that he is out of his depth.

But refer to whom? John's own limited training was entirely Roman Catholic. That meant that he had read and studied Aquinas, Aristotle, Augustine, Bede, et al, as an adult, but he hardly ever read the Bible (except the Jerusalem Bible which, he had recently been informed, was the *wrong* Bible). And, frankly, John hadn't ever paid much attention to the Bible since, while Catholics may be hip to secondary sources, they are pretty much encouraged to leave Bible reading to their priests.

As a boy, John had read Father Leo Byrne's *Boys Book of Saints*, which was essentially required reading for all Catholic boys. The Boys Book of Saints was an anthology of martyr stories. There, brave Catholic priests had their hearts ripped out and eaten before their eyes by Iroquois Indians, where burned at the stake by wicked Protestants, or they were thrown to the lions by Roman soldiers. As such, the stories were deemed adequate preparation for either of the two vocations available to Catholic boys, the priesthood or marriage.

John had attempted to introduce Mrs. Heartbreak to Roman Catholicism early in their marriage. But as a sporadic Methodist with Quaker antecedents, Mrs. Heartbreak wouldn't have it. "I feel like I just got out of Gym class," she reported after her first Mass. When John overheard her singing the Vatican Rag—"first you get down on your knees, fiddle with your rosaries, bow your head with GREAT respect, and Genuflect, Genuflect, Genuflect!!"—he knew that that cause was lost.

John suspected that Clara Jane, who grew up in Tisdale, Missouri just north of Berryville—an Ozark girl for sure—would be constitutionally and culturally incapable of any sort of comfort with Catholicism. What choice then? In what direction to aim her?

The Presbyterians might be a good fit for her since, up to this point, her existence has been predetermined by first, John Sanford and now, by me, the Authorial I, both creative gods of a sort.. There were, however, other aspects of Calvinism that John thought might not fit too well. For example, a sense that mankind is subject to the total depravity of human nature, unconditional predestination, limited atonement, irresistible grace, and the preservation of the saints. And there was certainly the problem of standing before the gathered congregation and relating in detail an acceptable conversion experience.

Or was that the Baptists? In either case, John couldn't see Clara Jane buying it.

John, admittedly, wasn't sure: there are as many different types of Protestants in Berryville as there are novels by Grace Livingston Hill or Danielle Steele (that's a lot). By last count, there are at least five, and perhaps even more, different Baptist congregations alone within sight of the Heartbreak's shop. John occasionally thought that the amount of Bible reading among Protestants accounted for their disputatiousness. Any way, it is hard to keep them all straight.

One of the intellectual architects of the Disciples of Christ, Walter Scott, was at least as much Enlightenment scholar as he was theologian. Although Locke, Bacon, and Hobbes were completely out of fashion by the time John entered graduate school, he remained enamored by them because of how they combined Golden Age philosophy with an optimism about the future and for the dawning of a glorious new age. The Enlightenment conception of man as an autonomous individual endowed with reason was a pronounced feature of Scott's theology. That appealed to John and fit well within his cultural and religious frames of reference. Unaided by the supernatural influence of the Holy Ghost as in orthodox Calvinism, one could read the Scriptures, weigh the evidence, and make decisions in faith that Jesus Christ is the Messiah and Son of God. Locke's *The Reasonableness of Christianity* was an apparent and frequent reference point for Scott.

To say nothing of the Disciples' fine maintenance of the church and responsible attention to cutting the church yard's grass. John recalls telling Mrs. Heartbreak, "That's the church for us!"

Naturally, John is thinking that the First Christian Church of Berryville is the right choice for Clara Jane, mostly because it affirms his own wisdom in choosing it for the present and future care and spiritual feeding of Mrs. Heartbreak. On the other hand—where there are different fingers—perhaps the Methodists are the right fit for Clara Jane. John has a feeling that Pastor Skipper French, the Pilot of the Good Ship Methodist in Berryville, would get along well with her. After all, Skipper is a huge fan of the Arkansas Razorback football team so he is no stranger to felons.

On the other hand (please be patient with the hands business: we'll use as many hands as necessary to skin this chapter and get through to its muddled conclusion) it is hard for John to forget Norman MacLean's joke that "a Methodist is just a Baptist who can read" that he told in his book, *A River Runs Through It*. (Did I already tell you that joke?)

John Turner's sermon last Sunday, "The Chains from Which God Saves Us", has caused John Heartbreak to think about how Clara Jane might be released from the circumstances and conditions that have made her life a fiction (ha ha ha) and kept her from knowing God, fellowship with her neighbors, and authentic living.

The point of Pastor Turner's sermon—the point as John understood it and which may or may not have been Turner's point at all—was that there is no GET OUT OF HELL FREE card. Expressions of faith and membership in a church are not guarantees of salvation. Instead, Human Beings must free themselves from various attitudinal, emotional, intellectual, and addictive shackles before entering the Kingdom of Heaven.

John is not certain about hell, but he has been to West Texas and to a Eureka Springs City Council meeting so he knows that approximate places exist. He is absolutely certain about heaven and is looking forward to asking some questions. Nevertheless, John is also aware that he himself, Jacob Marley-like and Clara Jane-like, must break free of a few chains if he is to get the chance to make a pest of himself in the Afterlife.

Turner identified seven chains from which God saves us—if we do our part. These chains are ignorance, guilt, sin, brokenness, meaninglessness, despair, and death. "Our" part, or at least John's and Clara Jane's part, is to break the chain of ignorance by knowing God, the chain of guilt through the righteousness of Jesus, sin by growth in Godliness, brokenness by wholeness, meaninglessness by purposefulness, despair by hope, and the chain of death by eternal life.

What does this mean? There are rhetorical and abstract qualities of certain words, such as "righteousness", for example, that goes over John's head, and would no doubt go over Clara Jane's head as well. If you are reading this (I guess you are reading this, aren't you!) and you are not churched, or not a Christian, or even if you are, the word righteousness almost certainly conjures up a war mongering politician or television evangelist since ordinary people hardly (never?) use the word except to describe a judgmental so-and-so who has a corn cob up their butt.

Gail DeWeese, for example, sent John the following poem after she read one of John's interminable pronouncements about the Town Square fountains:

BEST POEM IN THE WORLD

> *I was shocked, confused, bewildered,*
> *As I entered Heaven's door,*
> *Not by the beauty of it all,*
> *Nor the lights or its decor.*
> *But it was the folks in Heaven*
> *Who made me sputter and gasp—*
> *The thieves, the liars, the sinners ,*
> *The alcoholics and the trash.*
> *There stood the kid from seventh grade*
> *Who swiped my lunch money twice.*

Next to him was my old neighbor
Who never said anything nice.
　Herb, who I always thought
Was rotting away in hell,
Was sitting pretty on cloud nine,
Looking incredibly well.
　I nudged Jesus, 'What's the deal?
I would love to hear Your take.
How'd all these sinners get up here?
God must've made a mistake.
　'And why's everyone so quiet,
So somber—me a clue.'
'Hush, child,' He said, 'they're all in shock.
No one thought they'd be seeing you.'
JUDGE NOT!

Gail was almost certainly, but gently, suggesting that John pluck the beam from his own eye before commenting on the mote in the eye of his neighbor. It is a nice way of telling John he has a corn cob up his butt.

Righteousness in the context of John Turner's sermon—as John understood it—was a call to become righteous within one's self, rather than self-righteous toward others, and it is the message in Gail's poem. Thus, Gail's poem is a good poem, especially if one can discount or excuse the problem of making a living across from a small, never maintained monument to East German Communist Party inspired architecture.

But John is unrepentant in so far as the town square fountains are concerned, and his lack of sorrow precludes righteousness and any claim to it. Maybe someone will point out to John that his sin is judgment and impatience and intolerance and that no excuses are allowed. That he has plenty to feel guilty about. Maybe Clara Jane will be the one to do the pointing since she is certainly aware of these defects in John. She may be the one who saves him as he attempts to save her.

Or maybe not.

Clara Jane has her own problems. While John is certain of his knowledge of God, which he takes to mean his faith in the existence of God which he has come to him through the gift of reason, Clara Jane is not there yet. She may lend John a hand, certainly, but she must also break the chain of meaninglessness and discover her purpose before much else can happen. Up to now, her purpose has been Presbyterian-like, predetermined by one or another Authorial I. She has been off the hook up to now.

Now, she is on the hook.

Chapter 30:

Following the Crooked Path of the Reformation

John is standing on the Berryville Town Square in front of Mrs. Heartbreak's shop, watching traffic go by on Highway 62. There goes Fred West. There goes Dr. Fred Mayer, the famous musician-farmer. There goes Allen Rogers. Where are they all going? (John never goes anywhere.) .

He knows he should be inside working, but F. Scott Fitzgerald is on a tear just now and John can't stand the overrated little Honyocker. John isn't sure if Fitzgerald is re-experiencing the DTs, or is simply ranting at Ernest Hemingway, who is ignoring him from two shelves over. Either way, John isn't up to mediating quarrels this morning, especially since the basis of Scott's animus toward Ernest is unrequited love. Love is complicated.

John is having second—and third thoughts—about what has happened to Sodjerberjer, and if what happened is of any benefit to him. While it is true that Clara Jane may have had a moment of awakening to things that are unseen, John wonders if his assumption about Sodjerberjer's assumption into heaven is really valid. Yes, Sodjerberjer was smiling at Jesus, but was Jesus smiling back? After all, Sodjerberjer did burn down the apple tree and he did turn Paradise (on earth) into a corn field. Maybe Sodjerberjer is in hell this morning.

When John was a young boy he and his pals would speculate about who was bad enough to go to hell. "How about Judas?" they'd say. "How about Hitler?" John recalls that these conversations were thrilling.

Sometimes John and his friends would take these suppositions to Mother Gonzaga, the Head Screw at St. Michael's elementary school, where the boys attended from grades one through eight.

"No, boys," Mother Gonzaga would say, "We can't assume that anyone is in hell. Perhaps Judas was truly sorry in his heart before the noose snuffed out his life. Perhaps he repented in the last tenth-second and is now in heaven with our Lord."

"Were there no exceptions?" they'd plead. (At age twelve, John and his pals had a certain amount of blood lust.)

Mother Gonzaga would nod thoughtfully and consider. "Perhaps Martin Luther," she would slowly intone. "Still ... Luther might have been truly sorry in his heart for what he did ... it is possible—doubtful, but possible—that he made a PERFECT ACT OF CONTRITION with his dying breath. One never knows, do one?"

Protestants had complicated the Go to Hell business well beyond the Act of Contrition business. If you don't believe me, take a gander at "Sinners in the Hands of an Angry God" by Jonathan Edwards. That'll make you sit up straight and eat your spinach. It will make you wonder what happened to Sodjerberjer, too.

Still, John was pretty sure that Sodjerberjer is in heaven. He seemed, at least by Clara Jane's account, sorry that he had turned Iowa into a chemical dump, and sorry that he had become a USDA Welfare Queen. And he was expectantly waiting to meet Jesus. He took the meeting for granted, which seems like an aspect of faith (something that one takes for granted).

Across the Square, Mark Gifford stepped outside of Quality Tire and spent a moment to enjoy the morning. He waved at John. John waved back. John liked Mark for the evenness of his temperament and for his capacity to have fun. John knew he could learn a lot from Mark. Perhaps Mark might have an opinion about John's dilemma.

Which was: how can the Sodjerberjer-Clara Jane contretemps transfer to the larger population of Iowans infesting the Ozarks? It is well and good that Sodjerberjer is in Heaven, and that Clara Jane may be on her way to heaven, but how does John get a nickel out of the pockets of these Hawkeyes—at at least rid Berryville of their supercilious and miserly visitations?

It was doubtful that John could depend on large numbers of Iowans to come to Berryville for the sole purpose of dying in the Town Square Fountains. And think of the logistical problems! Since no one ever looked at the Fountains, or maintained them, or even knew that they were really there, Iowans would stack up like cord wood and stink worse than Tyson's on hot Thursday mornings. People would walk around town and ask, "What's that stink?" and someone would answer, "Oh, Tyson's is probably trying out a new chicken nugget process" … and dead Iowans would litter the Town Square like leaves on a late fall day. John knew that that would eventually be bad for business.

Worse, when the dead Hawkeyes were finally discovered, who would the cops be looking at? You bet. Good old John. Who else has such an extensive and documented history of Iowa-animus? No amount of Ozark Metaphysical Society meeting attendance (GASP!) would get John off the hook. Mrs. Heartbreak will be mortified. Truly, John needs to consult with Clara Jane about developing a SHAZAAM PLAN with more clarity.

As you can see, John and I are novices at navigating the Waters of Religion. While I have often been able to rely on John for advice on philosophical matters, he is—obviously—of no help at all when it comes to religion. I rack that up to the fact that he is functionally fixed in the 1950s and has both resisted and failed to grasp the ecumenical spirit of the last 30 years or so. No matter how hard I try to shift him away from the lessons of his boyhood, and the dourness of his world view, I know I am destined to fail. It is John's BIG problem.

My problem is a tendency to tell a joke that only I find funny. Any advice?

Chapter 31:

The Holy Ghost Trumps
the Leech on William's Thing

John continues to stand in the heat outside the shop, continues to stare lizard-like at the desultory traffic on the Berryville Town Square. Yodi and Sharon Sloan (the scholar and artist, not the movie star Sharon Stone) amble past him on the way to their shop on Church Street. They comment on the weather and their pleasure at having the Ozark Café open again after the owner's vacation. There are several cars parked in front of the Café and heat arcs off their hoods with an almost audible snap.

Heat like this always reminds John of Vietnam. It is not an unpleasant reminder: it was a long, long time ago.

When John was in Vietnam he was briefly paired up with a young Army of the Republic of Vietnam (ARVN) officer named William Nguyen. "William" was the name the young officer had chosen in an attempt at an American makeover. General William Westmoreland, who intimates called "Westy", was the source of William Nguyen's American name and, of course, Lieutenant Nguyen also and desperately wanted to be called Westy. Sometimes John would call him Westy and sometimes John called him Lieutenant Nguyen. John didn't give a rat's patootie what the guy's name was.

Pairing American and ARVN soldiers was part of Richard Nixon's strategy to shift the burden of defending South Vietnam from the United States to the Vietnamese. The idea was that American soldiers would provide on the job training for the ARVN. As a strategy it was a big joke: ARVN soldiers wanted to go to dental school in Ann Arbor, Michigan; most of them had even less interest than John did (who had zero interest) in dying for whatever it was that Richard Nixon thought they were supposed to die for that week.

This was what John and William were trying to avoid one hot August day—a day just like the one blessing the Town Square today. Except that back then, someone started shooting at them as they walked along a rice paddy dyke in a field between two tree lines. John rolled off the dyke and sat down in the water and tried to get very small. William followed. AK 47 rounds harmlessly thunked into the farther side of the dyke. John and William sat in the water for a long time. The bozo with the 47 kept thunking at them. At first it was scary. Then it was really boring.

After about 2 hours, William said, "Let's make a run for it." He pointed at the tree line to the East. "I'm tired of sitting in this water. I think I have a leech on my thing."

John thought he had a leech on his thing too, but he shook his head. "Nope," he said. "We better just sit for a while and wait for some fire."

William began to argue. And William outranked John, not that John cared much. He wasn't going anywhere, not even if Westy himself, the real Westy, happened along. Still, William persisted. John ran out of arguments.

"You can stay here," William said. "I'm going to run for it. Shoot at him and he won't pay attention to me."

John knew that William's doors would get blown off. "Don't do it, Bub," John insisted. "It's a real bad idea."

"How do you know?" William shouted. He was worried about the leech on his you know what. "What makes you so smart?"

John didn't know what to say. What he said next was a big surprise to him. "The Holy Ghost told me to sit here and wait. He wants you to wait too."

John had no idea why he said that. But William Nguyen's eyes grew large and startled. William was, like many Vietnamese, a Christian, but also superstitious and spirit and ancestor haunted. "Is that the truth?" he asked John. "Did the Holy Ghost really tell you to stay here?"

John nodded solemnly. "Yup," he replied. "The Holy Ghost said, "John, you and Westy need to stay put.""

"The Holy Ghost called me Westy?" William asked. He looked suspicious, but also pleased.

"Yup," John repeated. "He said, "You and Westy need to stay put.""

William continued to look suspiciously at John, but he stopped arguing and settled back down into the brackish water. Twenty minutes later air support arrived and napalmed the grove where the sniper was set up. After the Big Whoosh, John and William finished their walk across the dyke.

You will be glad to know—won't you?—that there was no leech on John's thing. There was a leech on William's thing. Ha ha ha.

John remembered this story now because it is hot outside, like it is often hot in Vietnam, and because he has been thinking about the Holy Ghost arranging Sodjerberjer's and Clara Jane's meeting on the Town Square. Or: maybe: probably: arranging their meeting on the Town Square. "Arranging or probably arranging" is still open to question, but John is certain that his mentioning the Holy Ghost saved William Nguyen's life.

Now, forty years later, John is more spirit ridden than William Nguyen ever was. He does not, for example, want to go back into the shop because F. Scott Fitzgerald will demand a conversation and confirmation about what a pig Ernest Hemingway is. But it is really hot outside and John would like to get into some air conditioning and cool off. He glances through the window and sees Mrs. Heartbreak staring at him from behind the counter. She may be glaring at him, but the light is refracted off the window, so he isn't sure. John decides that it really isn't too bad outside. He stays there and watches people go in and out of Wilson's TV and Appliance store.

Chapter 32:

The Case of the Chinese Cathouse

John continues to stand on Berryville's Town Square. He decides to spend the time helpfully directing visiting Iowans to the Public restrooms across the Square from Heartbreak's and next to the Carroll County Historical Society. It will be fun to watch them reel out of the Public toilets, clutching their throats and gasping for air.

In spite of the heat—it is the 9th of August, friends, and you know what August is like—the Square is full of people. John spies some Iowans among the crowd and, in fact, there seems to be a lot of them in town today. The majority of the cars parked around the Square have Iowa plates on them and the State motto, "I brake for hogs", is prominently displayed on each plate along with the cars county of origin.

The Iowans are easy to spot. Most of them look like the cars they drive, Buicks or Oldsmobiles, but the people have little round bloodshot eyes instead of headlights. See? There are a couple of them now, coming out of Dirt Poor, Berryville's best gift store.

Naturally, their hands are empty. They didn't buy a thing and they won't spend a dime during the entire time they suspiciously grope the town. Marcie Brewster, a fine gardener, has to step around a clump of them that have taken root, like mastodons in a tar pit, in front of Carr's. Marcie probably didn't notice that the Iowans instinctively and protectively grab their wallets as she passes them. Marcie is kind to everyone and thinks well of people, and she would be surprised to learn that she was the object of such suspicion.

Mrs. Heartbreak has started toward the front door to call John inside with the still hopeful but dimming expectation that he will do some work. Then, she sees what he is up too and decides not to interfere with the plan to shift the Iowans away from the Heartbreak's restrooms and to the Public Square's. Mrs. Heartbreak is glad to provide accommodations for her customers, but the Iowans are not customers so much as they are unhappy consumers of yards and yards and yards and ... okay, I'll stop ... of toilet paper. When they go into a restroom they exit completely wiped out.

John is certain that when an Iowan is at home, he or she gets the job done with a single abstemious sheet of paper. When confronted with free supplies, however, they whip through them like Paul Bunyan and Babe the Blue Ox. John knows that there is no toilet paper in the Town Square's toilets—there never is—and he is looking forward to seeing the looks of disappointment on their faces after they finish throwing up.

The Iowans, over by Carr's, lurch out of their existential tar pit and lumber in John's direction. I know that this does not reflect well on John (then again, what does?), but he smiles in anticipation. If it wasn't so hot out he would rub his hands together. Here they come.

There they go. Halfway between Carr's and where John stands, the Iowans turn east and head toward the Town Square fountain, away from John. John is certainly surprised. Then alarmed, when they gather around the fountain, point at it, and begin talking about something. Their faces are noticeably solemn and a thin woman in the group—the only thin Iowan John has ever seen except for some Mormons in Lamoni, Iowa—begins to weep.

One of the men sits down on the fountain's edge and trails his hand in the water. It is immediately covered with a hundred and eleven nearly drowned crickets that had unluckily leapt into the water last night and now find the hand a lucky escape route this morning. The man stands up and distractedly brushes the crickets off his hand into the chickweed surrounding the fountain.

He does not appear to have really noticed the cricket invasion; instead, he turns back to the fountain and stares disconsolately into its depths. All fourteen inches of it.

The Iowans fall silent, but begin to hold hands while staring at the ground surrounding the fountain, or into the water. The sun bounces off the water and slings back upward into the people staring in that direction. The people don't blink and they don't seem to care. They look like Zombies. More and more Iowans gather around the fountain. John gets the feeling that he is watching an old *Night of The Living Dead* film, or Federal employees at the Department of Agriculture on their way to work. It makes John feel uncomfortable.

John goes beyond uncomfortable when he sees Clara Jane coming toward the Square off Church Street. "Beyond uncomfortable" requires a big, scary word, but I can't think of one just now. Maybe panic? Let's go with panic for the moment. So:

John feels a surge of panic.

No. He. Doesn't.

We all know John by now. We know him well enough to know that he lacks the smarts or the wit to get shook up about anything. So let's just say that John, in character and consequently sloth-like, uncomfortably observes Clara Jane cross the Square to the fountain and begin speaking to the Iowans.

How's that? Okay?

The Iowans gather around her and John loses sight of Clara Jane as she stands in the middle of the small but growing crowd. The weeping woman has stopped weeping and listens intently to whatever Clara Jane is saying. She says a lot or at least talks for a long time, and then breaks through the crowd and points toward the Public toilets. She says something else, then turns and points at John, at Heartbreak's Pretty Good Books & RDC, and down Church Street toward Pritchard Avenue.

As soon as Clara Jane finishes pointing, she walks through the crowd and jumps up onto the fountain and then steps down into the water. Now John does feel a surge of panic. He imagines that Clara Jane has hypnotized these Iowans and intends to seize them up, one after the other, and dunk them beneath the water and hold them there until they stop wiggling. John rushes—okay, ambles or shuffles—across the parking area. He intends to leap between Clara Jane and her unwitting victims and snap his fingers repeatedly until each and every Iowan is brought out of their hypnotic trance.

Just as he is about to fling himself into the air and onto Clara Jane, he hears her say, "And now we'll sing a hymn." John brakes sharply and barely avoids bumping a stout and scowling woman off her feet. John has certainly been knocked off his feet!

Clara Jane, standing up to her knees in the fountain's pool (actually, fourteen inches up from the soles of her feet), raises her arms in Choir Director Imitation and begins to sing, "In Heaven There is No Beer."

The crowd of Iowans is startled. Good Lutherans all, they had expected something else and remain silent. Bravely, Clara Jane continues singing and John, in solidarity, begins singing too. One by one, in hesitant engagement, the Iowans sing and, by the third chorus, the Town Square resonates with robust Hawkeye singing. They even do a little arm swinging by the end of the "hymn."

"Thank you," Clara Jane said when they finished. "You know what to do. Go and do it."

The Iowans disperse. They are no longer weepy or solemn. One or two might even have been smiled, but it is difficult to tell. A naturally unhappy, stoic people, Iowans are hard to read unless they are eating. At which time they resemble contented and amiable farm animals. A few enter automobiles, which they resemble, and slowly exit the square. A few head toward Heartbreak's, filling John with concern. Mrs. Heartbreak's moods are often in inverse proportion to the number of Iowans that come into the shop on any given day. John expects Grumble Soup for dinner.

"Give me a hand, will you?" Clara Jane spritely asks. John hands her a hand, which he has thoughtfully kept attached to his arm and shoulder, and pulls her up and over the fountain's ledge. Clara Jane is smiling brightly.

"I thought that went pretty well," she said. "Thanks for helping out with the hymn. I didn't know that it wasn't a familiar tune."

"It's not exactly a hymn," John replied. "Although, we sometimes sing a lot worse stuff at church on Sundays."

"Really?" Clara Jane exclaimed. "I mean, about it not being a hymn. What's a better choice?"

John isn't exactly sure. All the hymns he knows really old, or are in Latin or Norwegian. And, John is a bit deaf, as you know, and has to pay attention to the sounds around him if he is to hear them. When he hears music he doesn't like, he tunes it out after the first few bars, or does something rash. Every once in a while Mrs. Heartbreak spins a few Loretta Lynn songs on the home jukebox, but she always and thoughtfully hides sharp objects first so that John does himself no harm. Mrs. Heartbreak still loves John, after all these years. Imagine that.

"Let me refer you to David Bell," John says. "He is a genial man, knowledgeable about music and other artistic matters. I believe he can teach you a hymn or two."

John steps away from the fountain and sits down on the unpainted (of course!), bench facing the water. Clara Jane joins him. She smiles sweetly.

"You know I have to ask, right?" he says.

"Ask what?"

"Number one, what did you say to that bunch and, number two, how did you get them here?"

"Oh," Clara Jane replies. "Number one, I told them not to listen to you about using the Public Square toilets because they are filthier than the floor in a Chinese cathouse. And I said you were an unreliable resource as far as tourist type information is concerned."

"What do you know about Chinese cathouses?" John asked, loudly.

Steve Shogren, who had just stepped out of Giraldi's, stopped fishing in his pocket for car keys and prepared himself to eavesdrop ... until he saw that it was just John, talking to himself again. Poor, Dear, Mrs. Heartbreak, he thought.

"I was between jobs," Clara Jane said, forthrightly. "But never mind that. And please remember that I'm a Serial Killer, not a sadist. I wouldn't send anyone into those toilets.

"I also told them that there was a clean, modern facility in Heartbreak's and that they should avail themselves of it."

"Thanks a bunch!"

"Cool down, John. I told them they had to spend at least a dollar in your shop."

John grimaces. A buck should just about cover the toilet paper costs. "Go on," he says.

"I directed them down Church Street so they could see where the First Christian Church is located in case they wanted to attend on Sunday. I am supporting your secret wish to boost FCC membership a tad."

"Thank you. Do you yourself plan on attending?"

"I'm not sure yet," she said. "I think the Methodists are the bunch I'd enjoy most. Although your church and the Presbyterians are still in the running."

"Good Lord!"

"Exactly. And the First United Methodists have been in Berryville for a hundred and fifty four years. That is longer than your Church has been around town—even though you say it's the oldest church in Berryville."

She added, "I think I need that kind of stability in my life right now. I like the idea of an old and established church."

"The Methodists weren't always First and they weren't always United," John retorts. "Once upon a time they were just Methodists."

"The Methodists helped me get the Iowan's to the Square this morning—at least, indirectly," she said. "They helped me answer the second question you asked, about how I got people here this morning."

John crosses his legs and settles back to hear all about it. He is unaware that Mrs. Heartbreak is standing outside the shop watching him talk to Clara Jane. Mrs. Heartbreak clearly sees Clara Jane—have you noticed that more and more people are able to see Clara Jane? Soon, it may be possible that people will also start seeing the fountains and how crappy they look—and she wonders why John is spending so much time with a strange woman. Mrs. Heartbreak intends to discuss the matter with him as soon as they get home tonight!

Clara Jane begins to explain how the Iowans got to the Square this morning. There is a lot of traffic on Highway 62 this morning. People are going to Eureka Springs to participate in Diversity

Weekend, or to attend the Passion Play. It is an interesting mix of folks who grumble at one another. The grumbling produces a lot of heat and no light. John leans toward Clara Jane and tries to hear her above the traffic noise.

"Last night I couldn't sleep," she began, "so I went for a walk around town. I ended up over by the Methodist Church and, since I was there, I looked around. They have a good parking lot ...

" ...anyway, I sat down on the steps of the Methodist Church and thought about two things the Authorial I said you said or did or thought. He said you think that faith is something you take for granted. Is that right?"

John nodded. "Yup. I think that."

Clara Jane nodded back. "I thought about all the things that I take for granted. Like turning the key in my car and expecting the car to start. Or hitting a light switch. When I turn a light on I take it for granted that it will go on. Is faith like that?"

"Yup. That's certainly part of it."

"But what happens when the car doesn't start, or the light doesn't go on? What happens then? Does faith come and go depending on your experience?"

"Faith does come and go, but it goes away less and less the more you use your brain. I mean, what do you do when the light bulb doesn't light up?"

"Change the bulb."

"Right. Your rational mind and your experience with light bulbs—or with faith—causes you to seek out an explanation and develop a plan to restore light, or faith."

"Faith isn't a feeling?"

"Faith is probably a feeling of confidence. Confidence is gained through experience and through thinking about your experiences."

"I have no experience of faith in God."

"But you're thinking about it. That's the first step. It's good that you're not waiting around to be struck by a bolt of lightning. I think the lightening comes later, if it comes at all and usually only after an awful lot of thinking."

"What if what you're thinking about is too complicated to figure out? Not all problems are as simple as changing a light bulb."

"You run the problem through your rational mind and through your life experiences and, if the answer isn't there, then you get a book, or you call a more experienced friend, or you call an electrician. The important thing is to get the light back on and not live in the dark."

John and Clara Jane settle into a companionable silence for a moment. Cars whizz by. There goes Brent Updegraff. There goes Marie Andresen. There goes the famous farmer-musician, Dr. Fred Mayer and his charming wife Linda. There goes Lisa Cone. Where is everyone going?

Clara Jane looks at John and says, "I also thought about the story the Authorial I told about you and William Nguyen and the Holy Ghost. Did the Holy Ghost really tell you to stay put?"

"No. Of course not."

"That's what I thought. But why did you tell William that?"

"I have no idea. It just popped into my head."

"But it worked. It saved William's life ... and it got me thinking about the Holy Ghost and other experiences in my life when I was really lucky or really oblivious to the miracles in my life. I began to think that maybe that luck and those miracles was the work of the Holy Ghost. Maybe the Holy Ghost took charge of me and William without my being consciously aware of it.

"So I became a better observer," John concludes. "My guess is that people who have strong religious faith are better observers."

"I am trying to be a better observer," Clara Jane says. "I am observing you and the people in this town and reading what the Authorial I is writing. My observations helped me get Iowans here this morning."

"Tell me."

"As I sat on the steps of the Methodist Church I decided to have faith that they would come—I would take it for granted that they would come—and I asked the Holy Ghost to go and whisper in their ears that they should be here this morning at 11:00 o'clock. And He said he would. And he did."

"People reading this book won't believe or understand that explanation," John said.

"I don't care what people think," she said. "That's what I did and that's what happened. That's my story and I'm sticking to it."

"Good for you, Clara Jane. It's a great story."

"Do you believe it?"

"What matters is if you believe it. But, yes, I believe it too."

"There is one thing, though," John offers. "I hope you gave them more think about then finding a better toilet. Specifically, finding my toilet."

"Oh, yes, John," she says. "I gave them a great deal to think about. But that's between them and me."

Chapter 33:

Such As?

When John got home last night, Mrs. Heartbreak was on the front porch reading her Bible. This is often not a good sign because it means that Mrs. Heartbreak has run into a situation that requires guidance of the sort that John is unable to provide—not that Mrs. Heartbreak ever follows John's advice.

John isn't much of a Bible reader as we know. He reads the psalms every day, but that's about it, and he has always been perplexed by Protestant tendencies to quote scripture at the drop of a hat. "And he threw his shoe into Moab ..." the Bible says and immediately they have a long confab about the shoe, the throwing, and the complexities of Moab's government during the administration of some guy with an unpronounceable name.

The Catholicism of John's boyhood was far more direct. Usually, guidance involved advice to suck it up and remember that lots of people have it worse than you. "Think of the Little Flower," Father Seitz would say. "There is dear St. Theresa, on her knees scrubbing floors while the world loaded insults on her poor, tubercular back. What are you whining about?"

Mrs. Heartbreak is not the sort of person who can benefit from the Little Flower's example. Mel Brooks probably had her in mind when he noted the difference between tragedy and comedy: "Tragedy is when I cut my finger. Comedy is when you fall into an open sewer and die." Consequently, any number of situations may have sent Mrs. Heartbreak to her Bible.

For example, there is a low-rent harridan on Church Street who is gossiping about Mrs. Heartbreak. The harridan requires mental health services, transport to a Gulag, a swift kick in the booty, or any combination therein. However, in a free society these measures are not readily available. So: John has counseled Mrs. Heartbreak to suck it up and to realize that small towns are full of Saints and Sinners; there isn't anything she can do about it anyway. We'll see if that works (but don't hold your breath).

But Mrs. Heartbreak was dealing with a different situation. "Just imagine, John," she says after setting her Bible down and motioning him to take a seat next to her. "I had fifty-six Iowans in the shop today and every one of them bought something!"

"Amazing," John agrees. "Astonishing."

Of course, John is not amazed or astonished. "Did they spend much?"

"That's the funny part," Mrs. Heartbreak replies. "Each one of them spent exactly a dollar. They went over to the dollar book table and bought exactly one book. It didn't matter what they book was about. We got rid of books that never should have sold. Of course, they were just dollar books."

"No kidding," John says drily.

"No kidding. And no insults, either," she added. "They were all nice as pie. Except, they wanted to argue about the sales tax.

"Sales tax?"

"A dollar sale comes to $1.08 with the sales tax. I had to explain that I wasn't getting the $1.08, that I was shipping the eight cents off to the government for such things as roads and public toilet maintenance."

"Did they complain that we weren't getting our money's worth?"

"Every one of them. But nicely. I've been in shock all day. Imagine. Getting money out of an Iowan. I wonder what got into them."

John was certainly relieved that Mrs. Heartbreak's Bible reading situation didn't require an intervention on his part. "I'm glad you had a nice day, dear."

"It was nice. Although, let me tell you, between ringing up dollar books and resupplying the bathroom with toilet paper, I am dead on my feet."

"Would you like to go over to the Grandview Hotel for dinner? Or we could go to Giraldi's."

As the Heartbreak's walked back up to the Town Square for dinner John noticed that the First Baptists had cut their grass again. John was pleased at the efforts they were making to assure that Berryville was a clean and tidy town. John thought, too bad Berryville's City Council didn't care enough to emulate them.

"Stop it, John," Mrs. Heartbreak said sharply.

"Stop what?"

"I know what you're thinking. There is more to life than books and a shaved lawn."

"Such as?"

Chapter 34:

The Mail Bag

John wonders if he should consult with Dr. Jim Young about the somewhat miraculous events of yesterday. John was satisfied with Clara Jane's Holy Ghost explanation of how the Iowans had arrived on the Square, but he is curious to know if there was some kind of mystical energy involved in getting them to part with money. Since John is fairly certain that God is uninterested in finance—the collecting of a dollar + sales tax, for example—perhaps there is a metaphysical foundation for yesterday's happy event? Jim Young, as a founder of the Ozark Metaphysical Society, may be knowledgeable about the influences of "dynamic energy" and etc. And: May the Force be with you! Jim, in case you are reading this.

It is a beautiful morning in Berryville, Arkansas, the Ozarks, USA, and Hooray! As John shuffles along Church Street toward downtown he cuts across Nelson Funeral Home's parking lot to Madison Street and lands in front of City Hall. Berryville is pretty today and John notices that Mary Margaret's cats are keeping him company as he walks to work. Halfway past City Hall they stop, sit, and watch him head toward Springfield Road.

Pam Bolerjack, who owns Jenny Jane's Bed and Breakfast, drives by on her way to somewhere. John waves, but Pam does not see him. She is mission focused this morning and takes no notice of John's lumpy, indiscriminate presence. Jenny Jane's B&B is, by the way, one of Berryville's most interesting and historic homes. It has a ghost of the unholy sort.

Across Springfield Road Hanby's Lumber is to his right and the Saunder's Gun Museum is to his left. John does quite a bit of business at Hanby's even though they haven't painted their building since 1854 when the business was founded. Across the street, the Saunder's Museum is respectably maintained and has the best gun and rifle collection in the United States. I bet you didn't know that, did you?

Braswell's Printing is closed; it is early and only the Ozark Café is open, down the street across from the Post Office and one building to the right from the corner. The Grandview Hotel is on the southeast side of the Square. Mrs. Heartbreak had enjoyed her dinner there last night so much that she forgot to question John about the strange woman with whom he has been seen hanging about. John had dodged a bullet he didn't even know was coming.

He turns at the corner and walks toward the shop, passing several hanging baskets of flowers that he will water shortly. These flowering baskets were a gift from Carroll County's Master Gardeners and John has enjoyed taking care of them. It is the one bit of work that he does each day.

As John enters Heartbreak's, he notices copies of *Tender is the Night* and *The Great Gatsby* lying on the floor. How typical. F. Scott Fitzgerald, piqued by John ignoring him all day yesterday, has flung himself off his shelf and has injured his spine and bumped a corner in the process. Now, $12.00 dollar books have become $8.00 books, all because Scott is such a spoiled poseur. John sighs and re-shelves the books.

John flips his computer on and combines piles of papers laying about into a single pile while the machine fires up. The box containing Fuzzy Markowitz's head is under a stack of Diane Mott Davidson mysteries. Maybe John will do something with the papers and Mrs. Davidson and Fuzzy today. Maybe. Maybe not. Probably not.

John begins to read his e-mail:

"Dear John," Vjosa Mullahatari, from Pristina, Kosovo wrote …

"...I don't know if you are in a ghost story or a science fiction story, or if what I am reading is a religious book. What is most surprising to me is that, in person, you seem like a normal person, but in the book you are extremely abnormal. Is such abnormal behavior tolerated in the United States?

"Please tell me as well if American Christians are all concerned with the Ghost, the "holy" Ghost that keeps showing up? Muslims have only one God and He is difficult enough to please. How do you please or even keep track of the Ghost and God and Christ? Who are you talking to when you talk to God?

"My trip to America is still on so I will see you in January. I want to look at your town and visit the fountains you keep insulting. I'm looking forward to meeting your wife. She is too good for you, you know, don't you?"

"Johnny," writes Monsignor Jerry Bachxner ...

"...I'm sure the Protestants in Berryville will resent the hell out of what you're writing about them. They're a thin skinned people, which is why they start a new church every five minutes. That aside, quit with the Catholic wisecracks. If I hear another reference to the Vatican Rag I'm going to throw my lap top at you. And another thing: I knew Leo Byrne *[The Boy's Book of Saints]* and he was a fine man and wrote a lot of good stuff. Boys would be better off today if they still read him ...

"...I don't think they're going to get the light bulb-faith analogy you used. The Calvinists among them will say "Of course the light is out! It never got it in the first place! To hell with the light (literally)." And Baptists aren't good with analogies or metaphors. They'll think you're just another smart__.

"Give my regards to your wife. She's too good for you, you know."

"John," writes Rod Britten ...

"...I think one big problem with the book is that neither you, nor the Authorial I, understand small towns. What you don't realize is that on the night of every High School graduation a small group of the new graduates—consisting of the head cheerleader, the two Rich Kids in town, the captain of the football team, and maybe the King and Queen of the Senior Prom—have a meeting to plan the town's future.

"Okee Doakee," says one of the Rich Kids. "Every since kindergarten all the other kids have been sucking up to us and wishing that they were us. They've sucked up for twelve years. Our job is to make sure that NOTHING CHANGES for the rest of our lives. As long as nothing changes, they'll keep sucking up and wishing they were us! Forever! The only thing we have to fear is CHANGE itself! Get this through your heads: Change BAD no change GOOD."

"This isn't paranoia speaking," Rod writes. "Think about how someone like George Bush can become President. Because he's so smart? Please. He's just part of the Lucky Sperm Club, that old American Aristocracy that has old money and Yale and Harvard University degrees, and influential mommies and daddies. It's also why High School assumes such importance in the lives of small town people. High School is their Harvard and Yale; it is the place where they first experience the power and bliss of being envied and sucked up to. It is one reason why almost ALL the tax money in small towns goes to the high school. It confirms and affirms High School as the place where the elites are identified and coroneted as Kings and Queens of the small town's future.

"The control of small towns is identical to how big corporations and big government is controlled—only on a smaller scale and perhaps more tightly. And the self-destruction in small towns is more self-evident since the only function of the control is to keep control—to keep everyone else in town sucking up and feeling envious. One reason you don't have any code enforcement in Berryville is because the Prom King probably owns all of the rental properties. Check it out.

"Anyway, good luck with the fountains and toilets."

Dear John," writes Hugh Jacobs ...

"...I wear size 50 pants. I am not fat. I am a large and intimidating presence. If you suggest again that someone who wears size 40 pants is fat I'm going to pound you into the sand.

"P.S. Your book sucks and your wife is too good for you."

"Dear John," writes Pastor Andresen ...

"...You really seem to have it in for Iowans. I mean, c'mon "I brake for Hogs" could be the Arkansas State Motto too. And your toilet paper tirade: "When they go into a restroom they exit completely wiped out." That's just wrong.

"As for what faith is; Hebrews 11:1-3 says:

"Now faith is the assurance of things hoped for, the conviction of things not seen. Indeed, by faith our ancestors received approval. By faith we understand that the worlds were prepared by the word of God, so that what is seen was made from things that are not visible."

"Feeling of confidence" isn't bad, though, as a description of faith ..."

"Dear Mr. Heartbreak," writes Tim Johannes, an aide to Senator Tom Harkin, D Iowa.

"Senator Harkin wants to inform you that agricultural subsidies are not "payments to Welfare Queens" and that the American corn and soybean farmer is a net contributor to both the GDP and to the fabric of American life, and to our way of life. Agricultural subsidies have brought some measure of security to rural America and, without such subsidies ...

"...I hope, Mr. Heartbreak, that this gives you a better understanding of commodities supports and that you will reconsider the content on the Coffee with John Heartbreak blog."

"Dear John," writes Sylvia Hojellie, John's aunt ...

"...I don't think you should say that "Norwegians are a violent and stupid people. It makes me feel bad, and it would make your mother feel bad too if she was still with us. And what's this "robot from the Planet Norway" business? John, please, *klareringsdockument kjoreglede forsningstropper malvokter,* for goodness sake."

Oh, my, John thought. *"Du skal ikke bedrive,"* he said, out loud (but to himself). John was feeling a bit abashed. He got up and made a pot of RDC. It was about time to open the shop.

John unlocked the shop and looked across Highway 62. Some local, small farmers were setting up for the Farmers' Market. They we all real nice folk and John liked them a lot. A group of musicians was setting up also. In a moment, music was treaded into the fabric of the morning. The Square was radiant.

Chapter 35:

The First Church of Popeye

Berryville's Town Square is beginning to fill up this beautiful Saturday morning. Across the Square, and catty corner from Dirt Poor, Marcie Brewster and Diane Schumacher are selling vegetables and flowers at a brisk pace. The famous musician farmer Dr. Fred Mayer is next to them, crooning melodiously to passing customers, "I got peppers, sunflowers, 'maters so fine, look at 'em shine." Mrs. Linda Jones superintends from the far end, keeping a watchful eye on the wheels of commerce, and nods approvingly as Pastor Judy Turner carries off a bag of okra.

John surveys from his window, feels content. Mrs. Heartbreak will be along shortly to count the money, and to watch John watch what John watches. Yodi, the Artist Formerly Known as Catherine Yoder, wheels her venerable Volvo onto the Square, parks, and begins her trek to Arts of Mud, her studio-shop on Church Street. Judge Kent Crow bustles out of his office, a stack of manila folders tucked under his arm, bustles off to separate the sheep from the goats.

Clara Jane's Taurus turns onto the Square and Yodi waits for Clara Jane to park and then smiles in her direction. Since artists see things ordinary people cannot see, John is not surprised that Yodi can see Clara Jane. John watches the two women exchange pleasantries, watches them mirror one another's expressions and gestures. This too, fills John with contentment.

John turns away from the window and heads back to his desk. He really must do something with Fuzzy Markowitz's head. John thinks about leaving it in a stall in the Public Toilet across the Square. He knows that it won't be disturbed for months unless some unlucky tourist picks it off the floor as Arkansas lagniappe. That would be fun—think about him opening the box that night in his motel room—except that the tourist would probably call the cops after opening his Big Surprise.

What do you think John should do with Fuzzy's head?

Clara Jane and Yodi wave goodbye to each other and Clara Jane walks toward Heartbreak's. The shop does not officially open until 9:30, but is almost always open by 7:30 because that's when John gets there. When she walks into the shop the Heartbreak's door squeaks and dongs and John looks up from his desk.

"Good morning, John."

"Clara Jane," John says evenly. "Good of you to visit. You and Yodi appear to have hit it off."

"She's a very sensitive person," Clara Jane says. "She treats me as though I were entirely real."

"It is the nature of artists."

"Well, it's a nice change. Sometimes I get a little blue about not being seen by people."

"Iowans have no trouble seeing you. And I've seen you from the beginning."

"You don't really count, John."

"Excuse me?"

"You begin to appear more and more unreliable to me. Actually, you seem more like me than you do like other people in this book. You seem a bit fictional, to tell the truth."

"I am a bit fictional, to tell you the truth back. But real people are a bit fictional as well. For example, Pastor Turner did not buy okra this morning, but she could have, or maybe will in the future, and may have in the past. Fred Mayer did not say "I got peppers, sunflowers, 'maters so fine, look at 'em shine" this morning, but my guess is that he will soon enough. The problem we're dealing with isn't fiction versus reality, it is time. It isn't about what or how things happen, it is about when."

"I think you're getting way off the Fleisch Kincaid scale," Clara Jane replies. "No one will understand what you're talking about."

"According to Google Analytics there are 590 people reading this book on a regular basis. My guess is that several of them have thought about time in a similar manner. It won't hurt you to struggle a bit with a few new concepts."

"What I'm really struggling with this morning is that the Authorial I reports that you don't read the Bible."

"I don't read the bible "much"," John says. "In the same way you didn't have "much" to do with Sodjerberjer's death. Let me remind you that the Psalms are in the Bible.

"In any case," John continues, "I'm not aware that you or your previous character found much use for the Bible."

"I used a Gideon New Testament as a silencer when I plugged Kiddo Tesco," Clara Jane protests. "I was in his room at a Holiday Inn in Madison, Wisconsin, and found it in a drawer next to the bed. Very thoughtful people, the Gideons. The editions they put in hotels are the perfect size for muffling small caliber weapons."

"They'll be glad to know that. Be sure to tell Dr. Lymon Squires when you meet him. He is a rather dedicated Gideon."

"I want to talk to you about the Holy Ghost."

"That can be a boring topic of conversation, or dangerous. In my experience it is better to let the Holy Ghost do the talking while the rest of us keep mum. Be aware please that there is a fine line between Holy Ghost hosting and schizophrenia."

"What I want to know is what the order of things is? What comes first?"

John is puzzled, and says so.

Clara Jane puts her fingers in the air and ticks off, in sequence, "faith, repentance, baptism, remission of sins, and last, (she holds up a thumb) the gift of the Holy Ghost. Which one comes first? Isn't there a logical order to these things? How come the Holy Ghost is around me if I haven't been baptized? Aren't I supposed to do or have done the first four things before the Holy Ghost arrives on the scene?"

John shrugs. "I don't know," he says. "It really is time for you to talk to one of the local vicars. My sense is that becoming a believing Christian can be a little messier than the Five Finger progression—look at St. Paul's conversion, for example—but, who knows? For whatever reason, God plucked St. Paul right out of the saddle of his horse, but ordinary people probably follow a path that has been broken open by generations of other ordinary people.

"Who knows?" John repeats. He walks over to the Ws and pulls *The Bridge at San Luis Rey* off the shelf. "Why don't you read this," he says. "It's a fine novel and it will give you a million questions to ask."

Clara Jane takes the book reluctantly. "I believe I should be reading the Bible and not spending my time on novels by old men named Wilder."

"You won't understand a word of the Bible until you have read a hundred novels," John said. "That's the main trouble with Fundamentalists. They're like monkeys playing with a nuclear warhead. They have the most powerful weapon in the world in their hands, the Bible, and they don't have a clue how to use it.

"What I know is that Christianity is centered in Christ and not in a creed or a theological system; it is not thoroughgoing rationalism, but it is rational. Scripture is rational but it has to be read by a rational, experienced, and thinking person for it to be useful and meaningful."

Clara Jane shakes her head. "The last five paragraphs are really boring. You're pontificating and you're not even a pontiff. Worse, you've avoided answering my question about the Holy Ghost. Why me? Why am I in communication with the Holy Ghost?"

"We don't know that you are, Clara Jane," John says. "The Holy Ghost is only one explanation. Perhaps these Iowans are drinking the water in Eureka Springs and its mellowing them out. Maybe they watched Joel Ornstein on TV last night and he told them to come to Berryville's Town Square."

"Who's Joel Ornstein?"

"A maniac posing as a Christian evangelist. He operates a First Church of Popeye."

"Huh?"

"The First Church of Popeye is a marketing gimmick that I've thought about incorporating," John explains. "Its theology can be summarized as I AM what I AM and that's all what I AM. I'M Popeye the Sailor Man!

"Popeye is the first Pope of the Church of Popeye. Its members consist of people who think they are God. Bill Clinton, George Bush, Vladimir Putin, and people who don't cut their grass and think the rules are for other people would want to join. These people worship themselves and are entirely focused on their own comfort and survival. These people are charter members of the Church of Popeye.

"I believe I could make some money off a deal like this," John says. "After incorporation I would preach the gospel of self-fulfillment, self-satisfaction, and self-involvement. I would put YOU AM at the Center of the Universe and, for a hefty fee, license churches across the world where all of the new YOU AMs would become I AMs. I'd make a pile simply by legitimizing the behavior of politicians, slum lords, and people who now have a reason not to cut their grass or clean their toilets."

Clara Jane's eyes widen. "Can you do that? Are you going to do it?"

"No Clara Jane. I'm going to sell books instead." John sighs.

He feels tired suddenly and wants to talk to Clara Jane about Larry McMurtry's new book instead of about religion. Through the front windows he spies Mrs. Heartbreak heading toward shop. It is probably time to introduce Clara Jane to Mrs. Heartbreak. Mrs. Heartbreak, in turn, can take a turn with Clara Jane; take her in hand regarding the Bible and its various uses.

"Anyway," he says, "I wouldn't worry too much about the order of things. The Turners, or Pastor Andresen or Pastor French can fill in the blanks for you. You'll have to make your own decisions about submersion and so on."

"Submersion!" Clara Jane is alarmed. She has been on the delivery end of submersion a couple of times and has seen the results of those on the receiving end. "I don't like the sound of that. You've introduced an entirely new idea here, Bub."

"It's an old idea," John retorts. "There's a rational basis for submersion. Whether it's rational enough to start wars over and new churches is another matter."

"Were you submerged? I mean, I guess if you were, and have survived, it can't be terrible."

"Clara Jane, the purpose of submersion is not to kill you, it's to baptize you. Your cultural and experiential context needs a bit of tweaking.

"Besides," he says, "I'm not a good example to follow. In that regard, you are right. I'm a bit unreliable. Here comes Mrs. Heartbreak. I believe she'll be able to see you. I hope you will accept her invitation to church tomorrow. "

Mrs. Heartbreak breaks through the front door. She is smiling radiantly. "Miracles!" she proclaims happily. "There are miracles happening on the Square!"

John and Clara Jane exchange looks, she smiles and does a little fist bump. John, in character, just looks stupid.

Mrs. Heartbreak sees Clara Jane. "Oh hi," she says. "I didn't see you standing there, I'm so excited!"

"Excited?" John asks.

"Yes! The Public Toilet has been cleaned. It looks fine! What a miracle!"

Chapter 36:

Confident, Humble, and Sincere

As John pondered the Miracle of the Clean Public Square Toilets, Clara Jane and Mrs. Heartbreak engaged in animated conversation. As he had predicted, Mrs. Heartbreak was able to both see and hear Clara Jane and, whether this was because Mrs. Heartbreak had simply removed the scales from her eyes or because Clara Jane was now "material" is not known. But: engage and talk they did.

John wandered back to his desk and checked e-mails. This popped up from Pastor Andresen:

"Dear John,

You are familiar with my varied career experiences before seminary. As you also know I am willing to tell a story from my days as a bar bouncer and manager (or any story for that matter) at the drop of a hat. Strangely, this is the perfect opportunity for one of those bar stories.

At closing time, just before the lights come up at 3:00 in the A of M, the wonderful dance of coupling is in full gear. There were two kinds of guys who went home alone, those who tried too hard and those who didn't know how to close. With Clara Jane, I think you're trying too hard to get her into the church.

We're a "doing" society. Most people have trouble sitting still; there is always something to do. I count myself guilty! A few months ago I went to a retreat at a lovely lakeside camp, had an afternoon off, and was anxious the whole time! I couldn't sit still. I know others are worse than I am, but I'm bad enough.

One of my favorite professors used to say in a pastoral care situation, "don't just do something, stand there." Simple non-anxious presence is important, effective, and deceptively difficult.

A member of the church is in the hospital. She's a nursing home patient, just turned 100 years old. She has Alzheimer's and she has no idea who I am. I tell her every time I see her, of course, and every time she tells me about how wonderful the church is and the people are. Somehow, she can still pick up enough of her experiences out of her disease tossed memory to remember the church fondly.

Yesterday, she was scared. She was unable to hear. She was weak. So what does the super-hero Pastor Son of Man (Andresen—son of man, get it?) do? I hold her hand. When she speaks I listen. I tell her she doesn't have to talk, it looks like it hurts a lot to speak. She says she's scared and I tell her I know. I don't try to reassure her. What is there to say? I offer to get the nurse when she says she is in pain, but when she says no, I just stand there. I just stand there and let the Holy Spirit do the work. And I tell her I love her and God loves her. I smile.

Do I know what shape the work will take, no, surely I don't. That's not up to me—and hope and faith remind me to let go of my expectations and let the Lord take charge. I don't try to close. I don't tell her Jesus will take away her pain. I don't tell her the streets of heaven are paved with Gold and all her loved ones are waiting for her.

I just tell her what I know. I love her and Jesus loves her. You can't go wrong with that.

When we try too hard, it's like badgering that poor woman at the end of the bar, the one who wants nothing more than ... well, let's be honest, who knows what any drunk-woman or man-wants at 3:00 in the A of M, still ... say she wants nothing more than one more cocktail or a better offer. The guy who tries too hard never makes the better offer. It's the end of a sad, sad evening to watch some guy get shot down like the RAF over Germany over and over again. It's completely discouraging to watch this poor slob strike out more times than "Casey at the Bat."

But it's because he has a program and it's worked before, once, maybe. So he keeps at it until it works on some fine young lady. Then again, who knows what was on her mind, but that's another story.

One author (Henry Blackaby) advises it is better to watch and see where God is working and follow from there than to try to do it yourself. When we work our plans, it's only a crapshoot whether or not we follow God's plan since we are paying more attention to ourselves than God's plans for our lives. And we Calvinists will remind the world that sin prevents us from figuring that out on our own. It's a paradigm shift, we go from being the master to being the servant. We go from active to passive.

This is another one of those Douglas Adams wrestling with language moments. Christians need to stop using active verbs. We don't initiate anything that lasts. When we follow, when we allow the Lord to work in our lives this is when we make a difference in the world. We shift from doing to being. Linguistically, we're moving from an active voice to a passive voice. Sure, it messes up the readability statistics, but that's the price we pay.

Also, it forces us Westerners to move away from this spiritual manifest-destiny we seek. That whole do something, make it bigger and better, "bigger, stronger, faster-Six-Million-Dollar Man" style of evangelism brings up the numbers and brings more money into the plate, but what is it doing for spiritual development?

God will use us. The praise song sings, "Make me your instrument, Lord." But tell me, which instrument would you rather be, a cowbell or would you rather be a violin? Both make music, music which bring glory to God, but one takes more to create and makes a fuller sound. Only those who allow the Lord to work in their lives will be able to be fashioned and used like a violin. Folks on their own program will be played like a cowbell–hit with a stick counting1-2-3-4.

You sold me a book a couple of weeks ago by the Swiss theologian Karl Barth (pronounced "Bart" for those of us who pronounce as we read) titled *"This Christian Cause."* It's a set of three open letters to the churches and people of France (Dec.

1939 and Oct. 1940) and Great Britain (April 1941). The letters are Barth's thoughts on the things that "stir us all" during this time in World War II..

The Americans have not entered the war, the Vichy Government was installed between the two French letters, and the Swiss are resolutely neutral. This quote comes from the letter to Great Britain:

"If Jesus Christ is indeed the reason for our present decision, then it will be made manifest in the humility and sincerity of the faith in which we do what we have decided."

(Don't get me started for what I think this implies about the American war in Iraq or Russian presence in Georgia!)

When our faith is practiced in a confident, humble (NO-not an oxymoron), and sincere way, when we let the Lord work in and through our lives toward the increasing of the kingdom of heaven, then the kingdom of God and God's good creation are blessed. And we are blessed in ways we can't possibly know or imagine.

The other day, I put up our on our road sign a note telling a member we were praying for her by name. While it was up, I got a phone call. It was a woman asking if the woman we were praying for was a woman with the same name who she knew. I told her I didn't think so, but isn't it wonderful how the Holy Spirit takes one prayer and multiplies it.

Later when I was changing the sign, a woman at the court house asked me if I was the one who changed the sign. I told her yes. (No, I didn't tell her that was a silly question.) She said a friend of hers at the county dispatch office who had the same name felt blessed by our prayers. We weren't praying for her in particular either, but the blessings of the Lord through the power of the Holy Spirit extended beyond my small intentions and touched and blessed the world in ways I couldn't have known.

Clara Jane is experiencing one of those things right now. The Holy Spirit is moving in her life, and it's doing more than causing a cackle of Iowans to spend a buck (plus 8 cents tax) in the store. She is being used as a messenger (the Greek translation of the word angel) by the Lord and helping Sodjeburger (MISS-spelled!) find peace on his way to his final resting pool. It is causing her to ask questions, questions you're doing a good job answering.

Just keep engaging her. Know that she is asking because she is being caused to ask. Maybe even take her out to dinner at Geraldi's or the Grandview (and yes, the red beans and rice is great!) with someone who you think can help with her questions, or at least say which ones are great even if the answer is unknown.

Tell her about the value of community. Buber wrote *"I and Thou."* Barth then expanded on this saying "I cannot be an I without a Thou." Where two or more are assembled ... means that it is impossible to be a Christian and a hermit. Without community, without a thou, we can't even be an "I." Don't try too hard, that will turn her off like the chica at the bar.

Of course, I was and probably still am one of those guys who didn't know how to close. That helps explain Sunday attendance.

There is one more thing I have to say about Clara Jane and her curiosity about why the Holy Spirit is so concerned with her right now. All I can speak from is my own experience, and from my personal experience I can say with truth and humility that I was glad God was concerned with me long before I was ever concerned with God.

Peace be with you, Paul."

Chapter 37:

The Little Town that Time Forgot

What time is it? Take a look at your watch, or the clock on the wall. If you are the average person you will spend the next 8 minutes and 9 seconds visiting this book. Please keep track of your time. Time goes missing, you know, and while you do get it back, the place where you get it back and how you get it back requires a complicated explanation.

The paragraph you just read is true, and the facts about time in the paragraph are facts and not science fiction. You can look it up, or you can take my word for it. Anyway:

You are reading in the present time about the Town Square in Berryville, Arkansas. As you read, the Fabulous Mrs. Heartbreak is walking to the back of the Heartbreak shop—Heartbreak's Pretty Good Books and Really Dreadful Coffee—and she is taking the reformed Serial Killer Clara Jane Smith along with her. As your eyes take in these words, Mrs. Heartbreak's feet take in the floor. You are both moving and time passes. Has passed.

Outside on the Square, cars pass. Mark Gifford stands in front of Jim's Quality Tire and rolls up his sleeves. Your eyes move over the words; Mrs. Heartbreak's feet move over the floor; Mark Gifford's sleeves were down and now—right now—they move up.

The only thing not moving is John Heartbreak. He sits at his desk and wonders what Mrs. Heartbreak and Clara Jane will discuss. Are discussing. Right now. Perhaps it will be—is— the state of Clara Jane's soul. Perhaps it will be—is—an invitation for lunch next door at Geraldi's. But lunch is in future time. Not right now. Where are you going to have lunch?

Okay. Sorry. I was just wondering.

Tracellen Templin-Kelly comes into the shop. She is an energetic woman who loves dogs and spends a million hours a day—why not a million? Why not googleplex?—taking care of them at the Good Shepherd Animal Shelter. She blows past John without noticing him. Typical. As she goes by, however, she glances at the box on John's desk, the box containing Fuzzy Markowitz's head, the box under a pile of Diane Mott Davidson mysteries.

John jumps up with a start. If Clara Jane sees the box she will be disquieted—okay, feel bad—because Fuzzy's head will remind her of the past when she failed to fit it through a wood chipper down in that pretty everglades fish camp where she killed him. She will feel bad about the failure—Clara Jane is a professional, after all—and she will feel bad because she is examining the past and has begun to experience guilt over it.

Guilt, by the way, is a sign of good mental health. Guilt is your conscience speaking. When it speaks it informs you that you know right from wrong. How's your mental health today?

John isn't feeling guilty right now. He is feeling sneaky. He picks up the box and walks past Ms. Templin-Kelly—who still fails to notice him—and he waddles out the squeaky front door. Mrs. Heartbreak and Clara Jane take no notice of him leaving. Typical.

John tucks Fuzzy under his arm and heads left toward the Post Office. Maybe John should mail the box to the University of Arkansas Medical School? They could use it as an instructional tool to teach new docs about how skulls look from the inside out. "Knock Knock! Who's there? Fuzzy?" Or, he could sent it to the Eureka Springs City Council with a note indicating that Fuzzy was discovered in an historic building and needs a permit for decent burial. That would keep the heat off John, and keep the ES City Council tied up, for several months.

Dave Buttgen walks into the post office with a stack of mail under his arm. Mr. Buttgen was once an undertaker and then an engineer, and now is a semi-retired businessman who goes to the same church John goes to. Perhaps Dave knows something about the adequate disposal of body parts since he has knowledge of the adequate disposal of all the parts. John considers asking his advice for a moment, but rethinks; he concludes that there is no reason to involve a third party. So: here is John, standing on the Madison Street side of the Square with Fuzzy's head under his arm. What to do, what to do ...

What John does is head across the Square in the direction of the Carroll County Historical Museum and the Public Toilet. He stops at the light—there are two on the Berryville Town Square—and waits for it to change. While he waits C. Allen Long drives by, Keith Ham drives by, and Ginger Oaks drives by in her Cadillac. None of them notice John waiting on the corner, like a deep stain in the concrete sidewalk, waiting to be scrubbed off. All together now: typical!

John stumbles across Highway 62 on the green light and walks across the front of the First National Bank. Most of the people who own the bank go to, or used to go to, John's church. John spends a moment thinking that he should move his money—gosh, it must be $40 by now—from Community Bank to the First National Bank—but he likes the girls at Community pretty well. John decides to leave his fortune where it is. For the moment. (Girls, you better keep on being friendly.) (Hi Joyce!)

John is moving toward the Public Toilet, possibly to see if Mrs. Heartbreak's claim of a miracle is true, and possibly because he has subconsciously convinced himself to leave Fuzzy's head in one of the stalls, whether the toilet is clean or not. Look at John walk toward the toilet. It sure looks like he is going to go in.

When Mrs. Heartbreak reported the miracle—let's see, that would have been about five or six minutes ago if you have picked up the story where it ended in Chapter 36—John assumed that the Quorum Court was simply reacting to a critical review of their poor bathroom hygiene which had appeared in The Ozark Observer. John doubted that proper maintenance would continue for very long, and that Mrs. Heartbreak's miracle would be a short lived one.

What John believed would happen is that the Quorum Court and Judge C. Richard Williams himself, would suggest that the

Berryville Downtown Merchants' Association should pick up the tab for the on-going maintenance of the County's responsibility. John giggled (Yes, I know. Thinking about an old white man giggling like some girl is kind of a revolting thought.) at the idea of those Good Solid Republicans suggesting a solution that was inherently a Communist Party or Utopian Society inspired strategy. "Yes, Comrades, let us all pitch in to get the job done. We'll collect the taxes and you mop the floors!"

John hoped that the people of Carroll County wouldn't fall for that old Maoist team work ruse. Then again, one never knows, do one? After all, Berryville had agreed to accept not one, but two, East German Communist Party styled fountains and had put them smack dab in the middle of town.

John peeked in to the Public Toilet. It was sort of clean, but a bit short of the miracle that Mrs. Heartbreak had claimed. John slipped in quietly and opened the door of one of the stalls. YEEECH! Less quietly, and hastily I might add, John dropped Fuzzy's head on the stool, closed the door, and left the building.

Meanwhile, time has come and gone. I had thought about what John would do with Fuzzy's head a few days ago. Now, John has just done what I had thought, and now, you are reading about it. This is time before, time now, and time later, all which can be explained by a range of subjects in cosmology, including the Big Bang, black holes, light cones and superstring theory.

Unfortunately, we've run out of time. Darn. Your 8 minutes and 9 seconds are up.

Chapter 38:

The Elf on the Town Square

John left the Public Toilet in a big rush, or at least in as big a rush as lumbering, creaky John can muster. Once on the sidewalk, he looks left and right and, unobserved, begins to whistle, begins to saunter, for the corner where Poyner Drug stands. John believes he is the picture of innocence.

Poyner Drug Store is a nice business, run by fine folks who have been in Berryville, Arkansas for a long, long time. The Poyner name crops up many times in the town's history; in the history of today it is the place to buy a birthday card and to get your prescription filled.

One of the things John likes about Poyners' is the elf picture hanging way up on the front of the building. John recalls that Christie Lee painted the picture. But maybe he is wrong. Whatever. John likes the Poyner building, which is tidy inside and out, and he likes thinking about the elf watching over the Town Square.

(I bet you didn't know there was an elf up there, did you?)

In the window of the drug store is a Razorback football game calendar. The calendar puts John in mind of Pastor Skipper French. Last Christmas, Pastor French bought his wife Char a beautiful old painting. It was probably the best picture in the Heartbreak shop. When John delivered the painting he carried it into a room decked out from top to bottom with Razorback doodads and rah

rah memorabilia; even the dust bunnies had little snouts. Pastor French obviously loves those Arkansas Razorbacks!

The Razorback football team has so many felons on the squad that the University can't decide whether to hire new assistant football coaches or prison guards. Pastor French's ability to overlook this important public safety matter is, John believes, a sign of his gentleness and equanimity, and it causes John to think that putting Clara Jane into his hands—if she is of a mind to go into anyone's hands—might be a good idea.

On the other hand—here we go again—Clara Jane's "life" experiences are awfully Calvinistic and pre-deterministic. Writers, first John Sanford *ne* Camp, and then I, have called her shots in manifestly direct ways up until now, and John, deaf and dim though he is, has also had a hand—this is the same hand as the one that started this sentence; so: we haven't switched hands yet—in shoving her along the path to Jesus.

John peers around the corner of Poyner's store where he can see the sign for Berryville's Presbyterian Church from where he is standing. It's a pretty church inside and the lawn, though awfully nondescript in John's view, is generally tidy. Maybe the Presbyterians can provide Clara Jane a Church home. The lawn care is good enough and, as we discussed, the theology will be familiar.

On the other hand—okay, this is the other other hand—Clara Jane has had what she believes to be, and what John also believes to be—fairly direct contact with the Holy Ghost. John isn't sure where the Methodists and the Presbyterians stand on Holy Ghost Business, but the Disciples of Christ are in favor of it. No one at the First Christian Church of Berryville Disciples of Christ would think Clara Jane odd for her Holy Ghost encounters.

John knows this because he picked up a "Spiritual Gifts Inventory" last Sunday after church. The "SGI" is a scored test that helps you figure out ... well, your spiritual gifts. John found himself to be a man of limited gifts, a failure at prophecy, speaking in tongues, interpreting tongues, and casting out demons, uttering wisdom, uttering knowledge, and exorcising devils. He did, however, score high on manual labor and could be relied on to keep the church grounds spiffy looking.

Less than two minutes has passed since John flung Fuzzy's head into a stall in the Public Toilet, yet all of these thoughts have been thought since he reached the corner in front of Poyner Drug. Time is astonishing, isn't it?

Time isn't very discriminating, either. Instead of thinking about what church would best suit Clara Jane and how it would help her on the road to Salvation and Everlasting Life, John could have spent the time thinking about buying a snow shovel, or about why his size 40 pants are too tight (gosh, what a mystery!). I guess we have to be careful about how we use time, don't we? Anyway ...

... what John thought now—and how he and you will spend the next sixty seconds or so if you finish this chapter—is whether or not he should follow Pastor Andresen's e-mailed advice to let Clara Jane figure it out for herself.

(You can find that advice in Chapter 37.)

It was—is—good advice. But the Authorial I (that would be me) has several plot lines to tie up, including the Problem of Unitarians, the Problem of Iowans, the Problem of the Town Square Fountains, and the Problem of Chaos Theory vs. Social Order Theory, all of which require Clara Jane's encounter with SHAZAAM.

How in the world can I let her to figure it out by herself?

Chapter 39:

You'll Just have to Guess

John steps away from Poyner Drug and crosses West Church Street toward La Cabana, toward Dirt Poor, and toward Its a Mystery. He hits the sidewalk, walks right, and peers into Bruce's Barbershop. It's time for a trim, but Bruce's waiting area is full this morning and John has no minutes to spare for waiting. He walks toward East Church Street and, just as he is about to cross Highway 62, catches sight of a County Truck pulling up in front of the Public Toilet. A County employee leaps out of the truck and slaps a padlock on the toilet door. John can hear the lock snick shut from 50 yards away.

Isn't that interesting? The challenge of maintenance appears too great for Carroll County's Quorum Court; better, these politicians think, to padlock the town square's sole toilet and let the people walk about with locked knees and tight, painful grimaces on their anxious faces. Isn't that interesting?

On the bright side, however, a locked Public Toilet is now a safer haven for the storage and much later discovery of Fuzzy Markowitz's severed head. John feels a surge of relief; no unwitting tourist will abscond with the packaged cranium, only to open it later in the day at the Motel 6 in Eureka Springs.

Alrighty then. It is idea time. Only you and I and John know that there is a head in the Town Square Head. Idea one: let the three of us keep it a secret, thereby assuring that John will stay out of hot water for a little longer. Idea two: why don't you spread a rumor that there is a decapitated head in Public Toilet—and that's why it's locked! Feel free to choose the idea that sounds like the most fun!

The traffic light turns green. John crosses the highway and passes Wilson's TV and Appliance and then jaywalks his way back to the Heartbreak Shop. Clara Jane and Mrs. Heartbreak are still at the back of the shop, Mrs. Heartbreak's pretty face an emblem of sincerity and concentration. Clara Jane is listening intently and nodding. Brent Updegraff, Heartbreak's new bookseller, stands behind the counter doing the work that John would do if John did any work.

I am standing behind Mrs. Heartbreak's fern, overseeing the operation of Berryville's small Universe and transcribing events as they roll back and forth in time. The record of these events now comprise (at the word "now") 68,755 words. *My Boys Book of Knowledge* informs me that most mass market novels are 85,000 words long ... so: we have about 30,000 words—more or less—to use to tie up all the "Problems" we listed at the end of the last chapter, and to bring Clara Jane to Jesus if such a brung is in the cards.

John has slumped behind his laptop but stirs when he hears the scraping of chairs. Mrs. Heartbreak and Clara Jane have finished their conversation and are getting to their feet. Interestingly, they hug and Clara Jane leaves the shop without noticing John or saying so much as goodbye. This irks John. While Clara Jane is becoming more and more visible to the people of Berryville, he appears to be disappearing, slipping into everyone's subconscious. If the trend continues, he will be no more in the conscious minds of people then are the Town Square's foundations. John's face becomes red and I can tell that he intends to speak to me, perhaps irritably, if I give him half a chance. (Fat chance. Ha Ha Ha).

Mrs. Heartbreak still notices John. She walks over to him and puts a hand on his shoulder. He feels material enough to her. "What an interesting woman," she says, meaning Clara Jane. "We had a really good conversation."

"About what?" John asks.

"Well, you for one. I asked her why the two of you seem to have become so chummy. Every time I look up the two of you are in conversation."

"And she said ...?"

"She said that you have been inviting her to our church and have had conversations about her options for a church home."

"Exactly. As is plain to everyone, I had but spiritual and no lascivious plans for Ms. Smith."

"For heaven's sake, John. How could you think that anyone could imagine anything else?"

"I know how your mind works."

"John, you are hardly a maiden's deepest desire. As much as I love you I doubt that an attractive woman such as Clara Jane would find an old, deaf, and impoverished pot-stirrer such as yourself much of a catch."

"A million thanks."

"You know what I mean."

"Precisely."

Mrs. Heartbreak rolls her eyes and moves away from John and toward the sales counter. "I did invite her to services tomorrow," she says over her shoulder. "She said she would think about it."

John glances in my direction, about to speak harshly to me no doubt, but I feint left behind a particularly abundant fern frond and disappear from casual sight. He sighs at my cowardice and realizes that much that is afoot (thank goodness we've switched from all that hands business) has become his responsibility alone to solve.

If memory serves, John's main responsibility is to intervene on the mendacity and tight-fistedness of the Iowans who visit Berryville. Sure, Clara Jane had some success with a few of them following Sodjerberjer's death, but did a $1.08 per Iowan constitute commercial victory? Certainly not, in John's view, especially since .08 cents of it went to the government for maintenance of roads and the Public Toilet. No, hardly a victory.

John reached up to the shelf over his laptop and took down the wrong Bible (that would be the Jerusalem Bible, Reader's Edition) and turned to the 121st Psalm, which Pastor Andresen had mention in a eulogy for Mrs. Elizabeth Beck, God rest her soul. John began to read it, a song of ascents:

I lift my eyes to the mountains:
Where is help to come from?
Help comes to me from Yahweh
Who made heaven and earth.

John nodded. That is pretty straight, pretty plain, he thinks. He realizes that one thing he has forgotten to do about Clara Jane was to pray for her.

No letting our footsteps slip!
This guard of yours, he does not doze!
The guardian of Israel
Does not doze or sleep.

John knows that praying for Clara Jane will help her. God is awake. Waiting for his prayer. Is God also waiting for prayers for the Iowans? John has not asked what was going on in her mind when Sodjerberjer was telling her his life story. Was she praying for him? Should he pray for them? (That would be hard.)

Yahweh guards you, shades you.
With Yahweh at your right hand
Sun cannot strike you down by day,
Nor moon by night.

Is this as a promise of success? But what is success? Among the many Problems left to resolve—the Problem of Iowans, the Problem of Unitarians, the Problem of the Town Square Fountains, the Problem of Chaos Theory vs. Social Order Theory (to say nothing of the Problem of the C. Richard Williams now Sam Barr Memorial Toilet)—will a resolution acceptable to John be "success"? Is separation of Iowans from their money the big victory? Or, is Clara Jane coming to Jesus the success?

Yahweh Guards you from harm,
He guards your lives,
He guards you leaving and coming back,
Now and for always.

John shelves his bible. Whatever the outcome, however success is ultimately defined, John is the Big Winner. "Oh, Lucky Man," John says happily.

Chapter 40:

John Goes to Africa

John feels unaccountably happy this morning, although "unaccountably" might be the wrong word. He can list a few reasons for his happiness, can account for the feeling: He has gotten rid of Fuzzy's head and it is now someone else's problem. Mrs. Heartbreak and Clara Jane have finally met, and they seem—as John had predicted—to get along like two peas in a pod. That is not surprising, given that both are Social Order Theorists, albeit ones with different modes of operation. Finally, the plot begins to move forward!

There is also the possibility of a new and rather exciting rumor on the cusp of circulation among Berryville's intelligentsia: there is a decapitated head in the Town Square toilet and that is the reason why the County has padlocked the bathrooms! Rumors incite more attention locally than money because money is, for most Berryvillians, a fantasia while rumors are personal and compound like interest. Let's see if "this" rumor has legs

John also decides that he does not mind that Clara Jane left the shop without so much as a Hidie-ho in his direction. He is aware that he is a mostly a non-presence on the Town Square, known mostly as Mrs. Heartbreak's slightly stupid and mostly invisible sidekick-husband. John's affiliations, like his with Clara Jane, might begin with him, but the affiliations automatically and appropriately shift to Mrs. Heartbreak because Mrs. Heartbreak is fabulous, while John is just deaf and lumpy. He might as well be in Africa instead of—right here right now—on his stool in the shop, for all that his physical presence matters to anyone.

"What a delicious thought," John thinks. "I might as well be in Africa or, I might as well be in Berryville, for all that it matters to anyone. I can take my pick!

"If I was in Africa, I could be thinking of myself being in Berryville and Presto! There I am (here I am!). Conversely, here I am in Berryville thinking about myself being in Africa and—there I am (here I am!)."

(No wonder people prefer to affiliate with Mrs. Heartbreak: she is always in one place at a time. The right place; the right time.

If John is in Berryville (he is) it is 11:30 AM. A lot has happened this morning, which you know about because you read all about these happenings in the three previous chapters describing John's morning. You know that John was followed to work by Mary Margaret's cats, at least as far as Springfield Road. You know that John hid Fuzzy Markowitz's head in the Town Square toilet, and that the County has locked said toilet. You know that John has read Elizabeth Beck's eulogy and that he read the 121st psalm in the Wrong Bible. And you know that Mrs. Heartbreak and Clara Jane have met and that Mrs. Heartbreak invited Clara Jane to church on Sunday morning. I'm sure we're all looking forward to that.

John stumbles back to the coffee pot and pours a long portion of RDC. Mrs. Heartbreak smiles at him as he pours, and he smiles back. Mrs. Heartbreak doesn't think he is in Africa, and if she did, it would be because that's where he would be. Not in Berryville, the right place, right now.

John carries his RDC to the front of the shop and peers out the window onto the Square. Mrs. Colleen Shogren parks her car and strides toward the shop. She has been swimming, and singing, and affiliating like mad in her new home, Holiday Island. She enters the shop and slides by John without noticing him. John thinks, I might as well be in Africa. Colleen and Mrs. Heartbreak begin to gab; John walks out of the shop and ponders time on the sidewalk

At the very beginning of this book, in Chapter One, I told a joke with the punch line "What is time to a Pig." What is time to anyone?

John stands and sips RDC. He has done this a hundred times in the past—in the exact same spot—and if he is lucky, he will do it a hundred more times in the future. But right now, he is sipping and looking out over the Square, right now. What is different between past sipping and future sipping, and right now sipping?

The date is different. And John's head contains memories of past sipping that he hadn't had before because the past sipping was, then, probably future sipping—like his sipping right now (which had been future sipping before it became right now sipping). I know this is boring to read, but it is about time travel, an exciting subject. You have time traveled yourself.

Christ was an experienced time traveler, whether you know him as God or know him as the adored Subject of 120,000,000 delusional wing nuts. The Actual Christ in life and history and the fictional Christ in books and movies both experienced crucifixion, and Lazarus rising, and Transfiguration, before the events happened, and during the happening, and after they happened. And so it goes, over and over and over: Christ is crucified today, and he will be crucified tonight and tomorrow morning. He might not only be in Africa, he is in Africa. What a time traveler!

Of course, you could say the same thing about Richard Halliburton.

Time, John thinks, is not a line going into the distance. It is the figure eight, constantly looping back on itself, over and over again. In this book John has been to Vietnam, he has spoken Norwegian to his Aunt Sylvia, and he has fallen freshly in love with Mrs. Heartbreak. These things have all happened to John, before they happened in a book, and they will happen again when John thinks about them, or re-reads the book. When were these events "real"? They seem real every time. They are real to John whether he is in Berryville, or in Africa.

Too bad John hasn't been smoking dope. That would explain things, wouldn't it? But he hasn't. Been smoking dope, that is. He just doesn't know what time it is.

Lina Blanchard pulls onto the Square and parks her white convertible. Gets out. Heads toward Heartbreak's. She nearly brushes against John's bulky form, but even with the near miss does not seem to notice him as she goes into the shop. "Isn't that interesting," John thought.

John drained the RDC and went back into the shop. Colleen and Lina and Mrs. Heartbreak were still gabbing at the counter. Then, they flew out, like hummingbirds, speed of light. Mrs. Heartbreak walked over to John and gave him a kiss. "Are you feeling alright," she asks. "You look pale as a ghost."

"Right as rain," John says. "What's up with Colleen?"

Mrs. Heartbreak frowns. "The Town Square Toilet is locked," she says. "And do you know why?

"Hmmn ..."

"Colleen says there's a dead body in the toilet. And it's missing it's head."

John feigns surprise. "No kidding?"

"No kidding," Mrs. Heartbreak replies. "The news is all over town. There is a dead body in the Public Toilet ... as rumor has it."

"As rumor has it," John agrees. "Well, maybe they'll clean it now." He pauses for a moment, considering.

"I wonder if they'll clean it if they only find a head instead of a whole body."

"Good Lord, John," Mrs. Heartbreak says. "Why in the world would you say such a thing? Sometimes I think you're on another continent."

Chapter 41:

Satisfied Thinking

It isn't even noon yet, and so much has happened!

Oh, come on. A lot has happened, at least if you are John. If you're not John, though, I suppose this is pretty thin gruel. What can I do to speed things up? Car chase through the Sonic parking lot? How about some naughty bits? Oh. I forgot. No SVSL allowed in this book. Sorry. And after all, this is Berryville, Arkansas, the little town that time forgot. Not much happens. I told you that in Chapter Two.

But did you hear? There's a dead body in the Town Square toilet.

No there isn't. It's just Fuzzy's head, not the entirety of Fuzzy. John wonders why people can't get the facts right. It bothers him a little bit, people not getting the facts straight. John wonders some more, this time about starting a rumor that a notorious local landlord has found Jesus and has reformed and is making sure that his properties are scrupulously—okay, minimally—maintained. Want to guess who the landlord is?

Nah. That's boring. You know who I mean. And it wouldn't be a rumor. It would be a miracle, and only a few miracles are allowed in this book. I don't want to go over quota.

John decides that it is time to advance the plot a bit (THANK GOD) and solve some of the outstanding problems. The hardest problem to solve will be the Problem with Iowans because it involves SHAZAAM and whether or not Clara Jane is integrated into a Church Home, or discovered as a serial killer and sent to the SLAMMER (or both). Therefore, John decides to leave that PROBLEM to last; the novel's finale, so to speak. What is the easiest problem to fix?

John, still flushed from Mrs. Heartbreak's kiss, goes to his laptop and sends Dr. Jim Young an email.

"Dear Jim," he writes:

"As you may be aware, I have for some time been perplexed by Unitarians and the somewhat paradoxical PROBLEM they present for a rational society. Here it is: Unitarians are a generally fine people. They oppose war, vulgarity, inhibitions, regression, aggression, don't ask don't tell, beef, orthodoxy, the National Rifleman's Association, chauvinism, Milton Friedman, fart and belch jokes, meanness, urban sprawl, the '80s, Albert Ellis, and my insistence that Richard Nixon was the Last Liberal.

"Unitarians are also for the Solstice, for fairies and brownies and elves, for peace, love, brotherhood, L.L. Bean, madrigals, the '60s, vegetables, honoring the feelings of others, sandals and peasant blouses, strands of pearls and sweater sets, the novels of John Updike, Volvos, political correctness, Fritz Perls, astrological charts, ethnic casseroles, the poems of Emily Dickinson, and the occasional martini.

"As you can see, Jim" John writes, "these are GOOD people, harmless in the best sense of the word, law abiding, hedge clipping, gentle, amiable folk with azure auras sporting daffy smiles or sweetly empathetic expressions as congruent as possible with circumstance. Unitarians are in fact not merely GOOD people but they could possibly be the BEST people. If one had the gift of choosing who his neighbor would or would not be, a Unitarian would top the would be list. Obviously, a Unitarian would TOP my list of potential neighbors had I the power to fill homes adjacent to my home.

"So you see the problem," John types. "These are the best folks in the world, but there is only a To Whom It May be Concerned residing in their heavens. There is no THERE there, no Jesus, no Allah Bless His Holy Name, no Yahweh, no Holy Spirit except photo-copied spook-clones summoned up by University sponsored

Phenomenologists working out of Women's Studies Departments. How can it be that such a vacuous religious sect holds the key to World Peace and Global Love and Universal Brotherhood, while genuine Christ-centered or Mohammed-centered knuckle biting, long suffering, Holy Book pedagoging, go to Sunday meeting folk can't tie a shoe without holding a massacre or two? What is the nature of this riddle, and how can we give answer to the PROBLEM therein?"

John hits the send button. Almost immediately, Dr. Young replies:

"What problem?"

John is slow. He thinks that Jim hasn't understood the question. He is about to expand on what he believes is an already comprehensive description of the PROBLEM when he realizes that Dr. Young has not misunderstood the question, but has simply rejected John's Unitarian conundrum as any kind of PROBLEM at all. He has rejected the entire premise.

If this were a poorly written book John would scratch his head in befuddlement: But I will avoid that cliché in favor of a more inspired chin rub and frown. "Dogma is not the end of thinking," John says out loud, quoting G.K. Chesterton. "Dogma is satisfied thinking." So why hasn't he satisfied the good doctor, or himself, for that matter? Why hasn't it satisfied Christendom in general? Could Chesterton be wrong?

Can it be that Christians are not satisfied because of Dogma, and that is why they are so disputatious? Conversely, can it be that Unitarians, a people without Dogma, are satisfied because of their very lack of Dogma? Or, should John swing into the abyss of his own good nature and, along with Dr. Young, let the Unitarians and the Christians puzzle out this paradox on their own?

John is about to consult with Ralph Waldo Emerson, an expert of sorts on these dicey metaphysical matters, but he resists. Is there a more vacuous thinker in American Letters than Emerson? John can't think of one, unless it was Elbert Hubbard himself. No. John needs to figure this out for himself.

But why?

Because Clara Jane is coming to Church tomorrow—John's Church— as a means to resume or expand her engagement of the

Five Finger Exercise (please see previous chapters, you malingerer, you). What good or harm will come to Clara Jane if she commits to membership, remits her sins (reports her sins!), is admitted into the fellowship of the First Christian Church, prepares for baptism, and is then hauled off to the slammer for the past she has shed, and for which she has been forgiven?

Obviously, the matter lies not between Clara Jane and the Unitarians—who will decide she had an unfortunate childhood and is therefore exempt of responsibility for adulthood shenanigans—and not with the Christians—who just might string her up—but between Clara Jane and God. And John suddenly decides that that is good enough. He will let the two of them (Them?) figure it out. He will take the Presbyterian Paul Andresen's and the Metaphysician Jim Young's advice and let it all get sorted out by SOMEONE else.

John is okay now, even happy again. His belief in God is unshakeable; he and God speak often: John knows from these conversations that God isn't particularly interested in the details. God is a Big Picture Guy who knows that the Devil is in the details.

Chapter 42:

Panic, Fall Helplessly into Despair

John falls into a fitful sleep. He dreams of Africa, but it is a short dream and of no consequence. But he did see an elephant in his dream. There, over to the right. That's the elephant he sees. Okay, enough. Sorry.

John's sleep is fitful because he is worried about Clara Jane coming to church in the morning, and of what might happen during the service. What if she responds to the alter call and decides to testify? How will the Heartbreak's church family respond? Oh my.

Oh my indeed.

If only the Heartbreaks were Unitarians, there might not be a problem. Surely, one way of solving a problem is to redefine it as something else. The good people of Salem, Massachusetts had the problem of witches in their neighborhood, and they went to a lot of bother spurning and burning them until society in part and government as a whole redefined the problem as mere superstition. That modern solution is called the TURNING THE PROBLEM ON ITS HEAD solution, and one of its curious outcomes is that Unitarians, as an outstanding example, are likely to not only accept witches into their church home, but to honor their history of suffering at the hands of a bigoted people as well. Perhaps they would do the same for a serial killer, especially one who had had a difficult childhood.

But the Heartbreak's are not Unitarians; they are Disciples of Christ, a people who resist turning problems onto their heads, a people who are not Modernists in any sense of the word. And, while no strangers to testimony, John doubted that they would tolerate a rough patch as any kind of justification for Clara Jane's past mayhem.

Then, there was the problem of music. Although John found Sunday services peaceful and restful and frequently inspiring, about half the hymns they sang wangled inside his head like bolts tossed into a tin bucket. John wondered where Protestants go all those hymns, and why their resistance to theological modernism didn't transfer when it came to music.

John dreams that he asks David Bell, the Music Director for the First Christian Church, to try out a few hymns from John's boyhood. "David," John dreams, "How about O Sanctissma? It's a swell song!"

> *O sanctissima, O piissima,*
> *Dulcis Virgo Maria.*
> *Mater amata, intemerata,*
> *Ora, ora pro nobis*
> *Tota pulchra es, O Maria*
> *Et macula non est in te*
> *Mater amata, intemerata,*
> *Ora, ora pro nobis.*
> *Sicut lilium inter spinas,*
> *Sic Maria inter filias*
> *Mater amata, intemerata,*
> *Ora, ora pro nobis.*
> *O sanctissima, O piissima,*
> *Dulcis Virgo Maria.*
> *Mater amata, intemerata,*
> *Ora, ora pro nobis*
> *Tota pulchra es, O Maria*
> *Et macula non est in te*
> *Mater amata, intemerata,*
> *Ora, ora pro nobis.*
> *Sicut lilium inter spinas,*

Sic Maria inter filias
Mater amata, intemerata,
Ora, ora pro nobis

Right. In John's dreams.

Wasn't it Alfred E. Neuman who rhetorically asked, "What, me worry?" from the covers of *Mad Magazine?* John recalls racing his bicycle down to the drugstore every 3rd Saturday morning—when the magazine came out—in order to get the single copy that Mr. Snider, who owned the drugstore, would churlishly order. Mr. Snider did not approve of *Mad Magazine* or of comic books in general except for Donald Duck, but he so disliked John, and the other warped boy in town, Donny Ganander, that he ordered the one copy so he could watch the slower 3rd Saturday boy cry when he failed to beat out the other boy. Sometimes it was John, who had the cry, and sometimes it was Donny Ganander who cried, but the weeping of either boy equally satisfied Mr. Snider. Mr. Snider, by the way, was a Nazarene, a matter of much gossip among the households in John's neighborhood, that were either Catholic or Lutheran or, less frequently both, in the cases of a few "mixed" (that is to say, doomed) marriages.

Alfred E. Neuman may have been the one who introduced John to Chaos Theory in the first place. And doubtlessly, 'Spy vs. Spy', the greatest existential riff every to appear in any magazine anywhere, reinforced the message—which John learned on a daily basis while growing up—that life is not all buttered scones. But why worry about that?

Why worry, indeed? Why is it, John thought, that I am consumed by PROBLEMS that no one else seems to give a second thought to? Is Berryville's smelly Town Toilet really a problem? Are the Town Square fountains horrific East German inspired kitsch, or merely an aesthetic, elitist conceit held by John alone? Does anyone care that there is a severed head in the Public WC? Does anyone besides John mind very much that Berryville's side streets resemble the alleyways of Calcutta?

Are any of these really problems, or, do they cease being problems if we just decide not to give a hoot about them?

But what if Clara Jane testifies and admits her past during testimony? John is sure that saying "sorry" won't be enough, that there will be some test of authenticity for what "sorry" really means, and for what "authenticity" might mean as well.

Well, John is sure the local pastors will derive some professional satisfaction at the chance to define authenticity in its varied and, yes, multi-varied forms. After all, as John Turner has preached, there is no GET OUT OF HELL FREE card. Turner meant that attendance at church is not by itself a ticket to heaven, and that mere admission of corporality and sorrowful expressions therein carry little weight until they pass God's sniff test. But there is that whole "render onto Caesar" gig to cipher through.

Pastor French has said much the same thing, writing that there are plenty of villains in Berryville's and Christendom's pews, but his views on serial killers is unknown, even though he is remarkably tolerant of the Razorbacks. Still, serial killing is not an ordinary occupation, and unlike other ordinary and organized crime, like banking, it is difficult pastime to over look.

Yup, John tosses and turns. He has plenty to worry about. His dreams are filled with panic!

Chapter 43:

Jane Russell Eats Bugs

Clara Jane is slowly walking up Pritchard Street toward the Heartbreak's house. She has decided to accept Mrs. Heartbreak's invitation to attend church services with her. She is not nervous (Clara Jane is never nervous), and in contrast to John, who is at home just up the street reading the Wrong Bible in preparation for that morning's services, she feels calm and a sense of anticipation. She has worked out a SHAZAAM PLAN to solve the PROBLEM of Iowans and is feeling pretty good about things.

It is a bright morning and Pritchard Street is beautiful. Mary Margaret's cats are laying about the neighborhood. They watch Clara Jane's progress as she saunters along and are incurious about who she is or what is going on inside her head. Too bad for the cats; they don't know that there is more to life than mice, a point that Clara Jane is mulling over just now. Up until recently Clara Jane's life has been all cat and mouse.

A car passes by. The driver, Sharon Sloan the artist and scholar, looks in her direction. Sharon stares at her and that too makes Clara Jane feel good: she has been seen; seeing is believing in Berryville; people are beginning to see her as real. What else will it be possible for Berryvillians to see? Will they begin to see their town?

John's sleepless night has been followed by a restless morning. He had been unable to enjoy Mrs. Heartbreak's gourmet breakfast and now the newspaper is full of bad news. "Bad news on the doorstep" Don Mclean had sung and ain't it the truth is how John is feeling. He hasn't noticed what a pretty day it is, or how lovely Mrs. Heartbreak looks as she gets ready for church.

John has never taken Mrs. Heartbreak for granted, not that she would ever allow such a thing, not for a minute, not for a single second. When John was dating—that would be decades ago—the women he went out with were apt to chase rabbits at inopportune times and could scratch behind their ears with their feet. It was interesting to watch, but a little off-putting too, to tell you the truth. Mrs. Heartbreak, prior to becoming Mrs. Heartbreak, did not chase rabbits and, while remarkably limber, didn't scratch behind her ears with her feet. Naturally, John was smitten and Mrs. Heartbreak, while not exactly smitten with John, had been able to overlook some of his deficiencies and, in the manner of all Social Order Theorists, believed that she could change the others in the fullness of time. Ha Ha Ha Ha Ha.

Meanwhile:

I've been wandering around the Heartbreak's spacious backyard, trying to figure out what to do next. I know what Clara Jane's SHAZAAM PLAN is, but I'm not sure I approve of it. And I am worried about John: he does less and less work and is spending more and more space in less and less time. (Go ahead, you can figure it out. Madame de Stahl did. Really. No kidding.) What John does or does not do—with space or time or with the $40 he has saved at Community First Bank—is entirely in my control, but I had no idea he would become such a dullard when we set out on this adventure.

I am also not sure if John's solution for the PROBLEM of Unitarians is satisfactory. Is a religion with "niceness" as its first and last Commandment a satisfactory religion? Probably not. But there is to be no (more) wrangling about words: all this ever achieves is the destruction of those who are listening. Have nothing to do with pointless philosophical discussions; I guess that's my point. I'm probably not the first one to have this thought. Am I?

Jane Russell Terrier is eating bugs off the concrete stoop behind the house. She seems to know exactly what to do. What I am going to do is follow John's example and let the PROBLEM of Unitarians go. It's a PROBLEM that I'll just eat.

I bet you're relieved. One PROBLEM down and four to go … the plot thickens.

Clara Jane turns up the brick path toward the Heartbreak's front door. She rings the bell. John shudders. Mrs. Heartbreak smiles and hustles to opens the door. "Dear!" Mrs. Heartbreak exclaims. "You decided to come!"

"Yes," Clara Jane says. "I'm looking forward to it."

Mrs. Heartbreak ushers Clara Jane in and shuts the door. "We have a few minutes," she says. "Would you like a cup of tea?"

Clara Jane nods. "That would be nice, thank you." She pauses and looks around the room. "Where's John?" she asks.

Mrs. Heartbreak is startled. "Why, he's right there," she says, pointing to a chair near the center of the room. "Say hello, John" she commands, over her shoulder. She is off to get tea.

John nods to Clara Jane. He notices that she is dressed in Church Lady attire; nearly identical in fact to what Mrs. Heartbreak is wearing. There must be a rule book somewhere, he thinks.

"Hello, John," Clara Jane says evenly. "I didn't see you."

"Ironic, isn't it?"

Clara Jane gets it right away. "It is a little weird," she admits. "I'm becoming visible and you're fading away. Do you suppose there's a kind of DNA transfer or something like that going on?"

"No," John says emphatically. "The jerk writing this book thinks it's funny or that it adds a level of complexity to an otherwise hackneyed and fairly tired plot line. I can't say I like it much."

"Where is the Authorial I?" she asks. "He's been quiet lately."

"He's in the back yard, watching the dog eat bugs."

"Is he coming to church with us?"

"He wouldn't miss it for the world," John says dryly. "I'm on pins and needles myself."

"No worries, John," Clara Jane says. "I'm just going to observe, get the lay of the land, locate the exits, and make myself blend into the furniture. I won't say a word. I just want to find out how these Christians operate."

"Does the Authorial I know that?"

"If he knows what's good for him," she says. "Besides," she continues, "I won't be able to effect the SHAZAAM PLAN if I wig out in church and get hauled off to the pokey. He's only got about 25,000 words left to bring things to a head and shut this turkey down. I doubt that he wants to delay things anymore than either of us wants him to."

John is peeved. "I don't sleep at all last night," he complains. "I've been beside myself worrying that you might be indiscreet and force the hand of our church family."

"Dear John," Clara Jane says, smiling. "I have reformed and won't misbehave again. But I also have a lifetime of learning about how to survive, and about knowing how to protect myself. You shouldn't have worried."

John is unconvinced. "Being a Christian means not worrying about surviving. It means giving yourself up to the protection of Christ. I worried that you might already be in that place. I doubt that most Christians can conceive of such bliss for themselves, let alone for others."

"I've got a ways to go before I get that blissed out."

John nods. "Yes," is all he can say.

"Yes, what?" Mrs. Heartbreak asks. She enters the room with a tea tray and biscuits.

"We were discussing what Clara Jane might expect at church this morning," John answers.

"Oh, such good things!" Mrs. Heartbreak says. "It's always wonderful!"

Chapter 44:

You Can Skip This Chapter.
Not Much Happens.

Clara Jane and Mrs. Heartbreak are walking up Pritchard Street toward Church Street. When they reach the corner—Mary Margaret's corner—they will turn right and walk about three hundred feet to the sidewalk leading up the steps of the First Christian Church. John follows them, about five feet back, taking note in a non-salacious way of the sway of their hips and of the mumble jumble of their conversation. He can't hear what they are saying but it is an amiable and animated conversation.

All the events of Mrs. Heartbreak's life are important. This walk with Clara Jane, their joint appearance in church, will become another exciting adventure in Mrs. Heartbreak's fascinating residence on earth. Mrs. Heartbreak will relive the adventure many times; it will be explicated, discussed, and mined for all possible nuggets of consequence and conjecture. John, Mrs. Heartbreak's mother, her sisters, and Mrs. Shogren, will participate in the adventure, albeit mostly as audience. Notwithstanding their relative passivity, they enjoy hearing about these adventures, and understand that their own drab lives pale by comparison.

For example, John might catch on fire in a rare act of spontaneous combustion, or he might go to Africa and return after a spin on the equator, but these are mere trifles compared to say, Mrs. Heartbreak's courageous management of a torrential downpour or Jane Russell's tussle with an opossum. John has grown to understand that Mrs. Heartbreak's life is Grand Opera while his is a tin whistle's tootle.

This is what John is thinking about as they turn the corner and near the First Christian Church. Lowell and Lorena Johnson drive by and they wave at Mrs. Heartbreak. They don't see John; otherwise they would wave at him too. John doesn't mind. His mind is catching sight of the idea of being unsighted, of being, and not being, not presently in view, merely a second thought. He is confident that he will be under any circumstances.

Clara Jane and Mrs. Heartbreak go up the steps, through the pretty red door, into the vestry; greetings abound. John follows, enjoying their slim ankles; absence of greetings—at first—then cautiously though squinted eyes as if peering into the great beyond. "Oh. It's John," they think. John might as well be in the Great Beyond, since he has to be—will be—somewhere. "Hi John," they say, smiling. "Now" John is in church. That's where he will be. In case you're looking for him. For the next sixty minutes.

Maybe this will help with all this "be" business:

A guy is following a parade of elephants. He is carrying a shovel and pushing a cart with a barrel on it. The circus has come to town and his job is to scoop up the elephant poop. It's a hard, smelly job and, as you might guess, it requires heavy lifting. Elephants are not dainty poopers, without putting too fine a point on it. Poop, scoop, poop scoop, poop scoop, that's life.

A man in the crowd watches the guy. He feels sorry for him. He rushes up to him and offers him a job. "Work for me," he suggests. "I've got a great job for you. Indoors! No poop!"

The guy is incredulous. He stares at the Good Samaritan, dumfounded. When he is finally able to speak, he exclaims, loudly, "What? And give up show business?"

Mrs. Heartbreak is in show business. John is just glad to be there for the show.

Hymns are proof that time is elastic. Today's opening hymn is *Great is Thy Faithfulness*, a tune of several hours duration that John is unable to fake but which Mrs. Heartbreak engages as a duel to the death. Clara Jane is following along silently but with apparent interest. It may be the first hymn that she has heard, or at least has paid attention to. She is mouthing the words and may be on the cusp of joining in. Her concentration seems deep.

So far, so good, John thinks. Everyone appears able to see Clara Jane. Perhaps she is fully material, fully realized. Naturally, there are some gaps in her character development. We know she is from Tisdale, Missouri, just a few miles up the road. She is pretty in a non-descript way but has used her sexuality to lure men into compromising situations. This resulted in their deaths by various means, all violent. That is what John Sanford, her creator, has told us, minus exciting verbiage involving car chases, wounds of a critical nature, and the odd boyfriend or two.

John has given us a sketchy summary as well, focusing on Clara Jane's ordinariness and, in occasional lapses of emphasis, on how well tended her yard is. He has watched her "grow" in the consciousness of others such as in Mrs. Heartbreak's consciousness, in Yodi the AFKA Catryn Yoder, and now in full blossom, fully grown, before the people here at the First Christian Church of Berryville.

John does not find it ironic that Clara Jane is essentially born (has become fully material and is seen by everyone who cares to see her) at the FCC. What is remarkable about this "point in time" is that between Clara Jane being and when she will stumble into not being—as we all will stumble—is "becoming." I know this is boring, but hang in there. Think of an arrow in flight. When you first see it at a certain "point in time" it is no longer at that point in time. It has come and gone. We will also come and go. Unless certain hymns are being sung. Then we will stay and stay. Infinity may be a hymn.

Among the ladies at First Christian Church are a few that are wondering if Clara Jane has been born again. John is unable to comprehend the meaning of "born again." He understands it to be defined as a discreet event where one comes to believe in Jesus Christ in a deeply meaningful way. But John's experience is of being born just once, of being and becoming; that is Clara Jane's practical experience: becoming born again is a lifetime's labor.

Pastor Judy Tuner officiates today: her sermon is on 1st Thessalonians 5:12-24. Clara Jane pays close attention. Turner's message is that prayer must be unceasing; "Pray always," Saint Paul says. "Give thanks in all circumstances, for this is the will of God in Jesus Christ for you."

This is the message of *The Way of the Pilgrim,* an old Russian book that John loves. J. D. Salinger also passed the message along in *Fanny and Zoey,* an odd little book that John tries to keep in stock. What is the message? "Lord Jesus Christ, have mercy on me, a sinner."

Turner's sermon is a fine sermon. John feels calm and edified. Clara Jane remains attentive. Mrs. Heartbreak is calm, edified and attentive. There are better adjectives and adverbs but these are good enough. The service is over. A hymn is sung—this one is as long as it should be; it is a good hymn. Several of the ladies invite Clara Jane back. She smiles. She is non-committal.

Mrs. Heartbreak and Clara Jane reverse their steps; now they walk arm in arm. John follows at a short distance. It is a beautiful day in Berryville.

Chapter 45:

I Come as a Thief

Sunday afternoons can be a problem for John. Since he is ordinarily a man of leisure he finds himself at sixes and sevens with time that is designated for leisure. What will he do differently with a free afternoon? Read? Stand on the front stoop and sniff at the world? John does these things habitually; forced relaxation makes him nervous and now, this Sunday afternoon, he feels compelled to read and sniff, which makes of the reading and sniffing nothing except work, the thing that John avoids habitually and which is now unfairly forced upon him during a designated rest period.

Things have ramped up a bit on the old Fleisch Kincaid Reading Scale, which I'm sure you've noticed. You're reading at the 10th and 11th grade levels and, once in a while, like in the paragraph above, you've been shoved into the 12th grade, a grade level rife with passive sentences and changes in tenses that are confusing and not much fun to read. But why should you have fun all the time? What about poor John, all sixes and sevens this afternoon?

Church had proved anti-climatic to John; he had anxiously awaited the wigging out of Clara Jane and she had behaved no worse than anyone else at services this morning. Gil Hrdlicka, a priest in Bloomington, Minnesota, had e-mailed John his disappointment. "The Authorial I had built up Clara Jane's visit to church so much," Father Hrdlicka wrote, "that I expected an old fashioned Come to Jesus, or at least a bit of Southern Gothic Revival. But nothing happened!

"And by the way," Gil finished, "it looks like the Razorbacks couldn't beat the Little Sisters of the Poor this year. Florida certainly cleaned their clock!"

Unlike Father Hrdlicka, John is not disappointed; he is relieved. It is easy for other people, people on the outside of Berryville looking in, to hope for melodrama and SVSL, but if you live inside Berryville you hope for peace and calm and you accept the cultural Jansenism of the place as right and proper as long as it is polite Jansenism, and understated. Berryvillians do not push the river, a fact that John knows is hard for Yankee Catholics like Father Hrdlicka to understand.

John's relief is tempered by Clara Jane's parting request to "have coffee" with him tomorrow. Having coffee is a new behavior or activity for Clara Jane. As Clara Rinker, she did not eat, go to the bathroom, or drink coffee insofar as John can recall. John Sanford had given Clara Jane a fast paced life that allowed little time for the ordinary activities of human kind. John wondered if Clara Jane was irked by these new obligations, or viewed the consumption of a cheeseburger or the purchase of oven cleaner as novel and exciting adventures. *Life its Ownself,* as Dan Jenkins intoned is comprised of little steps—like eating cheeseburgers and buying oven cleaner—and big pratfalls—like hiding decapitated heads in public toilets, or sending Iowans to their Maker. Some rich lady, probably Diana Trilling or Lady Astor, said that life is "short, nasty and brutal." John couldn't remember which lady said it, but he didn't agree with her. Life is pretty good, John thought, although Jenkins had it about right.

John's interest in cheeseburgers is unabated. He wishes he had one right now as he sits on his Pritchard Street stoop, pondering coffee with Clara Jane tomorrow. His interest in cheeseburgers is important because it is proof that he still exists, that he hasn't faded entirely away and is still material in a, well, material way. On the other hand—yeah, I know—John hasn't ever purchased oven cleaner and he wouldn't know how to make a bed. Mrs. Heartbreak handles the practical matters of life, both because she is a Social Order Theorist with an overweening need to control the details associated with the Operation of the Universe, and because John is wholly uninterested in details. SOMEONE has to run the world, thank you very much.

John assumes that Clara Jane intends to reveal her SHAZAAM PLAN tomorrow. He assumes this because he has read, in an earlier chapter of this book, that she has in fact formulated a plan and is ready to act on it. More to the point, though, John knows that I don't approve of the plan, and this has heightened his interest in it and, sadly, has increased his appreciation for it sight unseen though it is.

John's joy at my discomfort is unseemly and, like his enjoyment of the impoverishment of Razorback victories, is not very Christian if the Christian view is to comfort the afflicted and to empathize with the sorrowful. Still, if America is a Christian Nation then we can assume also that hell is a Christian Nation as well. Think about it. Then you can forgive John his transgression. I certainly will.

John gets off the stoop and goes inside. Mrs. Heartbreak is on the phone, talking with Mrs. Shogren. Mrs. Shogren has recently played the part of Bambi, a cheerleader, at the Holiday Island Theatre Company, and Mrs. Heartbreak wants to know how it went. Mrs. Heartbreak ignores John and may not even be aware that he has come into the room. "So," Mrs. Heartbreak says to Mrs. Shogren, "there were no vegetables or whistling involved, then?"

John picks up a copy of Louis Auchincloss' book, *I Come as a Thief,* and goes through the house, exiting into the back yard. Jane Russell is hunting for bugs among the hostas growing under a pecan tree. John sits, opens the book, and then lights a cigar. (He gets one every Sunday.)

John reads several chapters of Mr. Auchincloss' very dense prose before he realizes that this entire chapter has been written in the manner of Louis Auchincloss. John wearily shakes his head. Some guys will go to any lengths for a joke.

Chapter 46:

Rainy Days and Mondays

It is Monday morning on Berryville's Town Square. John is standing in his usual spot, just left of the front door, facing the grassy area from where the fountains hiccup periodically. The sun is shining, but there is a chill in the air for the first time since spring. John notices that the parking spaces are filling up with cars with Iowa license plates. "I brake for hogs," the state motto, is fixed permanently across the bottom of nearly every license he sees.

John feels a bit conflicted as he watches the Iowans cruise around the Square angling for a parking spot. He is curious to see if they conduct themselves any differently now that they are the target of a SHAZAAM PLAN, but he isn't certain that Mrs. Heartbreak has lain in enough toilet paper to meet their special needs. If they can't get wiped out precisely to their satisfaction they will give her a hard time and that will make her feel bad. That will make John feel bad.

Bits of music snake out of their cars as they cruise; John hears snatches of *Muskrat Love* from one car and *Rainy Days and Mondays (Always Get Me Down)* from another. John worries that his eyes will begin to bleed: He remembers a time when he drove seven Chinese bankers from Modesto, California to the airport in San Francisco in a five seat Toyota ... and

... natural (compulsive) over-achievers, these bankers believed that every minute spent in the US should be invested in assimilating as much of America's popular culture as possible. As soon as John hit the freeway out of Modesto the boss banker handed out mimeographed sheets covered with both the lyrics and music to the then very popular *Rainy Days and Mondays,* which those China boy loan sharks set out to learn for the next 300 miles.

One of Berryville's Merriest Pranksters had recently loaned John a CD titled *If I were a Carpenter* which was a compilation of greatest hits sung by tribute bands. It was an unsolicited loan, but oh my, the memories.

Okay. Back to the Square:

John surmises that Clara Jane and perhaps the Holy Ghost may have summoned the Iowans, much as she (they?) had summoned them before. But he could be wrong. The chill air reminds John that the off-season is just beginning which means that hotel rooms in Eureka Springs are going for $29 a night instead of the more extravagant $32 tourist season rates. As you might expect, Iowans will drive many hundreds of miles to save $3 bucks a night, so they mostly visit the Ozarks at this time of the year.

It is also possible that Clara Jane and the Holy Ghost have simply timed their plans to coincide with Iowan travel schedules to take advantage of the economies of scale therein: cheap rooms equals more Iowans. However, that might be a leap of faith (so to speak), since John is unable to come up with a single story of how or when the HG acted on the basis of seasonal discounts. One never knows, though, do one?

Yodi, the artist formerly known as Catherine Yoder, walks past John. She is in an unseemly rush. "You look positively washed out, John," she says, over her shoulder. "You need some color, maybe a dash of crimson in your cheeks!"

John thought not. He wasn't about to get all tarted up just for the sake of being more observable. Anyone who needed to see him, John thought, could see him. He hoped.

John has taken up his sidewalk post a bit earlier than usual. When he opened the shop this morning Norman Mailer had been walking around the stacks, shouting imprecations at Gore Vidal, an old talk show enemy. Mailer, newly dead, had yet to learn the protocols of the dead and was acting, as he had in life, the bumptious fool.

Matters were not helped when John informed Mailer that he was in Arkansas, a matter of interest to Mailer since his 5th wife was from Pine Bluff, down in the central park of the state. Mailer immediately adopted the Big Daddy accent from *Cat on a Hot Tin Roof*. Both Vidal and Tennessee Williams, who shared shelving tier to the far right (V and W) of Mailer's (M and just south of MacLean, Norman) shelf in the middle of the shop, giggled a bit.

"That New York Jew a pistol, in'nee," Williams laughed. "I 'clare, he sump'in."

"Shut up, you fruits!" Mailer roared (roaring, as you know, is how Mailer speaks, even when he isn't Big Daddy).

"Mr. Mailer, please," John had said, attempting to intervene. "Please be civil."

To no avail. They—Mailer, Vidal, and Williams—continued to squabble. John continued to intervene. To no avail certainly, but with a good deal of spirit and resolve. In fact, John was prepared to intervene indefinitely, and would have, except that Mrs. Heartbreak and Jane Russell chose that moment to enter the shop.

"John!" Mrs. Heartbreak shouted. "Stop it!

"Who do you think you are talking to now?" And, "Do you have any idea how foolish you look? Why are you waving your hands in the air?"

That was three too many questions for John. He simply shrugged, shoved Mailer back to the Ms' (Mrs. Heartbreak wondered why he seemed to be dragging a foot), and walked out the door. Where he is now. Feeling sorry for himself.

"Why don't people understand that just because a writer is dead doesn't mean that he stops speaking?" John asks, plaintively, looking at the sky. "And if they speak to you, why is so strange to answer them?"

"Because you'd waste thousands of hours a year in conversations with hopeless drunkards and atheists and wife beaters—WHO AREN'T REALLY THERE. Which is what you do!"

Mrs. Heartbreak has snuck up on John and scared him with a LOUD answer to what he intended to be only a rhetorical—and silently spoken—question. John hangs his head and apologizes, but Mrs. Heartbreak isn't having any of it.

"I worry about you," she says, shaking her head. "Sometimes I don't think you're all there either."

Mrs. Heartbreak spins on her toes and goes back into the shop before John can defend himself. John turns around to face the Square and back to watching Iowans search for parking or stumble in and out of the Ozark Café. They are powering up on pork this AM, all the bacon, ham, and fat fried spuds you can eat for $4.99. That reminds John of a pig joke:

So this guy goes to court, see, and he tells the Judge that he wants to change his name. The Judge asks the guy why.

"My name is Joe Pig," the guy says.

"I certainly understand why you would want to change a name like that," the Judge sympathetically says. "What do you want for a new name?"

"I'd like my name to be Edgar Pig," the guy answers.

Naturally, the Judge is dumbfounded.

"I don't understand this at all," he says. "Please explain yourself!"

"Certainly," the guy says. "I'm tired of people coming up to me and saying, "Hey Joe, whaddaya know?""

The sympathetic Judge thinks that being named Pig is a terrible thing while Mr. Pig is bothered by something else entirely. Perception is what it is. Sometimes it is everything.

John is thinking about the Joe Pig joke (it is a very old joke) and pondering its meaning in light of Berryville's Town Square. He knows that a hundred or more people that come to town today will say they love the Town Square fountains if somebody asks them. But they won't be able to say how big the fountains are, or what color the bottoms are (robin's egg blue), or what they are made of (brick). They love the fountains, even though they haven't really seen them, except in their memories, except in a different time, in years. Their perception is that the fountains look just fine, whatever they look like, whatever they are made of.

John sees the fountains every day, and they are frozen in time for him too. But they are frozen in today's time, every day—and not in yesterday, or in his boyhood. He has no experience of them as bottle rocket launching pads, or of having courted a girl from a fountain-side bench back in the days when the benches might have been painted regularly. His memory of them is like time lapsed photography: sometime they appear in his memory under a bright sun, or in a less bright sun as a cloud passes overhead, or in the rain. But the essential qualities of the fountains remain the same; they appear to John in every memory as derelict, worn out, impoverished evidence of how little Berryville has invested in its downtown, and how careless it is of perception. "Hey, Joe, whaddaya know?"

Not much.

More and more Iowans fill the Town Square. Where is Clara Jane?

Chapter 47:

Chaos Theory

It is nearly noon and Clara Jane still hasn't appeared. When she asked John to coffee this Monday morning he had assumed, as all Yankees assume, that "morning" means a time between 5:00 AM and 8:00 AM, and on the day named—in this case, Monday. He had forgotten, for a moment, that Clara Jane was Ozarks born, and that time was (is) relative to hill people in the same way that it is supposed to be relative to Native and indigenous peoples the world over. The relativity of time in cases like this one is sometimes referred to as "Indian Time," no ethnic slur, political incorrectness, or boorish insensitivity intended. I am just reporting.

John does not hold the fact that Clara Jane is time challenged against her. Nor does he hold it against his neighbors that they habitually arrive late, or arrive far too early on the designated day, but on a day that is one or two or three weeks later in the designated month. As you know, John has some unusual ideas about time, and he really doesn't expect Clara Jane to keep schedules created by old, insomnia-ridden Yankees like John, even if the Yankee is reformed of his workaholic ways and means, as is John.

To tell you the truth—let's assume that I am starting now—John has forgotten all about his appointment with Clara Jane and is content to simply stand on the sidewalk in front of the Shop and watch what happens out on the Square. From this vantage point he can watch Iowans stuff themselves with cholesterol, suspiciously guard their wallets, or simply nurture their various and sundry grievances. A few of these Hawkeyes have passed right by John as they wandered into the Shop. One or two have mistaken John for a Cigar Store Indian and have poked him in the belly before going inside. John has enjoyed watching them stumble backwards when he scowls at them and says "UFF DA!"

They never stay long in the Shop, and when they leave they all clutch small plastic bags containing a single book off the dollar table. Mrs. Heartbreak is busy inside, ringing up $1.00 sales, plus the .08 cents tax that is divied up and goes to our city, county, state, and federal masters. Oink, oink, oink, you Jerks.

John is impressed that Clara Jane's "buy something" instruction to the small group of Iowans who had come to the Square after Sodjerberjer's death has been followed by all visiting Iowans since, and that it was not simply and only restricted to that original and smaller group. And since it has—probably—been impossible for Clara Jane to communicate directly with every Iowan milling about the Square this morning, it must mean that DIVINE INTERVENTION has played a part. This causes John to stand even more aimlessly out on the sidewalk, pondering the Holy Ghost—while Mrs. Heartbreak is inside, working her pretty tail off to meet the heightened demand for dollar books.

John is sure of the Holy Ghost's existence, territory which we have already covered, but he is less sure of how and why the HG might operate in Berryville, especially within the context of a SHAZAAM PLAN focused on the niggardliness of a bunch of dour Iowans. Would the Holy Ghost, for example, take advantage of seasonal discounts on hotel rooms to achieve certain economies of scale contributing to a critical mass of Iowa-pigeons? Or, would S/He (the verdict is still out about the HG's gender) think about parting them from their money as the best vehicle by which to help them travel the Salvation Road and consequently become a happier, more cheerful, and generous people?

John has heard enough sermons to know that separating sheep from goats and pigeons from gelt is possibly the main work of the Holy Ghost, or at least a main sign that S/He is at work in one's life. John is not cynical about this: he can't recall a single time when Jesus recommended that we all get good jobs and go to work every day, or to otherwise spend much time working and saving. In fact, if it weren't for Christ's frequent advice to deny the flesh the Protestant Ethic would pretty much be a Big K on life's Score Board.

Sadly, the Holy Ghost has decided (if S/He has decided at all, mind you) to effect a SHAZAAM PLAN on the cheap—or has taken Clara Jane advice and believes that the transfer of $1.08 from the Iowans to Heartbreak's Pretty Good Books and RDC as an adequate sign of their reformation. As we've discussed, a buck eight hardly covers the costs for toilet paper. John intends to bring the matter up with Clara Jane when she shows up for their coffee date. Perhaps the HG will be amenable to upping the ante a bit if she offers the suggestion.

The question of whether or not the Holy Ghost is working through Clara Jane is still open, of course. Clara Jane has not been baptized yet so, for example, would S/He speak to and or through Clara Jane at all? The Holy Ghost is certainly the paracletus of persons, even of sluggards and dullards such as John, but would S/He work through someone who is fundamentally still a pagan? John seems to recall that the Holy Ghost makes a first appearance in the New Testament, and then only to those who have been baptized, and who believe, big "B".

John is a Big B person, but his intercourse with the Holy Ghost has been periodic and not dramatic; John is unable to speak in tongues and he is several bricks shy of a full load of the Fruits of the Holy Ghost such as wisdom, piety, fortitude, and so on. He does believe that his ability to converse with dead writers is a divine gift and not merely a deficiency in psychotropic medications. Just this morning G.K. Chesterton told John how much he admired Robert Louis Stevenson. "It is the great glory of Stevenson," G.K. said, "that he was not crushed by the Calvinistic creed of his forebears, or by the even emptier fatalistic creedlessness of his contemporaries."

John hadn't had a clue what Chesterton meant by that, but perhaps it has something to do with his current confusion about Clara Jane. Stevenson wrote fine great fantasy fiction, like Dr. Jekyll and Mr. Hyde, and many great adventures. Stevenson wouldn't think twice, John was sure, about allowing a rule or two to get in the way of a story. Perhaps he should just accept that Clara Jane is conversant with the HG and is not psychotic and is not scamming him. After all, Iowans are still streaming past him into the shop and coming out clasping dollar books. Something has happened to cause them to bust open their tightly grasped wallets and John bets that Mrs. Heartbreak has broken into a sweat and will tell him all about it tonight over one of her gourmet dinners.

John wonders if he should ask Mrs. Heartbreak what she thinks are the causes of the day's events. Perhaps she has, unbeknownst to John, fostered and implemented a marketing campaign directly targeting Iowans, and is now having some success. Or, maybe, she has secretly been praying for improved business and reformed Iowans and the two main objects of her prayer have come together in happy coincidence. It is possible that all of John's noisy scheming and all of Clara Jane's planning don't amount to a hill of beans and that it is the quiet prayers of Mrs. Heartbreak, or of Yodi the AFKA Catryn Yoder, or of Gail DeWeese at Dirt Poor that is causing the Hawkeye Hub Bub.

Of course, the other possibility is Chaos Theory. Perhaps a minor event in the far off universe, and not the Holy Ghost, has triggered the heedless tossing about of spare change among visiting Iowans. John recalls Lorenz's paper: *Predictability: Does the Flap of a Butterfly's Wings in Brazil set off a Tornado in Texas?* The paper suggested that a flapping wing, representing a small change in the initial condition of a system may cause a chain of events leading to a large scale Fandango.

You can skip the next paragraph.

Sensitivity to initial conditions is often confused with Chaos Theory in popular accounts. John certainly confuses it often enough. But sensitivity can also be a subtle property since it depends on a choice of metric or the notion of distance in the continuum of the space of the system. For example, consider the simple dynamic that is produced by repeatedly doubling an initial value defined by iterating the mapping on a line that is x to 2x. This dynamic—now a system—has sensitive dependence on initial conditions everywhere since any pair of nearby points will eventually become separated. It is, of course, very simple behavior—you knew that, right?—as all points except zero trend to infinity. Unless we view the result as a circle and restrict the system to bounded metrics that are closed bounded invariant subsets of unbounded systems, then many systems abound! And you thought it was all beans, Ha!

By the way, did I tell you yet that Chaos Theory has been discredited? I'm sure John hasn't told you, if only because he views Chaos Theory as the last defense against Social Order Theorists such as Mrs. Heartbreak, public school administrators, Marxists, Fascists, Republicans, Democrats, Dixiecrats, Dixie Chicks, Chick Filet franchise operators, Operators as a general rule, and Ralph Nader and Bob Barr as very specific rules. How, then, can you expect John to abandon a perfectly good theory simply because it is stupid?

Anyhoo, here is John, standing in front of the shop watching Iowans not simply arrive but now swarm around the Town Square. Dr. Jim Young drives by in his Volvo, looking for a parking space. But he won't find one because all the slots are filled with sensible American made automobiles bearing "I Brake for Hogs" license plates. Sharon Sloan, the artist and scholar, not the actress Sharon Stone, drives by, fails to find a parking slot, and drives on. James Jones the farmer, not the dead writer, drives by, drives on. Mrs. Colleen Shogren, fresh from Play Practice—a passionate and lively pursuit recently taken up now after the long hiatus between High School and Retirement—drives by and ... you get it: Iowans have taken over the whole dang town.

Mrs. Heartbreak slips out of the shop. She is in a dither, her brow shining with the excess of effort. "John," she exclaims, "We are running out of dollar books! Will you please get in here and scout up some more?"

Mrs. Heartbreak rushes back into the shop and begins ringing up more $1.08 sales. John follows, slowly wedging himself between and through crowds of Large People toward the back room. He feels excitement. Today is the likely day that he finally unloads *I Told You So* by Rush Limbaugh, *Border Waltz* by James Waller, and *I Was Wrong* by Jimmy Bakker. John, in the back room, fills his arms with these and other notable titles and lugs them to the dollar book table. They are snapped up immediately and John's excitement turns to elation. He returns to the back room and invites a host of celebrity writers—Roseanne Barr, Whoopi Goldberg, Rosie O'Donnell—anyone, actually, who has ever owned a keyboard, to leap into his arms. They accept. Hooray!!

John has forgotten Clara Jane, and his appointment with her, so he is surprised to see her standing near the front door, next to the oversize book shelf. She smiles and gives him a little wave over the shoulders of the crowd.

Clara Jane is wearing what looks like an old fashioned nurse's uniform, right down to the white hose and white shoes. The only thing missing is the hat with a little red cross on the crown. John is reminded of Katherine Hepburn in *The African Queen;* he thinks Clara Jane looks dishy in a disorienting sort of way and he wonders if anyone else in the crowd has taken notice of her getup.

Clara Jane motions him forward and exits the shop, expecting John to follow her. He does, shouldering his way past several men wearing John Deere caps who are murmuring "Louis L'Amour, Louis L'Amour" over and over again like chanting Buddhists. John finally shoulders his way through and out onto the sidewalk. Clara Jane is still smiling.

"It doesn't look like we'll be able to get any coffee at your place," she says. "What a crowd!"

John nods. "It is a crowd," he says. "Are you responsible?" He wants confirmation about the Holy Ghost's involvement: Rule in, rule out is John's drift.

Clara Jane raises her eyebrows and looks upwards. "It seems like a miracle, doesn't it?"

John is hoping for a more definitive answer, but Clara Jane has grabbed his arm and turned him to face the Grandview Hotel and post office building before he can pursue it.

"Look at that," she says, pointing.

A large truck is parked catty corner from the Grandview and a crew of men are hauling junk out of the old drug store and stuffing it into the back of the truck. A bucket truck is parked next to the junk truck and two men are jockeying a large sign into place above the drugstore's awning. John can't read the sign from where he is standing.

"What's going on?" he asks.

He begins to walk toward the corner for a closer look. Clara Jane companionably hooks her elbow into his and they walk arm and arm down the street. They have to weave in and out of small groups of Iowans so it takes them a bit of time and, because of the crowd and all of the excitement stemming from selling unsalable books, John does not notice that an Arkansas State Crime Lab van has pulled up in front of the C. Richard Williams now Sam Barr Memorial Toilet across the Square. Two Berryville squad cars are already there and one of the local cops is stringing yellow tape around the perimeter of the building.

Clara Jane hasn't noticed the action across the Square either. She is jiggling with excitement—not an unpleasant thing to observe—and points again to the sign, which is being installed high up on the front of the old drugstore. "Oh, John," she exclaims. "Don't you just love it?"

John believes that Santa Claus is jolly because he knows where all the bad girls live, and he believes that Forest Rangers have no place they go when they want to get away from it all. John also believes that atheism is a non-prophet organization, and that there is no other word for synonym. But he is having a hard time believing what he reads on the sign toward which Clara Jane is pointing.

John's chin begins to quiver, and he feels like crying.

Yet, on a positive note, perhaps the following evidence on behalf of Chaos Theory will cause another and friendlier review from the world's philosophers and mathematicians. This is what John read:

IOWA VISITOR'S WELCOME CENTER

Chapter 48:

Flap, Flap, Flap

John is crying now. His tears are by no means a landslide of grief, and no audible blubber accompanies the imperceptible rivulet that courses down his left cheek. When Norwegian males are born the attending physician removes their tear ducts (the foreskin is an afterthought, actually) and slaps their bottoms, not to get things pumping, but to prepare them for the future. Thus, John's invisible wailing and gnashing is observed by no one and he alone witnesses the infinite well of despair into which he now descends.

Clara Jane's eyes remained fixed on the spanking new WELCOME sign being bolted onto the front wall of the old drugstore; her eyes shine with pleasure and anticipation. The crowds of Iowans milling around the square don't see John either. They are asking one another where the "dollar" bookstore is, or if the $3.99 all you can eat breakfast buffet at the Ozark Café is still on. They have no time for anyone's existential crisis.

The satisfaction of breathing a bit of life into Chaos Theory is of the bleakest quality, and John feels no validation. He had flapped his tiny butterfly wing in expectation that Iowans would be driven back to their rectangular, flat state, forevermore. Clara Jane was that wing, the Deus Machina that would, in his scheme, non-violently hurl them from the Ozarks and back to Des Moines, Boone, Manly, Ames, and Sioux City. At John's direction, the Authorial I (that would be me) gave her fifty thousand dollars to affect that hurling, but he (me!) stupidly stipulated that no physical harm come to them, all due to the NO SVSL stipulations—stupid!—of this book—which is, if not increasingly stupid, has admittedly gone a tad bizarre, a soupcon array, "off" Brits might say with a sniff.

The NO SVSL butterfly wing flap had led Clara Jane to a SHAZAAM PLAN that was frankly MIRACLE based and had, in turn (maybe, or maybe not)—flap flap flap—caught the attention of the Hoy Ghost—flap flap flap flap— which had caused John's subsequent invitation to Clara Jane to attend services at the First Christian Church of Berryville Disciples of Christ—flap flap flap flap flap!

The Texas-like tornado that John had expected, and which would blow the Iowans out of Berryville forever, had instead resulted in an IOWA VISITOR'S WELCOME CENTER not more than six or eight doors down from the entrance to his and Mrs. Heartbreak's Commercial Universe. Yes friends, Chaos Theory lives ...

When John started out in the book business (Stop laughing. It is a business. Really. No kidding. Well. Sort of.), he carried a line of long playing phonograph records in addition to books. He almost immediately ran into trouble though, because music doesn't really catalog the way books do.

For example, John catalogued Peter Frampton F under S for Excrement E. Similarly, he catalogued Charlie Rich R under Migraine M. For reasons unexplainable to John, customers found this system confusing and, along the lines of "you can lead a whore to culture but you can't make her think", personally offensive. It wasn't long before John got out of vinyl, but through the experience, became even more convinced that Social Order theorists invariably mistake nuance for chaos and will find fault with what is only the brute reality of the matter in hand.

Thus, John cannot find fault with Clara Jane's plan. He had willed one thing and got another. The thing that he had gotten was the last thing he wanted, and that seemed cruel. But to resist it or to resent it would merely cast him among the roaring, ever more volatile tide of Social Order Theorists responsible for corn subsidies, social promotion, vegetarianism, prohibition, 'Sesame

Street,' lotteries, margarine, late twentieth century hymns, adjustable rate mortgages, Jerry Springer and James Dobson, chemical dependents vs. tosspots and drunkards, pantyhose wearers, decaffeinated coffee drinkers, mega church goers, self-esteem wieners, white collar unions, compassionate conservatives, and the popularity of soccer. No, John has his theory, and he is sticking to it.

But it is tough. John feels his pain, and alone. (Former President Clinton has, curiously, not stepped forward to feel it for him.) Clara Jane continues unaware that John is discommoded, hors de combat, and flat on his psychological butt. She is radiant and fully, humanly, happy. She hugs his arm and pulls him toward the old drugstore's front door.

"It will be a lot of work," she says, pointing into the building's dim interior. "But by the time we get it cleaned up it will be wonderful."

"What do you mean "we"?"

Clara Jane looks at John for the first time since she left the shop. She notices that John's face is red and kind of squished up, but assumes it is because of the wall of cat urine wafting out of the old drugstore. The smell roils out the door like automatic weapon fire, nearly felling the work crew hauling trash out, which they proceed to pile in the back of the parked truck. The crew is wearing surgical masks and their eyes are watering.

""We" means you and me, John, and all the citizens of Berryville. We want to make the Square as welcoming as possible for our visitors, don't we?"

John notices that Clara Jane is speaking corporately: she has become a Berryvillian, and in the throes of first love with her new affiliation, assumes that good will and a bit of civic elbow grease will bring Mohammed to the mountain. John knows that this isn't the time to discuss the condition of the Public Toilet, the festering open wound that the Grandview Hotel was for years before Alexander and Sandra poured their fortunes and hearts into it—and it is certainly not the time to bring up the East German Communist Party inspired architecture of the Town Square Fountains.

"I am doubtful of much civic participation," he says, kindly, putting his consternation aside. "Folks here are not too concerned with the physical appearances of buildings."

"It may take a while for them to warm up to the idea, but I'm sure they'll get excited, eventually."

"You could be right. Especially if you are willing to define "a while" as ..."

"Stop it," Clara Jane interrupts. "Stop being so cynical. Look at all of these Iowans. They've come to town by our invitation. Notice that I say "our" invitation. You can't pretend that you haven't been at least partly responsible for what's going on. That puts you back into the "we" business."

"I liked you better when you were just a serial killer," John says. He steps away from the front door of the now former drugstore and out of its shriek of cat urine. "But you have a point."

The IOWA VISITOR'S WELCOME CENTER sign is firmly in place now and a small crowd of Iowans are gathering around Clara Jane, drawn as if to a magnet. John detaches himself from the elbows of two burly Hawkeyes wearing seed caps and shuffles back in the direction of his shop. He is feeling a little better. Well. Just a little. Hopelessness has replaced despair. That's a step up, isn't it?

Chapter 49:

Pilgrims Progress

As John makes his way back to Heartbreak's Pretty Good Books & RDC his gaze shifts left and he sees the CRIME SCENE tape around the entrance to the Public Toilet. One of the two Berryville squad cars parked at the scene pulls away with lights flashing, but the cop doesn't have his siren on for some reason or, John can't hear it: he is getting so deaf ...

He stops in front of Geraldi's and watches the action.

In a minute, a wheeled stretcher emerges from the bowels of the toilet (sorry) pushed along by a couple of fellows in official Arkansas Crime Lab uniforms. Under these circumstances, one expects to see a body on such a stretcher, or at least an oblong lump under a sheet if the body in question is deceased. There is something under the sheet on the stretcher, certainly, but it is a small round ball about the size of a cantaloupe or large gorgonzola.

They've found Fuzzy.

A crowd has gathered around the front of the Public Toilet. Not all of them are Iowans. John spots a few notable Berryvillians rubbernecking among them. Sheriff Bob Grudek, the administrator of Carroll County's fine jail, has just pulled up. It is not clear to anyone how closely the local police work with the Sheriff's Department, but Bob is a smart guy who looks just like John Larroquette, the television actor. He spies John as he gets out of his car and waves. John waves back, and hopes that he does not look guilty.

John does not look guilty and, frankly, he probably feels less guilt than he ought too. John's been around, you know, and he didn't become such a non-productive idler without years and years of practice. Nor sir, you do not become John Heartbreak overnight without there being plenty enough guilt to go around. But John won't get around to feeling it today. He continues to look across the Square and feels bemused and curious, and a slight uptick in anxiousness. But no guilt.

Steve Hanna is circling the Square, hoping to find a parking space. He is followed by Marie Andresen, in a Japanese car, and by Linda Jones in her green Escort, and by Dr. Fred Mayer, the famous Musician Farmer, who is tooling about in a white van of foreign descent. None of them can find a parking spot because all the spaces are taken up by cars from Iowa, or by crime fighters, or by the trash removers down at the new IOWA VISITOR WELCOME CENTER. John begins to move away from Geraldi's and toward the shop when he hears someone call out to him.

"Hold on, Pilgrim," the voice calls. 'Allow me to interrupt your progress."

John turns and sees a bald, middle-aged guy wearing shorts and a University of Iowa tee-shirt. The guy has the hairiest legs John has ever seen. The legs seem to lack knee joints and to pour into a pair of topsiders where, almost as an afterthought, they hook up to sockless feet. Also hairy. If the man had not been standing upright, John might have assumed that his style of locomotion could only be in phases like an articulated bus, that his front end would arrive several seconds or minutes ahead of his back end. Why a man with such articulated legs and plentitude of hair wore shorts—particularly on a day that contains a bit of chill air—is the biggest mystery you will encounter in this book.

"You can't interrupt me," John says pleasantly, dropping into what Mrs. Heartbreak would describe as a "Customer Service" moment. He has noticed the University of Iowa tee-shirt and, assuming that Mr. Hairy Legs is an Iowan, intends to support Clara Jane's hospitality efforts in any way that he can. He will be nice to Iowans (but then, hasn't he always?).

"I'm here to help," John says with gritted teeth. "The "dollar" bookstore is just next door. Mrs. Heartbreak will be glad to direct you to the sales table. Or, you can follow me in and I'll point you in the right direction."

"I believe your book sale is over," the man says, grinning.

He points toward the entrance to the Heartbreak's shop. People are streaming out past its squeaky door and hustling over toward the Square's fountain. There, Clara Jane is being helped up onto the Fountain by a man in a cheap suit, so that everyone can see her. She has added a white cape to her outfit and looks spectacular and angelic while waiting patiently for the crowd to assemble. She smiles radiantly, and John smiles too: he is reasonably sure now that she won't drop a bomb on the crowd, and he is only slightly anxious about what hymns she may have chosen for the occasion.

"Don't worry about it," Mr. Hairy Legs says. He is standing next to John now, and they are both staring at Clara Jane.

"About what?"

"About the Hymns she's chosen," he said.

"She's either going to go with 'O God Our Help in Ages Past' or 'Come, Holy Ghost, our Souls Inspire.' I love that one. What a tune!"

John nods approvingly; these are not bad choices at all. It takes him a minute to catch on that his companion has just read his mind. It's a brief read, of course, but is still a neat trick. He turns and faces the guy.

"I didn't catch your name," John says.

"And you're John Heartbreak. It's amazing to find you in Berryville, Arkansas."

John nods. Dubiously. "Have we met before?"

"From time to time. Here and there. Strangers on a train, so to speak."

"Frankly, I don't remember meeting you. And I don't recognize you."

"We were in Viet Nam together. And we've had peripheral encounters here and there, from time to time, yon and hither. So to speak."

John believes the guy is full of horse hockey. They have never met before, especially not in the Army. How would a guy with legs like that even get in? John nods, smiles, plans to get away.

Clara Jane is speaking to the crowd now, smiling down on them and John and the guy turn to watch. The audience is nodding their heads at what Clara Jane has to say and they clap from time to time.. Then, they begin to sing 'Royal Oak'.

"That Clara Jane," the guy says, admiringly. "You never know what she's going to do. I thought she might suck up a little and go with 'Come, Holy Ghost'.

John is getting the picture. Maybe he has "met" the guy before, here and there, yon and hither, so to speak. John notices that the guy's shirt has a radium glow. The letters I O W A shine like the dial of a luminous watch in the dark. The shine gathers under his chin and illuminates his face in a peculiar fashion.

Hairy Legs seems to know exactly what's going on. And he obviously knows Clara Jane. John wants to ask him about the SHAZAAM PLAN, but then he worries that the tentative assumptions he is drawing about the guy may be wrong, or that he will look foolish if he asks the guy about the PLAN—and why it is *the* plan. What if he doesn't know what John is talking about?

"You don't have to worry about that," the guy says. "You have no idea what fools I've encountered. You are small fry indeed, Mr. Heartbreak."

Hairy Legs smiles broadly at John. "You not a contender for the World's Greatest Fool trophy ... and, to tell you the truth, there is foolishness, and then there is foolishness. What goes on in Berryville is small potatoes indeed."

Clara Jane continues to speak and stops only long enough to point in the direction of the IOWA VISITOR WELCOME CENTER. John notices that she also pointed once at the Heartbreak's Shop, and once toward Geraldi's. John strains to hear what she has to say, and picks up ... "and it won't kill you to pay $6.50 for a meatball sandwich, praise Jesus. The meatballs are really big, and Andy has a family to support, so cough it up.

"Okay, now, how about 'Come, Holy Ghost, Our Souls Inspire' now?

John sees Hairy Legs shiver. The sun has drifted behind a bank of clouds, and the short pants he wears are no match for the temperature drop.

"Do you want to go inside?" John asks.

'I'm not cold. That song always makes me shiver. Anyway, I've got to get going. There's a lot to do, and I'm interested in seeing what happens."

John is perplexed. "Don't you already know what's going to happen?"

"Sure I do. But it's still interesting. I mean, I've seen *The Maltese Falcon* at least twenty times and I always laugh when Bogart says "you're a good man, sister" to Lee Patrick. What does knowing have to do with interesting? Things—people, art, governments—are only boring when they're bad. Otherwise, this is a pretty interesting place, and the people are really super.

"Although," he says, "your Town Square Fountains are totally bad. For some reason they keep reminding me of stuff I saw in East Germany when the Commies where running the place. Now that was a boring bunch."

"I know," John says, agreeing about the fountains, of course, but also about how boring bad is. He understands immediately what Hairy Legs has said, about how banal evil is. It is Goodness that takes our breath away, that astonishes us.

John is hesitant to see him go. "I have a few questions to ask," he says. "I'd like to know if you're interested in economies of scale like discount hotel rooms in Eureka Springs, or whether or not Christians should overlook past indiscretions among new members. Did Sodjerberjer go to heaven? How did you hook up with Clara Jane? And ..."

" ...I don't really answer questions. I'm more in the suggestion business, in the pointing out stuff business.

"Let me give you an example," he says. "I hooked up with Clara Jane when she was Clara Rinker. She was driving through Blue Eye, Missouri, on her way to Hot Springs. She looked at Blue Eye and said to herself, "What a God forsaken town."

"That was my invitation. I jumped into her head and pointed out that God does not forsake towns. People do. By the time she got to Berryville she had become Clara Jane Smith.

"Here's one for you," he says, pointing toward the square. "See the guy in the cheap suit, standing in the crowd, watching Clara Jane? He's an FBI agent. The Arkansas Crime Lab folks called the FEEBIES because Fuzzy's face is pretty well-known in organized crime circles. They ran a shot of his decapitated head against the National mug shot data base and up popped Fuzzy twenty-five minutes after being discovered in your Town Toilet.

"Let me say" he said, "that human beings are really amazing ..."

Chapter 50:

In The Mood

John so intently watches Clara Jane instruct her gaggle of Iowans that he misses hearing the Man with Hairy Legs' call out "tootle loo" when he left his side. When John sees him next, he is standing at the back of the crowd, nodding at what Clara Jane is saying. Actually, he appears to be lip-synching along with her. John, who like many deaf people is an adept lip reader, sees that both Hairy Legs and Clara Jane are giving the same speech. He can tell from the rapt expressions on the faces of the Iowans that it is a pretty good speech.

John is sorry that he missed a chance to grill the guy about the SHAZAAM PLAN; obviously, he is a mover and shaker in its execution. John knows now, of course, that Clara Jane and Mr. Hairy Legs hooked up in Blue Eye, Missouri—didn't he say so himself?—and that His Hirsute Self was responsible for transforming Clara Rinker into Clara Jane Smith, the newly arrived citizen of Berryville, Arkansas. But how John was subsumed (sucked) into the role he has been playing—as Clara Jane's sidekick—and, he supposed, as the mystified factotum in the playing out of the PLAN, are still matters of curiosity to him. He had wished simply for politer, less thrifty (tight) Iowans—or for them to disappear altogether—and instead, he had been hiding criminal minds, and abetting them, ever since.

John also regrets not seeing Mr. Hairy Legs move from Point A to Point B, from John's side to the backside of the gaggle of Iowans. John has assumed that the man is the Holy Ghost and his assumption includes consent, of course, that the HG's locomotion is of any mode that He chooses. In point of fact, John knows that the HG was standing by his side and that He was standing at the backside of the crowd simultaneously. It occurs to John that He is probably still standing at his side. As Peter Hook said, playing Lucifer in the movie *Bedazzled*, "God is everywhere! He's in your pants, He's in the air, He's everywhere! Bugger!"

Still, it would have been cool to see a bit of "Beam me up, Scottie," a little supernatural razzel dazzle for a change. The sudden appearance of the IOWA VISITORS WELCOME CENTER on the square was certainly unexpected, but it fell short, in John's opinion, of a miracle. It would have been nice to see a Divine Dove flying about, to hear a heavenly voice—The Voice—to observe blue flames sprouting over the heads of Berryvillians as they spoke Mexican and Latin and Esperanto to one another. But that was not happening. That was not to be. Yet. Well, maybe. Probably not. Not. Well, maybe.

All of this is so much *fiksfaksereir*, John's Aunt Sylvia would say. *"Kiekkelig klikkevensen opplesning samvittighetsfull!"*

Of course.

At the same time, maybe all the *fiksfakserier* (if your Old Norse is a little shaky *"fiksfakserier"* means "hanky panky." I apologize for presuming that some of you may not be up to speed vis-à-vis the Mother Tongue. Yet, it is surprising how many of us haven't kept up …

Clara Jane has finished speaking. The FBI agent who helped her get up onto the fountain is Johnny on the spot and helps her down. The Iowans begin to disperse and John sees several of them headed toward Geraldi's. They have obviously taken Clara Jane's admonition to pony up for the $6.50 sandwich to heart. John hopes that Andy has laid in an adequate supply of meatballs to handle what will surprise him as a robust lunch crowd. If the Iowans take to the meatball sandwiches the same way they scarfed up Heartbreak's dollar books, it will be a banner day for the restaurant.

In The Mood

John feels a bit of disquiet about the Feebies proximity to a known (to John) serial killer, but he and Clara Jane are earnestly, and apparently happily discussing some matter that John can't quite pick-up. In any case, Hairy Legs is hanging around somewhere and, if he (He?) is as John suspects, the HG, Clara Jane can come to no harm.

John is less sanguine about his own situation. He is responsible for sequestering Fuzzy's head in the Public Toilet and, if all the CSI jazz on TV is even remotely connected to reality, then surely the FBI agent will connect him to Fuzzy's decapitated noggin. How he explains Fuzzy to Mrs. Heartbreak is really what is foremost on his mind. He doubts that she will go bail for him and, if she does, it will certainly come with a ration of grumbling about the inconvenience and the money.

Clara Jane and the Feebie walk toward John. They are laughing and talking animatedly about the new IOWA VISITOR'S WELCOME CENTER. They seem very friendly to one another. John stifles an urge to flee. But where would he go? Yes, John is caught between the Federal Bureau of Investigation and Mrs. Heartbreak; he suddenly sees the world as a long, dark hallway with him standing in the middle.

"John," says Clara Jane, gesturing to the Feebie, "This is Special Agent Harold Staley. He's on assignment in the Ozarks to assure that Beaver Dam isn't targeted by El Qaida terrorists. Isn't that exciting!"

"You bet," John says. He wonders what cock up Staley authored that got him assigned to Northwest Arkansas.

"I'm delighted to meet you, Sir!" Staley shouts. He grabs John's hand and crushes it. He pumps John's arm up and down twenty-six times. John wonders if he can file assault charges.

"And meeting this little lady," Staley continues. "Well, what an honor!"

Clara Jane inserts her arm into the crook of Staley's elbow and smiles broadly. "Harold is originally from Forrest City, Iowa," she says. "Home of the Winnebago!"

"The RV, not the Indian," Staley says, still shouting. "And let me say that I am pleased as punch at how this Little Angel here is

255

taking my fellow Hawkeyes under her wing. What a grand thing for Berryville to do."

Clara Jane has never struck John as a "little" lady, nor as a "little" angel, although she does look attractive in her nurse-like get-up. The all white costume, with its flowing cape, is actually quite spectacular, and John sees that it has attracted notice from people passing by. Dr. Sharon Sloan, the Kings River Computer Whiz and Mistress of Cyberspace, gives Clara Jane a long glance as she hunts for a parking space; other Berryvillians are craning their necks and staring at her for a long moment (but none of them have blue flames over their heads. (Yet.)

"Yes," John says drily. "We are all pleased as punch. We couldn't be happier. Fine books have been flying off the shelves. You Iowans are quite the readers."

John spots Mr. Hairy Legs standing in front of Wilsons TV and Appliances. He is doubled over in laughter. When he looks up, he smiles widely and gives John a thumbs' up sign. "We couldn't be happier!" he mouths to John, and then laughs some more. Sarcasm from a Higher Power is an unattractive quality.

"Do you know what is most exciting?" Clara Jane asks. "Harold is in hot pursuit of a very bad apple. The police discovered a human head in the public toilet this morning—and Harold knows to whom the head belongs."

" ...to whom the head belongs?" John stammers. "You've worked very hard not to end that sentence with a preposition. Do you mean, " ...and he knows whose head it is"?"

"Yes! The head belonged to Fuzzy Markowitz, a terrible man who deserved killing!"

"Now, Clara Jane," Staley interjects, "Markowitz was certainly a bad apple, but it's up to the law to do the killing. We can't have just anybody out whacking Public Enemies and leaving their remains lying about in public toilets. It's the JOB of Federal, State, and Local Authorizes to do the whacking.

"That's why we get the BIG BUCKS," Staley finishes, with a hearty laugh.

Clara Jane arches her eyebrows but chooses to remain silent, except for a skeptical "Hmmm" sound. John sees that the local pastors still have some work to do helping her through the "repentance" part of her conversion experience. On the other hand—yes, here we go again—if a very bad person is stuffed into a wood chipper by another person, even if the "another" person is also a bad person (but on the path to redemption), is there a sound in the forest?

Edmund Burke aside, (oh, let's not go there).

"Do we know how Fuzzy's head got into the Public Toilet?" Clara Jane looks pointedly at John when she asks the question. She is hip to the fact that John has let her down. Jeepers, first Mrs. Heartbreak and now Clara Jane!

"Yes!" Staley shouted. "We know that Fuzzy was killed by Clara Rinker, a heinous serial killer in the employ of John Sanford ne' John Camp. Apparently, she was on her way to Hot Springs, Arkansas, a well-known and historically designated den of sin and inequity. For reasons yet to be discovered, Rinker stopped here in Berryville and dropped Fuzzy off in your Public Toilet."

"How thrilling," Clara Jane said, in a breathy voice. She put her hand on Staley's arm and batted her eyes at him. "Do you think you'll catch her? This Rinker woman, I mean?"

"Without question," Staley said emphatically, loudly. "Unfortunately, Rinker has obviously left the area and her pursuit will be taken up by our Little Rock office. I will refocus my time and energy on protecting Beaver Dam and the Good People of the Ozarks from El Qaida. But I assure you, she will be brought to Justice."

"Oh, Harold," Clara Jane said, smiling up at Staley.

John felt a tad queasy. Geez …

Hairy Legs is no longer in front of Wilson's, but Mrs. Heartbreak is standing in the shop's window, tapping on the glass to get John's attention. Iowans have left Geraldi's and have been streaming into the shop. She needs his help. Right now!

Reluctantly, John offers his hand to the Feebie. "It was nice to meet you, Agent Staley," he lied. "Good luck with all your pursuits, hot or otherwise."

"Harold," Clara Jane said, "Would you like some lunch?"

"Wonderful!" he shouted. "I'm in the mood for a meatball sandwich!"

Chapter 51:

The Mail Bag (III)

The day passes with hardly a break until 2 PM. John has been uncharacteristically helpful to Mrs. Heartbreak, who has been busy ringing up not only $1.08 books, but the occasional $5 and $10 dollar book as well. The Iowans have nearly depleted John's supply of celebrity autobiographies, and the Ann Coulters and Chris Matthews are gone, gone, gone. One man, wearing a Wartburg College sweatshirt, bought all the Lutheran hymnals in stock.

Mrs. Heartbreak is cheerful. Not only has she been playing the cash register like Horowitz on Steinway, her customers have been polite too, if not exactly bubbly. True, she had gotten into a tugging match with a woman from Keokuk who had handed her a five dollar bill and then couldn't quite bring herself to let go of it, but that was the extent of any unpleasantness. Surprisingly, given the high volume of flushing, even the toilet paper supplies have held up satisfactorily.

Clara Jane and Agent Staley have not reappeared. They had chummily entered Geraldi's and, as far as John knew, where still inside, munching away on meatball sandwiches. John felt disgusted with how adeptly Clara Jane had played the empty-headed, helpless female, and by how easily Staley had fallen for the ruse. John has assumed that Clara Jane had given up her wicked wily ways (that was fun) and has entered into a more decorous and less mendacious period of life.

Yet, why should John think that? Clara Jane was obviously making a life for herself in Berryville. She kept a neat yard, was about to embark on a career as the (probable) Director of the IOWA VISITORS WELCOME CENTER, and was very likely looking for and would eventually find a church home. Yes, she was embarking on the common human journey and would make use of what tools she possessed. There was no reason to expect that she would avoid any of its mistakes.

It is even probable, John now surmises, that Clara Jane would fall in love, would marry, and would complete the tragic cycle of life. She certainly looked attractive in her white nurse-like uniform, and no doubt many men would find her so, as well. John recalls seeing a film when he was in the army that involved several student nurses and ... never mind.

Mrs. Colleen Shogren enters the shop. Because of John's manifest customer service deficiencies she has agreed to draw time away from the whirlwind of her cultural affairs to assist Mrs. Heartbreak, on an occasional basis, with the operation of Heartbreak's Pretty Good Books and RDC. She ignores John—typical—and begins an animated conversation with Mrs. Heartbreak. John shambles away toward his computer, stopping only to get a cup of RDC.

Gmail delivers a batch of insults, imprecations, and offers of a dubious nature. Among them are a few e-mails that may interest you:

Vjosa Mullahatari writes, "The man with hairy legs is God, right? That is what you mean by the Holy Ghost, one of the three parts of how Christians understand God? I don't know, John. That seems strange to me. Allah would not appear to anyone. He would send a jinn or an angel. Jinns are evil and made of fire. Angels are good and made from smoke. I think the man with hairy legs is an angel. He does behave like an angel because he knows things no human will know. And angels would probably find the woman Clara Jane a worthy challenge. I don't like her very much, though. Perhaps she is a jinn? But then, an angel will not help a jinn, at least in our tradition. I don't know why you have involved yourself with her."

Ernest Leonard writes, "You should come back to Laos, Bub. You need a little song, a little dance, a little seltzer in the pants. Bookselling sounds like stone dead monkey business. What is going on in your head?"

"The meeting between John and Mr. Hairy Legs looks a little like the meeting between Kurt Vonnegut and Kilgore Trout," Paul Andresen writes. "Is Mr. Hairy Legs the "Authorial I" perhaps?"

"Johnny," Monsignor Bachxner writes, "The guy with hairy legs isn't the Holy Ghost. He may be an incarnation of your deepest desire to hear from God, or he may be the Spirit of God working through you, or you may simply be deeply troubled in a psychiatric sense.

"St. Athanasius tells us that the Holy Ghost is united to Jesus by relations just like those existing between Jesus the Son and God the Father; that He is sent by the Son; that He is His mouth-piece and glorifies Him; that, unlike creatures, He has not been made out of nothing, but comes forth from God; that He performs a sanctifying work among men, of which no creature is capable; that in possessing Him we possess God; that the Father created everything by Him; that, in fine, He is immutable, has the attributes of immensity, oneness, and has a right to all the appellations that are used to express the dignity of the Son.

"Of course, the Holy Ghost spoke almost on a daily basis to William Blake, which I believe is a fact even if Blake was goofy. And, as you know, my mother used to say to me, 'Jerry, be nice to the old wino on the corner. He may be Jesus in disguise, testing your charity and humility.' But as you also know, my mother, God bless her, was as loony as St. Eulalia, the one who thought she was a loaf of bed and kept trying to bake herself.

"But who knows what actions the Holy Ghost might take, or with whom? All we really know for sure is that He tells us to avoid despair, presumption, impenitence or a fixed determination not to repent, obstinacy, resisting the known truth, and envy of another's spiritual welfare. And we know that the fruits of the Holy Ghost are not habits or permanent qualities, but acts. So who is say that

He is not acting through Clara Jane, regardless of how hard that is to believe?

"Let me conclude by saying that I wish your interest was in something more elevated than chiseling Iowans out of a few bucks. You ought to lay off those people. Most of them are Good Catholics, and the balance is Lutherans who you can depend on at least, to behave themselves. They're not out divorcing every five minutes like some of those dismal Southern Tribes that occupy that town of yours."

"Dear Mr. Heartbreak," writes Thomas Ernst, from the Iowa Corn Council, "If you drive Iowa's roads this fall, you will be surrounded by more than 12 million acres of corn. Iowa's excellent soil and growing season are ideal for corn production, and Iowa's farmers are some of the best in the world. The result: Iowa leads the world in corn production.

"It has come to our attention that you have "issues" with Iowans, and in particular with Iowa's corn farmers. Several of our members have referred me to "The Death of Sodjerberjer," a chapter in *Coffee with John Heartbreak*, a book in which you appear. The book in general and the Sodjerberjer chapter in particular, have disturbed these members and, after reading it myself, I too felt disturbed. I can only say that I found the book to be a one-sided, highly inflammatory account of our members, and how they make their livings. Sir, Iowa's farmers are not "Welfare Queens" but honored constituents in that body of patriots Jefferson called the Yeomen Citizen

"Most of Iowa's corn will travel far from the field to be turned into ethanol, starches, sweeteners, plastics, grits, meal, and more. In thousands of industrial and consumer products, these corn-based ingredients contribute qualities that improve our daily lives. In short, Mr. Heartbreak, without Iowa's corn farmers you and the fair citizens of Berryville—who I am sure DO NOT share your opinions—would be eating grass and sleeping on straw mats.

"In the interest of fairness, I ask that you cease and desist.

"At the same time, we realize that the Iowa Corn Council has an obligation to educate the public, and to offer a friendly caution to the occasional critic of Agribusiness. That's why we, at the Council, invite you and your charming (and sensible) wife, Mrs.

Heartbreak, to come and visit us at our headquarters in Lamoni, Iowa—at no expense to you. We'll put you up at the Chief Lamoni Motel, and buy you dinner at Barth's Dairy Cup! We'll even buy the gas (ethanol only, please). All we ask in return is for an hour or two of your time to tell you the "the real story" about Iowa Corn.

"What do you say, Mr. Heartbreak? Can we count on you?"

"Sincerely," and etc.

John thought not. He hit the delete button and pushed back from the keyboard. He wanted to get another cup of RDC, but he was sure that Mrs. Shogren was staring at the back of his head and he was unable, at least for the moment, to turn and face her withering glance. John understood that fewer and fewer people thought that they could count on him, irrespective of the Iowa Corn Council's hopefulness.

John suddenly felt misunderstood. People didn't realize how hard it is to be a character in book, and to know that you are a character in a book. There is also the matter of the Authorial I observing your every move, or inventing your every move, before you even begin to think about moving. It was sort of like living in a Calvin inspired hell, albeit a comfortable one with doses of Mrs. Heartbreak's gourmet cooking to leaven the day.

John also felt that he was fading away. The end of his ability to hear was beginning, and the only speakers he could clearly hear anymore were all dead writers. Yet his conversations with them embarrassed everyone who listened to him talking with them. And, thanks to Mrs. Heartbreak, everyone in Berryville thought John was a ventriloquist—if they thought of him at all.

No one really wants to associate with a ventriloquist either; they are party boors or marginally employed.

The thought fills John with loneliness. Ventriloquists have no union, and since Vaudeville died in the early 1930s, they can work on the Ed Sullivan Show, or between acts at the Boom Boom Club in Las Vegas—if they are lucky. All of which is beside the point: John is not a ventriloquist, and he would be hard pressed to throw a tantrum, let alone his voice. PS. Ed Sullivan is dead.

John avoids Mrs. Shogren's stare and stumbles to the front of the shop, directly opposite of where the RDC is located. He stares out the window and wishes he had the courage to get a cup. But he does not; he stares, instead:

Shelly Buttgen has found a place to park, and is probably on her way to the Post Office since she is carrying a bundle of mail. The Iowans have mostly dispersed, and the Square begins to resemble the half vacant, empty shoe persona it normally wears.

Gail DeWeese has come out of her shop, Dirt Poor, and is talking to Melinda, owner of the It's a Mystery Bookstore. Lowell Johnson drives by in his pick-up truck. Mary Ann Bell walks her dog, Bear, over to the First National Bank. Carol Ann Engskov, Berryville's Librarian, drives by. It is possible, John thinks, that her husband Paul might know a little Old Norse. He plans to check it out.

These people all know John, and he knows them. But John also realizes that he is atrophying, burning out like a distant star. The Whoopee is going out of his Cushion; there is less there there all of the time; and his duck is definitively lame. John is disappearing before his own eyes and he stares with worry that he will fade entirely from view before the resolution of several pending matters.

There were so many problems to solve. The Problem of Unitarians has been solved, to be sure, but not in any satisfactory way; they, the Unitarians, remain happy and satisfied and completely confident in To Whom It May Concern as their Spiritual Guide and Consort. Any threat describing how they will get beat about the head and shoulders in eternity falls on deaf ears. They respond to threats with piffle sounds and prune their well-tended orchards between cocktails and Historic Preservation Meetings.

And yes, John has revived Chaos Theory and its possibilities for endless Silver Linings. But no one cares. Social Order Theorists ignore the Revival and will continue supervision of the Universe, no matter how Chaotic circumstances become. To them, it ultimately makes no difference whether Wal-Mart or the Brothers Grimm ultimately rule, as long as they supervise the end result. John supposes there are worse things than fading away.

What has not faded away is the disreputable condition of the Public Square's fountains; even John's Supernatural Visitor, Mr.

Hairy Legs, has commented on their lamentable appearance and, certainly, John himself hoped that He has bigger fish to fry then Berryville's Commie inspired public architecture.

And Iowans have not faded away, but have instead come forth and multiplied. What Fresh Hell hath Clara Jane wrought? How will the SHAZAAM PLAN play out? John certainly hopes he will be around for the big finish.

Chapter 52:

The Helpful Mr. Rilke

Special Agent Harold Staley enters the shop at five past five o'clock. He comes in alone, smelling not unpleasantly of Italian meatballs and an aftershave of common provenance. He nods in the direction of Mrs. Heartbreak and Mrs. Shogren, but it is apparent that he seeks John—for whom he makes a beeline. Mrs. Heartbreak is astonished; no one seeks John except impoverished widows and orphans who are intent on selling him "priceless" collections of Zane Grey novels left to them by recently deceased loved ones.

"I need to talk to you about Clara Jane," Agent Staley says abruptly.

"Ah," John says. Busted, he thinks. He wonders if Staley will frog march him out in cuffs for aiding and abetting.

"I believe I'm in love," Staley shouts, abruptly and breathlessly.

"Ah," John says. Not busted. Amazed yes, but still at liberty.

"She is the most remarkable woman I've ever met! So service oriented, dedicated ... so exciting!"

"Uh huh."

"I'm not an impetuous man, Mr. Heartbreak. But the moment I saw her I knew she was the one for me. What style! What grace!"

John nods. Slowly. He has begun to understand why the Bureau assigned Agent Staley to the Ozarks. "Yes," John says. "Clara Jane is a competent woman. By any definition."

"Mr. Heartbreak," Staley says, "Clara Jane tells me you are her best friend in Berryville. What can you tell me about her?"

"A competent woman. Keeps a tidy lawn. Clean about her person. Full of surprises."

"Yes, yes, of course," says Staley impatiently. "But what can you tell me about her? Where is she from? What is she really like?"

John is stumped. Perplexed as well. Hmmm. What to say?

Then, out of the corner of his eye he catches a glimpse of Rainer Maria Rilke standing in the poetry section. "Tell him that she is like the summer rain," Rilke says. "She comes from heaven and sweetens the earth with her tears."

"She is like the summer rain," John says. "She comes from heaven and sweetens the earth with her tears."

"Yes!" Staley shouts. "Yes! You've got her in one!"

"Tell him that she is the best hour of the best morning of the best day," Rilke says.

John says it. Mrs. Heartbreak and Mrs. Shogren are staring at him. Mrs. Shogren is astonished. Mrs. Heartbreak is thoroughly annoyed (Why is John talking about another woman that way?). Agent Staley is in rapture. He grabs John's arm and pumps it violently.

"Heartbreak, you've made me a happy man. I'm going to marry that girl!"

"The death of love is the progeny of every nuptial," Rilke recites. "Death is the shallow kiss, the ..."

"Not on your Nellie," John says emphatically. "Now is not the time."

"What?" Staley asks. "Are you objecting, Mr. Heartbreak?"

John had forgotten about Staley, even though he is still gripping John's hand like a turkey neck about to be wrung. The sight of the elusive Rilke had unnerved John; the poet rarely showed himself, and he was never known to be very helpful. Thus proving the case just now.

"Now is not the time for Clara Jane to be ... distracted from getting the IOWA VISITORS WELCOME CENTER off the ground," John stammers, pulling his hand out of Staley's vice. "It will take a lot of work and ... time."

"John ... may I call you John? I realize that you and Clara Jane have poured your hearts into getting the Center started ..."

"!"

" ...and I want to assure you that I'll do nothing to interfere with your dream, and Clara Jane's dream, of making Berryville a little Iowa away from home ..."

"Rose, oh pure contradiction, joy of being no one's sleep, under so many lids," Rilke says.

" ...as a matter of fact, you have my word as a Government Official, that I'll do everything in my power to make that dream come true."

Is proof of hell proof of God's existence?

Chapter 53:

Yesterday and Today and Tomorrow

John does not mind that he is disappearing. His memory is almost full. His growing deafness feels inconsequential to him. He has heard what he has needed to hear; anything he hears from now on will probably just be noise.

John can also see nothing (which is quite a trick if you think about it). He has shut off the 'Open' sign at the front of the shop, and he is turning out the overhead lights. Now he stands in the dark. The only light is the dim glow from the screen of his lap top. It beeps the entry of a message into his in-box, but he ignores it. John has talked to enough people.

Jane Russell and Mrs. Heartbreak have gone home. Mrs. Heartbreak will prepare one of her gourmet dinners. Jane will hunt for bugs beneath the pecan trees. When John gets home he will read T.C. Boyle or Thomas McGuane. John has still not read enough. And Boyle and McGuane are still alive, and so, can be relied on not to interrupt John with demands for conversation. He won't have to talk to them.

John has had enough time. Berryville's motto is "Yesterday, Today, and Tomorrow." That is about right: John and Berryville have been here yesterday and today, and he and Berryville will be here tomorrow, which will be like today, which will be like yesterday too. Time loops back on itself; it is not a line into infinity. John has gone around the loop so many times he can see himself coming.

On his way out the door John notices that the fountains have been drained for the season. In his mind's eye, John has seen Clara Jane baptizing Iowans in the fountain's waters as the means to turning them into more decent, happier people—and subsequently more cheerful consumers. At other times he has seen her holding them under the waters until they were dead, or agreed to get out of town, before she would pull them up from the depths. Either approach has an historical and practical basis: Christians have applied it to Jews and Muslims, and Catholics have applied it to Jews and Muslims and Protestants; and Protestants have applied it to Jews and Muslims and Catholics. Now, Iraqi Muslims, in their new, newly paid for democratic society, are applying it to Chaldean Catholics. You get what you pay for.

But now the fountains are empty of water, the one necessary ingredient to baptism, whether by Spirit, or by sword. Fuzzy has fled the Public Toilet: the building is empty. The Iowans, so plentiful during the Town Square's commercial hours, have left Berryville for their heavily discounted hotel rooms in Eureka Springs: there are plenty of places to park.

John realizes he is the only man in town. It isn't the first time of course; John wanders around Berryville at all hours. But think about it! How often are you the only man, or only woman, in town? It is a lovely feeling, really. John feels it.

John sees nothing and hears nothing and he sees everything and hears everything. He sees Berryville as it is yesterday; pretty girls are shooting bottle rockets across the Square; couples kiss in the gazebo; the Town Square in the rain, the snow, the sunshine, the heat, the lovely ice of a storm, dark and light, under the somber grey of a thunderhead. He sees it today, he sees it tomorrow, he sees it all. Time loops, John loops with it.

When John gets home Mrs. Heartbreak greets him at the door. She looks the way she looked yesterday. She looks the way she looked when John first saw her.

Epilogue

A year has gone by on the Town Square. It may have gone by yesterday, and we just missed it, as it slipped by. Or, gosh, it may be passing by today or it may not pass by until tomorrow. When the year goes by is unimportant. It is enough to know that it has/will go by, whether you notice it or not.

Quite a bit and almost nothing has happened in the past year, whether you've noticed it or not. After Fuzzy Markowitz's head was removed from the Public Toilet, C. Richard Williams, the County Judge at the time, commanded its renovation and clean-up. It is now a sparkly and wholesome place in which to take care of your personal matters. Thank you, Richard.

Almost everybody except Berryville's City Council enjoyed the le' Affaire Fuzzy Toilet since the rumor about a body in the toilet was confirmed and the joint was cleaned up. Only time will tell if Carroll County's new Master, Sam Barr, will keep it clean. (Stay tuned).

The majority of tourists visiting Berryville these days are from the Great State of Iowa. They like Berryville's low country prices, its affordable stock of one dollar literature, and the chicken fried steak at the Ozark Café. What they especially like is the Iowa Visitors Welcome Center. Here (there) they can sit a spell, enjoy the company of other Hawkeyes and exchange corn recipes, compare corn subsidy checks, and listen to old Lawrence Welk and Karen Carpenter tunes streaming from the Center's sound system.

The Welcome Center is staffed by volunteers from Holiday Island's Iowa Club. They are glad for the opportunity to serve their fellow Statemates, and for the chance to exchange corn recipes and to invite visitors to services at Emmanuel Lutheran Church, conveniently located near the Holiday Island Social Security Office, where further subsidies can be had.

A large portrait of Clara Jane Smith, commissioned by the Iowa Corn Council and photographed by Stephen Shogren, hangs in a place of honor over the coffee pot. Clara Jane is dressed all in white and bestows an angelic smile on everyone who looks up at it. The portrait, which has been photo shopped to look like an Old Master's painting, bears the caption, "Our Founder". Postcards of Clara Jane's picture are available at Heartbreak's, where it sells pretty well. For a buck. Plus eight cents tax.

A pamphlet, 'The Clara Jane Smith Story' is available next to the coffee pot, free for the taking. The biography section is a bit sketchy, but the pamphlet lists Clara Jane's favorite hymns, and her hobbies, which include gardening and collecting small hand guns and Israeli manufactured weapons of all types.

Clara Jane is (was) universally liked and more than 200 people attended services at the United Methodist Church, in Berryville, when she was baptized and received into membership. When she became engaged to Special FBI Agent Harold Staley and moved with him to Forrest City, Iowa—where the couple now own and operate a Recreational Vehicle Dealership following Agent Staley's retirement from government service—her loss was keenly felt.

Mrs. Heartbreak continues to manage the Universe and remains optimistic that her interventions will yield positive results. Sales are up, despite the recession that has proven so surprising to the government, and her efforts to recruit new members to the First Christian Church may soon bear fruit.

If she has any worries at all, they are about her husband John, who remains immutable, but less so, if that is not a contradiction in terms. John is simply and everyday less and less of the unchanging same. If he appears (if he appears) a bit loopy, it is because he is looping, and through time. Where, incidentally, deafness is not a handicap and no one mistakes him for a ventriloquist.

The PROBLEM of Berryville's Town Square Fountains remains a problem for those that can see them.

But nobody can. So there you have it.

A Note from the Author

Thank you, to everyone who participated in the making of Coffee with John Heartbreak. I started the book on December 21st, 2007 and concluded it on December 17th, 2009. Your feedback, brickbats, insults, and laughter have made the year a lot of fun.

About 1,200 people have "tuned in" to John Heartbreak at one time or another when the chapters appeared on my blog 'Coffee with John Heartbreak'. Four hundred and ten (410) of those visitors stayed for less than a minute and never came back. One the other hand, 790 people have read every "page" of the book at least once. Whoever you are, God Bless; may you live long and prosper.

If you are interested in writing a book I highly recommend blogging as a great first draft tool. Knowing that people are reading—and may comment on—what you write is a real help in keeping you on task. It also helps to "see" what you've written, not only for tracking down pesky typos and misspelled words, but to locate sentences and paragraphs that don't quite work.

A lot of sentences and paragraphs in John Heartbreak don't quite work. I know it is a poorly constructed book, and I beg your indulgence; I am still trying to make a living and I don't have the time to write (good) books. What was I thinking, you may ask? I wasn't. But as Chesterton said, "Anything worth doing is worth doing badly." I have taken him at his word so I have avoided a (necessary) second draft.

If you have purchased this book, I thank you. As a bookseller I have mixed feelings about tossing yet another book on the poor world's back; there are too many books and too few readers today.

But John Heartbreak is the only book that I know of that takes place almost entirely on Berryville, Arkansas' Town Square. Like the talking dog, it is remarkable not for what it says, but that it says anything at all.

Printed in the United States
by Baker & Taylor Publisher Services